Walk Into My Parlour

Tania Park

ISBN: 978-0-6485565-8-9 (Paperback)
ISBN: 978-0-6485565-9-6 (e-book)

 A catalogue record for this book is available from the National Library of Australia

NATIONAL LIBRARY OF AUSTRALIA

Tania Park Publishing.
For all enquiries contact:
goldpark3@gmail.com

The Spider And The Fly

'Will you walk into my parlour?' said a spider to a fly;
'Tis the prettiest little parlour that ever you did spy.
The way into my parlour is up a winding stair,
And I have many pretty things to shew when you are there.'
'Oh no, no!' said the little fly, 'to ask me is in vain,
For who goes up your winding stair can ne'er come down again.'

'I', sure you must be weary, with soaring up so high,
Will you rest upon my little bed?' said the spider to the fly.
'There are pretty curtains drawn around, the sheets are fine and
thin; And if you like to rest awhile, I'll snugly tuck you in.'
'Oh no, no!' said the little fly, 'For I've often heard it said,
They never, never wake again, who sleep upon your bed!'

Said the cunning spider to the fly, 'Dear friend, what shall I do,
To prove the warm affection I've always felt for you?
I have, within my pantry, good store of all that's nice:
I'm sure you're very welcome – will you please take a slice?'
'Oh no, no!' said the little fly, 'Kind sir, that cannot be,
I've heard what's in your pantry, and I do not wish to see.

'Sweet creature!' said the spider, 'you're witty and you're wise.
How handsome are your gauzy wings, how brilliant are your
eyes! I have a little looking glass upon my parlour shelf,
If you'll step in one moment, dear, you shall behold yourself.'
'I thank you, gentle sir,' she said, 'for what you're pleased to say,
And bidding you good morning now, I'll call another day.'

The spider turned him round about, and went into his den,
For well he knew, the silly fly would soon come back again:
So he wove a subtle web, in a little corner, sly,
And set his table ready, to dine upon the fly.
Then he went out to his door again, and merrily did sing,
'Come hither, hither, pretty fly, with a pearl and silver wing;
Your robes are green and purple – there's a crest upon your
head;
Your eyes are like a diamond bright, but mine are dull as lead.'

Alas, alas! How very soon this silly little fly,
Hearing his wily, flattering words, came slowly flitting by;
With buzzing wings she hung aloft, then near and nearer drew,
Thinking only of her brilliant eyes, and green and purple hue;-
Thinking only of her crested head – poor foolish thing! At last
Up jumped the cunning spider and fiercely held her fast.

He dragged her up his winding stair, into his dismal den,
Within his little parlour – but she ne'er came out again!
And now, dear little children, who may this story read,
To idle, silly, flattering words, I pray you ne'er give heed:
Unto an evil counsellor, close heart, and ear, and eye,
And take a lesson from this tale, of the Spider and the Fly.

Mary Howitt (1828)

Walk Into My Parlour

With eyes glued to the front door of the house across the road, Rachel took a sip of the now tepid coffee and glanced at her watch. 'Any second now.' She nudged the man next to her. When the cream wooden door moved, she straightened. The moment it flung wide her lungs stilled and gut tightened.

'Is that him?' The newspaper fell off Sgt Dylan Marshall's lap.

'Yes.'

'He's going running dressed in…'

'Yes.' Rachel had to stifle a giggle.

'It's bright pink.'

'So it stands out.'

'In case a car hits him?'

'So people will look at him.' When the eyes of the man across the road swung their way, Rachel turned her face towards Dylan.

'Why? The last thing I'd want is for anybody to see me in such a garish tight-fitting outfit.'

'Watch. He'll preen when he spies the woman coming up the rise.' And sure enough, Kyle Jacobs stretched to his full five feet nine, thrust out his chest and sent the woman a smirk with a finger flick through his thin brown hair.

'There's a sock in his groin.'

Dylan spun his head and stared at her. 'Excuse me?'

This time her giggle escaped. 'To give the impression there's more there than Mother Nature endowed him with.'

'Are you sure?'

'Take a look.' As though her mind had been read, the early morning sun hi-lighted the area in question. 'Cyclists come into the café on a regular basis and the male runners in the Olympics and Commonwealth Games… everything… uh, moves. Jeeze, this is so embarrassing. And none of the bits are exactly the same size or shape. He,' she pointed to the man strutting in a slow trot towards the corner, 'has a padded roll jutting out, which in no way looks natural.'

With several shakes of his head, Dylan folded the newspaper and tossed it onto the back seat. 'I don't want to know. Please, can we call it in now? Anything to get rid of the visions in my head.'

Rachel laughed and put the half-empty cardboard mug in the console. 'Sure, he's gone and won't be back for an hour. It will be best if the van parks on the verge.'

Dylan rolled his window down and waved to the other two vehicles. 'Let's go. Van on the verge,' he called to the nearest man who sat on the passenger side of the smallish removalist van.

Engines roared to life. Vehicles moved. In mere seconds Dylan parked his car to the far right of the expansive brick paving of the house they had been studying, with plenty of room left for the removalists to carry furniture and for the owner's bright yellow car to drive out. Thank goodness it hadn't been parked in the garage under the house. They would be here a while.

Next to their car, the line of shrubs against the low side fence needed a trim, the straggly growth reached in all directions as though each new shoot demanded it was the best and wanted to take pride of place. The lawn on the other side was wild with areas of weed determined to overtake the sparse growth while other patches were matted long strands of rich green as though fertilizer had been dropped in those areas alone.

After she climbed the five wide concrete steps, Rachel met the locksmith at the front door, Dylan close enough behind his breath fanned on her nape. The locksmith wasted no time. A quick study of the lock, he fiddled with his tools and was about to poke when the handle turned.

All three gasped aloud when the door swung open.

A blonde woman, dressed in a tightly belted cotton gown, gaped. 'Wha… who are you?' A heavy waft of perfume accompanied the words.

More than shocked, it took a few seconds before Rachel found words. 'The sergeant, here, has a court order to remove a list of items from these premises.' This will be interesting, an anomaly she had no idea about. 'Do you live here?' she added when her brain cells aligned and the heavy silence needed to be broken.

'No, but I stay some nights.'

'And your name is?' Rachel asked.

'Angel.'

'Really?'

The woman frowned and planted her hands on her hips. The twist of the robe exposed a pendant nestled against pale brown skin. 'Yes, Angel. Why doesn't anyone ever believe me?'

Not daring to comment, Rachel reached for the pendant and turned to Dylan. 'Photo number five of the jewellery.' She studied the pendant and eyed the woman. 'Where did you get this?'

Angel jerked backwards and patted the pendant against her skin when it was torn from Rachel's fingers. 'My fiancé gave it to me for my birthday.'

'Your fiancé?' Wow, the shocks kept coming. And Rachel thought she had been thorough in her research. 'I assume you mean Kyle Jacobs.'

'Yes, of course. This is his house.'

'Technically it's not and the pendant wasn't his to give. It's stolen property. You need to take it off and give it to the sergeant.'

Angel stepped backwards with a shudder and screwed face. 'No way.'

The second her hand went to the door to close it, Dylan stepped forward with his mobile phone showing a photo. 'Here's a photo given to us by the owner. It's stolen property. If you don't hand it over, you can be arrested for receiving stolen goods.'

'Stolen? He stole it?'

'Yes,' Dylan and Rachel chorused while Dylan planted his foot against the door and held out his hand.

Moisture appeared in hazel eyes but Angel lifted her hands and looped the chain over her head. She wore so much perfume, every movement sent out a strong whiff. It was a nice perfume but so much overpowered the senses.

When Rachel spied something from the corner of her eye, she caught the woman's left hand and studied the engagement ring. Sweet mercy. 'This ring is also stolen.' She turned to Dylan. 'Photo one.'

Dylan swiped, held out his phone. 'It's identical.'

'But… but… are you sure?' With panic in her eyes Angel stepped further back into the room.

Rachel followed and stifled a gag at the sudden conflict of aromas. The air freshener was as strong as the perfume but they clashed with violence. 'I'm certain. I'm sorry but you need to take it off.' Her heart twitched for the dilemma the woman was facing so softened her tone. 'I'm sure you don't want to be arrested for a crime you had no idea about, but the ring is one of seven pieces of stolen jewellery. Has your fiancé given you any more pieces?'

'No.' With a whimper, Angel twisted the ring off, stared at it and finally held it out to Dylan. It was obvious she was both confused and upset.

'Can we come in?' Rachel asked. 'We need to explain why we are here.' She leant towards Dylan and whispered. 'Don't let on.'

He raised his eyebrows in question, nodded and mouthed, 'Okay.'

With a screwed face of worry, Angel waved one hand in the air. 'You can come in but I don't understand.'

'This court order outlines the list of items that belong to Mrs Jacobs,' said Dylan who stepped aside when the two removalists followed them in.

Rachel pointed to pieces of furniture in the front room. 'Those two leather chairs, the coffee table and sound system. In the dining room, there's an antique oak table with nine expansion leaves and twelve matching chairs. There's also a long sideboard to match. What's in the sideboard will need to be sorted. Many of the items stay.' She turned to the locksmith. 'In the study: last room on the right at the end of the passage, is a locked filing cabinet. If you can find the key, fine. If you can't, the cabinet needs to be opened. You might want to check if any of the desk drawers are locked.'

Angel's eyes were wide and her mouth moved like a guppy in the final throes of death. 'But Mrs Jacobs is dead. She left everything to her husband.'

Stunned, Rachel spun around to face the other woman. 'Dead? When did she die?'

'About a year ago. She had cancer.'

This needed careful questioning. Rachel sorted through confused brain cells. 'Where is she buried?' was the first question to hit.

'I don't know any details but I think Kyle said she was cremated and her ashes scattered on the ocean.' Angel shuffled to one side when a leather chair brushed against her side. 'Why are you taking our furniture?'

'It's not yours. The judge was more than satisfied with the evidence to prove ownership. Here is the list of items we'll take today.' Dylan held out a sheaf of stapled papers underneath the official court order.

While Angel read the pages Rachel was more interested in what she'd learned in the past couple of minutes but more information was needed. A few friendly questions might gain more details. 'Do you have a wedding date?'

'Four weeks - Saturday.' Angel kept her eyes on the papers.

'A big wedding?'

'No.' She turned to Rachel. 'Since Kyle had been married before, he wanted to keep it small. We've invited twenty friends.'

'No family? What about your parents?'

'They live overseas.'

'Still, I'm sure they would want to be here.' The way Angel shrugged indicated it wasn't what the woman wanted. An idea struck. 'Where is the ceremony?'

'A private room at the Hilton.'

'What time and date. I presume you'll have a wedding celebrant.'

'Yes, of course.'

While Angel gave the details, Rachel searched her phone, dialled the number for the Hilton Hotel and asked for the function manager, not sure if they would be available at such an early hour. When she was put through she repeated the details and turned the speaker on so everyone could hear.

'I'm sorry, but there is no small function booked at that time,' came the tinny response after a three minute search.

'I might have got the time wrong. Can you check the entire day?' Rachel added with a glance at Angel who had lost interest in the list and fidgeted while they waited for an answer.

'There is only a big convention over the entire weekend and evening. We wouldn't have booked any other function with such a large convention. What name is the booking under?'

Rachel sent a raised eyebrow towards Angel.

She screwed her face. 'Kyle organised it.'

'Kyle Jacobs. Can you check any other day for the booking?' With a quirked eyebrow, Rachel shrugged her shoulders towards Dylan who stepped further into the lounge room to keep an eye on the removalists.

'Sorry, there's nothing. Are you sure you've got the right hotel?'

'I'll ask. I'm ringing on behalf of the bride. Give me a minute.' Rachel pressed the phone against her chest. 'Angel, are you sure?'

'Yes, he showed me the details printed on a Hilton Hotel form.'

'A printed copy or a real master copy?'

'Oh, I suppose it was printed from an email. I don't know.'

'Didn't you make the arrangements yourself?'

'No. Kyle said he would make all the arrangements. He paid for the entire service and meal for twenty guests. I paid half of it.'

'How much did you pay?

'Eight thousand.'

'Eight thousand?' Dylan spun back around with a shocked face. 'You mean room hire and dinner for twenty would cost sixteen thousand? That's close to a thousand each. Must be an amazing meal.'

Angel twisted her fingers and squirmed. 'Well, there's the decorations - and photographer - and drinks and the celebrant.'

Shocked at the steep price, Rachel lifted the phone to her ear. 'The bride believes there is a receipt for the function, which includes a meal for twenty guests. Are you able to check? You can ring me back on this number if you find the details. I appreciate your time. Thank you.' Rachel ended the call and eyed Angel whose tears were real, despite the obvious fight to keep them at bay. 'I'm sorry. There is no booking. I was sure there wouldn't be.'

'Why? How would you know?'

'Because Kyle can't marry you. He lied to you.'

Angel hissed. 'How would you know? He would never lie to me. He loves me.'

'Kyle is still married to his wife.'

'Huh? No way. How can he be if she's dead?'

'She isn't dead and never had cancer. Kyle hasn't yet applied for a divorce.'

'You're lying,' Angel screeched. 'You wouldn't know.'

Dylan stepped forward and placed a hand on Angel's forearm. 'Elise Jacobs was in court when the judge granted her every item listed on this court order. There were witnesses to verify her claim and plenty of photographs to prove the items belonged to her prior to the marriage, which was so short, Kyle has no claim on any of the items.'

'But… but… what court? Kyle didn't know about it. She must be an imposter. She's dead.'

'No, she's alive and well and Kyle did know. I served him the papers myself. I went to his place of work over six weeks ago, where I watched him sign to say he had received them. In those papers was a subpoena to appear in court. He refused and didn't turn up.'

'I don't believe you. He would have told me and who are you?'

'Sergeant Dylan Marshal.' He removed his I.D. from the top shirt pocket and flipped it open. 'I'm a police officer on secondment to the court to serve official documents and ensure court orders are carried out. I'm here today to ensure only the listed items are taken. I'm sorry but this isn't the first time Kyle has lied to a woman and taken her on a fantasy ride. He's after your money.'

'My money? But I don't have much.'

'You've already given him eight thousand dollars,' Rachel butted in. 'Do you work?'

With a determined face, Angel turned to her. 'Yes, of course.'

'Where does your pay go – your account or a joint account?'

'Mine but we were going to change to a joint account before the wedding.' There was a sudden pallor to her face as though realisation had hit like a sledgehammer.

'He tried the same tactic with his wife but she refused. She's glad she did because he tried several times to clean out her account until she changed banks and put most of her money into a term deposit so it can't be touched. How much a fortnight do you pay him for bills and food? No don't answer. It's $355 isn't it?'

'Huh, how do you know?' Angel's face had paled further under the light tan of what might be Mediterranean skin. She was a beautiful woman, although the hair had to be bleached.

'It's the same amount his wife paid. I hate to tell you this but $205 pays half of his housing loan. You are paying for half of this house when your name isn't on the title deed or the bank loan.'

'Huh, no way.'

'I promise you and when I get into the study I will prove it to you. Are you going to work today?'

'Angel glanced at the wall clock and jolted. 'Yes, and breakfast. Kyle will want his breakfast as soon as he comes in from his run. Oh, God, I have to hurry.'

'Can't he get his own breakfast?' Dylan asked.

'He likes me to cook when I'm here.'

'I wouldn't worry about breakfast,' said Rachel.

'But he insists.'

'Not today he won't. You go. Have you got your own car?'

'We sold it?'

'Why?'

'Kyle drops me off at work and picks me up.'

With a shake of her head, Rachel closed her eyes for a second. 'I know I shouldn't have to ask this but how much did you get for the car and where is the money?'

'Fifteen thousand. Kyle invested it for me.'

Rachel hid her head in her hands. Poor woman doesn't have a clue. 'Go and get ready for work and you'll need to call a taxi.'

'I don't believe you. I'll prove it when Kyle gets back,' Angel shouted before she turned, spun around in a full circle as though not sure what to do and fled towards the main bedroom.

'Poor girl is in for an almighty shock,' Rachel said to Dylan. 'The control and manipulation has already started. I need to get to the office and search the files before the bastard gets back.' She headed for the office. Proof time.

The locksmith stood at the open study door when Rachel reached it.

'Did you find the key?' Rachel asked.

'No, but it's open. Wasn't hard. I've reset the lock. All you need to do is push the drawers closed and listen for the click but make sure you leave them all ajar until you've finished. The bottom desk drawer was locked. The key was taped where all keys are taped – underneath the drawer above. Any more locks?'

'No. I appreciate your time. Thank you. I presume you have the details to send the bill.'

'Sure. I wish all of my jobs were this easy.' He waved over his shoulder as he walked away.

Rachel studied the pristine black and white room. A black leather office chair was precisely placed close to the back wall and tucked under the front of a modern black desk. A laptop stood open in the centre – still warm. One tap of the mouse and the screen sprang to life. Delight brought a wide grin. He hadn't shut it off. A quick scan of the folders and she clicked on Angel to find no password protection. Idiot was too up himself to assume anyone would dare touch his computer.

The folder opened to reveal dot-pointed dates with a few sentences after each. She pressed print and checked the printer was on. It took mere seconds to spew out papers while she continued a study of the room.

Four different coloured pens were in neat alignment to the right of the laptop with three various sized notebooks stacked behind them, the front right hand corner aligned with each other. The printer sat on the end of the desk and a tall metal filing cabinet was pressed against the wall within easy reach. A huge monochrome print held centre stage opposite the desk. To her, it was offensive with the grotesque modernistic view of a semi-naked woman. White walls and ceiling, white tiled floor with a black shaggy rug under the furniture. Curtains were white with black wavy vertical lines. It said a lot about Kyle Jacob's nature. Pernickety about detail, obsessive, and from what she had learned – overly possessive.

The bottom drawer with a key in the lock grabbed her immediate attention. Locked drawers meant held secrets. To be sure no important item was missed, she studied the contents of the three smaller drawers. They were O.C.D. neat but held nothing out of the ordinary. On her knees, she took her time to pull out the bottom drawer. The sight of a small metal cash box caused her stomach muscles to tighten. It was a surprise to find it opened with ease, but with the drawer locked it made sense.

Wads of cash held together by elastic bands were crammed inside. Small sticky labels sat on top of each bundle. *Angel – wedding* was written on the top bundle. Rachel didn't have to count the cash but did in any case. Eight thousand. The next label read: *Angel – car.*

She didn't bother to count. Underneath were three more bundles, two with Elise and one with Adam. Why a man's name? She placed all five on top of the desk and went back to the computer when the printer stopped. The next folder she was interested in had the name, Elise. Again there was no password so she opened it and scanned. It appeared Kyle wasn't a verbose person for again it was dot-pointed with brief sentences. She pressed print and went back to the drawer.

Three passports. Three? Why were there three? She frowned. It was possible he already had hold of Angel's. She lifted out the top one, opened it and read the details on the first page. It belonged to Elise Esquilante and since it was on the list, she removed it and put it with the cash. She hadn't been married long enough to get it changed to her married name. The second one had Kyle's smug mug and details. The third caused her to gasp. There was Kyle's photo but with entirely different name and details.

'Wow.' Overcome, she fell back on her heels and stared at the name – Keith Jackson. It took too long to come to her senses. A stack of A5-sized notebooks, all with black covers, filled the space at the back. Underneath them sat a lap-top, one she recognised as it was on the list so she levered it out. A small calico bag came out with it. Inside, she found the five missing pieces of jewellery. The bag went into the pocket of her jeans. It took only a quick scan to realise how important the notebooks were but it created a dilemma. They weren't on the list. Therefore she would have to secrete them out.

With time short, she left them and turned to the filing cabinet to search for vital paperwork. A pause while she studied the barely open drawers. Which one first? Her eyes trailed up and down and landed on drawer three. The folders were super-organised, with headings in meticulous printed letters. She flipped through to *Certificates,* took out the file and opened it out on a clear area of the desk. The two she wanted were on the top: both labelled Elise. Her birth certificate and wedding certificate dated fifteen months ago. Now, she wondered how legitimate the marriage was if she took into consideration the other passport. Curve balls were being flung at a rapid rate.

Two more birth certificates sat at the bottom of the pile. She scanned both. Only one looked genuine, the other appeared to be dodgy but she couldn't figure out why so studied them in more detail. The wording and signatures were exactly the same but names and dates were different. It both scared and worried her how the one for Keith Jackson sent out the genuine vibes. Not sure what to do, she took the real certificate and Kyle's passport to ask Dylan. One of them had to be fake. Before leaving she opened another file on the computer with the same man's name as the fifth wad of cash. A single press on *print* and the machine whirred.

Back in the lounge, there was an unreal atmosphere with furniture already gone and items from the top of the sound system now lined against the white, dust-laden wall underneath. The room gave the impression of being twice the size and spooky. The murmur of voices drew her into the dining room where piles of glassware, crockery and cutlery were being laid out on the floor along the far wall.

'Dylan, can I have your attention for a moment?'

'Sure, you find what you needed?'

'So far but check out this passport. Is it genuine?'

He took it, opened it out and flicked through before studying the front pages. 'Looks okay, why?'

She held out the birth certificate. 'It doesn't match the details on this and there's a passport with this name as well. Both passports have the same man's photo.'

Kyle's eyes swung between the two. 'Phew, I understand what you mean. Could he have an alias?'

'Possible, but what can we do about it?' She paused. 'My gut is sending me scary messages. Why would a person need to have an alias? The only reason I can think of makes this whole situation a lot worse. He's hiding a lot more than we have discovered. There must be something awful in his background. And there are two piles of cash with Elise printed on top.' No way was she going to tell Dylan about the other three piles. They weren't listed so he wouldn't let them leave the premises.

'Have you counted the cash?'

'Not yet but I will.' To keep Dylan's mind away from the office, she scooted towards the piles and indicated with one foot. 'The dinner set with the gold rim, the four sets of crystal glasses and stainless steel cutlery in the canteen are the items on the list. The rest stays. She moved back to Dylan and took the paperwork. 'What do you want me to do with these?'

'I'll think about it. I might have to get one of the detectives to research but technically, and legally, we can't take them. How about jotting the details on paper for me?'

'Will do. I'll count the cash but you'll need to check it.'

'Sure, later.' He waved her away.

Back in the office, Rachel checked the printer and removed the small stack of printed papers. There wasn't time to read them despite a desperate need to find out every detail. She stashed them under the notebooks. With both passports flattened on the printer, she closed the lid, pressed for two colour copies and scooted back to the filing cabinet. They might not be able to take the actual documents but there was nothing in the court order to say she couldn't copy them.

The title deed was exactly where it should have been – in a file with the same name. She opened it out; read the details to ensure it was for this property and dropped to the floor in shock.

'Wow, no way,' huffed out. 'Well this makes a huge difference.' Too stunned to believe it, she studied every word. It still said the same. Kyle's name wasn't on it. The house belonged to one person – Elise Esquilante. Why would he put it in her name when he made the payments, although both she and Angel had made half the payments? It didn't make sense. And how could she prove it without taking the document?

Overjoyed, she scrambled upright, took the passports from the printer and placed the title deed on the printer glass - slightly skewed, and made two coloured copies of each page, one for her and one for Dylan. Instead of putting the originals back in the file she set them aside next to the money. The copies went back in the file. The barely noticeable skew would prove they weren't the real deal. After doing the same with the mystery birth certificates, she replaced all the papers where she found them and went on the hunt for more juicy bits of evidence.

A profanity slipped out when she opened the file headed W*edding,* for it was stuffed full. It only took a quick glance before she grabbed the lot and headed for the main bedroom. Without knocking she opened the door to find the room empty. 'Angel,' she called at the scuffle from the en-suite.

'Yes.' When the woman stepped through the doorway, Rachel's jaw dropped. Angel was dressed in a power suit of crimson. Her hair was tied back in a neat bun and faultless make-up enhanced already beautiful features.

'You look amazing,' she said after getting her brain cells into gear.

'Thank you. What do you want? I have to hurry.'

'You wanted proof.' Rachel dropped the file on the bed and opened it out. A pile of stamped and addressed envelopes spread out. It didn't take a genius to figure out what they were. She lifted one and held it out to Angel. 'Your handwriting?'

The poor woman stared and paled. 'Y... y... yes. But these were posted. Half of the people emailed back their acceptance.'

'To your email or Kyle's.'

She lifted moist eyes. 'Kyle.'

'Did you see the replies or did he tell you?'

Angel plopped onto the bed and sifted through the envelopes. 'Told me.' Her eyes lifted again. 'He didn't post them, did he?'

'No. I'm sorry.'

Angel searched through the other papers, lifted them one at a time to read and dropped each, not caring where they landed. Despite good manners meant it was rude to read over a person's shoulder; Rachel scanned them at the same time. A Hilton

Hotel letterhead featured on several blank sheets along with several scanned copies with figures and words.

'Oh, God,' stumbled out of Angel's mouth. 'These are all fake aren't they?' Eyes rose again, flooded with moisture this time.

With her heart on mission to squeeze all the blood from her body, Rachel sat next to Angel and put an arm around her shoulder. 'I'm sorry. Everything he's told you is a lie. There was never going to be a wedding. All he wanted was your money. He would have ditched you before the big day. It could have been when you arrived at the hotel expecting to be married. If you had set up a joint account as you intended, he would have cleaned out the account before you realised he wasn't going to turn up. You're not the only woman he's done this to.'

Moist eyes stared at Rachel. 'What am I going to do?'

'Not sure. My advice is to call in sick and spend the day packing all of your belongings. It wouldn't be wise to stay here.'

'Why not?'

'As soon as Kyle gets back and spots the furniture van, it will be obvious his secret about his wife is out.'

Tears tumbled down a distressed face. 'Why? Why would he do this to me? How can anyone be so cruel? What about my money? I paid for this wedding. My car?' Her head shook. 'He didn't invest the money, did he?'

'No, he stole it all. But wait, I'll be back in a jiffy.' After a quick glance along the passage to ensure she wasn't caught, Rachel ran, grabbed the two wads of Angel's cash and shot back. 'This was in the locked bottom drawer. Both piles have your name and where the money came from. I counted the wedding pile. The entire eight thousand is there. I didn't have time to count the rest. You count it but don't say a thing for this money isn't on the court order list and the sergeant out there will only let listed items leave this house. Lucky for you, it doesn't prevent you from taking what belongs to you. Hide the cash in the bottom of a bag. It's yours and thank your lucky stars we came today. We nearly didn't.'

'But what if Kyle comes looking for me? He knows where I live and work.'

'I can't give you an answer, only advice. If it were me, I'd find another place to live. Stay with a friend for a while, where you can be protected. And make sure everyone at work knows to not let Kyle in the premises. It might be a good idea to tell them the partial truth: he turned out to be abusive, which is true in one sense because he's been emotionally and financially abusive. I presume he has never physically harmed you.'

'No, of course not. He never would. He's not an abuser.'

'He is. His wife ended up in hospital.'

'No way.'

'If anyone crosses Kyle, he lashes out. When his best friend assisted his wife after she fainted, Kyle beat the man to a pulp. You might have to get a workmate to see you safely in and out of the work premises. Buy another car. Find a new home. With what I've found out today, it might not be for too long.'

'Why? How come?'

'If my suspicions are correct, he might find himself arrested.'

'Are you sure?'

'I can't say for certain but it's possible. I need to search more to find evidence. Look, send me your contact numbers. Have you got a mobile?'

'Yes, of course.' Angel spun around and took a phone from the bedside table.

Rachel stared when she recognised the model.

'Where did you get this phone?'

'Kyle gave it to me. It's an old one of his but much newer than the one I had before.'

'Show me.' Rachel whipped it from Angel's hand to study.

'Hey, that's mine.'

'It might not be. It's the same model listed on the court documents. I'm certain this belonged to his wife and I know why he's given it to you.' It took mere seconds to find what she was looking for. 'See here.' She pointed.

'Sure, it's an APP.'

'Do you know what for?'

'No, I hardly ever use APPs.'

A quick scan of the room and Rachel found what she was looking for. With utter joy for Kyle's stupidity, she climbed over the bed, grabbed his phone, wallet and car keys from the other bedside table and turned his phone on, delighted when it also wasn't password protected. It took a while to find what she wanted. 'Okay, you keep an eye on this mark – here.' Her finger stabbed at an icon.

'Why? What is it?'

'Watch it.' With Angel's phone in her hand Rachel walked around the room, into the en-suite, out again and went along the passage and back. 'What is the mark doing?'

'Moving, but why?'

Rachel returned. 'He did the same to his wife. It took her two weeks after their marriage to figure out he was tracking her movements. It was as though he knew where she was all the time and would ring when she was at her brother's house, with a friend or if she went to a local café for lunch. Kyle asked specific questions. Where was she? Who was she with? Why was she there? Yet he never called her at work.'

'He's done it to me as well. I went for drinks after work a couple of times. He rang a few minutes after I arrived and wanted to know every detail. Why? And what is this?' She stabbed at the mark.

'The APP tracks the phone. It was designed to find where your phone is if you lose it. His wife had a work colleague figure it out. She also discovered he logged her calls so she bought a pay-as-you-go phone, which she kept at her workplace. When she went out for lunch or coffee, she left this phone on her work desk. She gave the new phone number to family and friends and always left it at work overnight to ensure she received no calls at home. He never found out. He also gained access to her computer and read all of her emails so she bought another one, created a new email address and only used it for personal contacts. She also left it at work so he would never know.'

'How do you know this?'

'All of these details came out in court. He also put a tracker on her car because she refused to sell it. When she discovered it, she removed it and left it on her desk at work if she wanted to drive during the day. On Saturday's, when Kyle played golf, she planted it behind a paint tin in the garage so Kyle could check his phone and see the tracker hadn't moved. She almost got caught once when she forgot to put the tracker back under the wheel hub.'

'But why? If he was out, why couldn't she do the same? And he never plays golf on a Saturday. It was the only day he spent with me until his wife died.'

'Spent with you?' Oh, wow, another curve ball, from the far left this time. 'He does this to isolate his partner from her family and friends.'

'Why?'

'It's a form of abuse where the partner wants total control. They call it coercive control, which a few states have already legislated as illegal. Why did he urge you to sell your car? It was to ensure you became dependent on him to drop you off and pick you up so he can control where you are at all times. This isolates you from close family and friends because you can't visit them without his permission. Did you want to sell your car?'

'No but his arguments made sense. Well, at the time they did.'

'And now?'

'Now I'm so confused I don't know what to believe. He was always so nice to me. A real gentleman and caring. He bought me flowers every week. Nobody ever bought me flowers before.' She plonked on the bed with her face buried in her hands.

'It's how coercive abusers begin. They shower the victim with affection and love to create a sense of intense intimacy and dependence. Some call it love-bombing. When they've got their victim in their clutches they control the social interactions to isolate the victim from their support network so they become dependent on the abuser. I suspect Kyle had reached this stage with you when he was able to talk you into selling your car. This also involves the control of your finances, which he's done with theft of your cash, and he would have had further control if you'd put your money into a joint account. His wife refused. He wasn't happy and began the next stage of criticism, to chip away at her self-esteem and confidence. Things like criticising her appearance, telling her what to wear or not to wear.' She paused at Angle's whine of distress. 'He's done similar to you?'

'Yes, all the time.'

'Do you understand, now? With the evidence of the money and the papers in the wedding file, you must realise the truth. And the lies he told you about his wife.'

'I know, I know.' She waved her hands around in the air. 'It's so hard to believe. What am I supposed to do?'

'First, ring work and call in sick, or urgent private business. Is there a landline in this house?'

'Yes.'

'Use the landline because I need to show this mobile to Dylan to make sure it's the one on the list. If it is, he will take it. Kyle might check any numbers you ring from the landline as well. But it's your work number so you might get away with it, although it won't make any difference now.'

Angel reached out. 'All of my contacts are on this phone.'

'I'll ask Dylan to download them. Is the phone connected to your computer?'

'The one at work, yes. It's the only computer I've got now.'

'Kyle?'

With a new bout of tears and a loud sniff, Angel nodded.

Unable to believe how a person could give up their personal computer, Rachel gave her a hug. 'I'm sorry but it's a good thing you found out now before he could wreak any more havoc with your life. How about you make the call and gather all of your belongings ready to pack? There are still items to search for in the office. If you need a packing box, the removalists might have a spare.'

A loud snort and gulp was followed by a nod. 'Okay.' The tears flowed again.

With a final hug, Rachel turned away and was at the door when an idea struck. 'Tell me, do you know if any of the wife's clothes are still here.'

Angel stood and swiped the moisture from her face leaving a long dark streak of make-up across the right cheek. 'There might be women's clothes in the bedroom next door. In the end of the wardrobe. I'm not sure. I only went in there once.'

'I'll check what I find against the list.' Delighted, Rachel pocketed Kyle's car keys and wallet, closed the door and hurried to the next room.

The second bedroom was cool and dark with an aura of disuse despite the neatly made double bed with the quilt so straight and smooth it gave the impression an iron had been run over it. Two pillows were hidden under the quilt. A teak dressing table with two rows of small drawers underneath increased the sense of abandonment with nothing on top apart from a layer of dust. The blinds were down, the drapes drawn, the dim light added to the depressive atmosphere. There weren't any bedside tables or lamps to give life to the room. In the doorway a shiver swept across Rachel's shoulders at the musty scent. She shuddered, huffed and crossed the carpet to the two-door built-in wardrobe across one end wall. The room wasn't large enough to be comfortable with the double bed. A single would give more sensation of space but it would need a complete décor change to give it life.

The left hand door revealed a row of white melamine shelves containing nothing but dust bunnies. The other door had a high rail with empty hangers bunched at one end. On the floor sat a cardboard box tucked behind an unzipped fabric suitcase with parts of clothes hanging out under the lid. Whoever had tossed the clothes in, hadn't taken any time or care. She suspected Kyle had been in a fit of rage and with the amount of dust on top, this had occurred on the day he kicked his wife out or not long after.

First she peered into the box to find a group of DVDs with no cover pictures. Each had a small label stuck to the top right hand corner. She lifted one and studied the neat printing. Olivia. 'Oh, wow, why Olivia?' The second was titled Laura. When she read Elise on the third and Angel on the fourth, her brain cells went haywire and gut clenched at the certainty these were important but she didn't like the message her gut was sending to her brain. With eyes shut, she lifted them out and spread them across the floor. Nine DVDs with nine different names. Unable to draw breath, she stared. It took too long before she gathered them up and set the pile next to her. She had to take them without Dylan's knowledge.

With a shudder to clear her mind of unsavoury ideas, she dragged the case onto the floor and lifted the lid. She didn't need the list to know to whom the clothes belonged. With time short, she wanted to bundle the ends in and zip the zipper but regret had her haul the lot out for a more orderly fold until an idea came when she spotted the internal zip in the bottom lining. What better place to hide the items from Dylan? She doubted he would check. If he did she could claim they must have been there all along and she hadn't noticed because she never took all the clothes out. It sounded plausible. A quick squizz along the passage before she ducked into the office, grabbed the money, notebooks and copied paperwork. Another check before she dashed into the bedroom and spread out the items along the base so there were no lumps. To prevent rattles she wrapped the hard plastic covers in knickers.

It wasn't until all the clothes were packed she remembered the wife's money was on the list and Dylan wanted to count it. Removing the money made what was hidden less noticeable, thank goodness. The clothes were of good quality but sober apart from the underwear which was expensive and lacy. No outer garments were overtly sexy or gaudy, much like the owner. Six pairs of quality shoes went upside down on the top, which made it difficult to get the zip sealed and left small lumps in the tough fabric lid. These weren't all of the clothes for what woman's wardrobe would fit into a single suitcase? Her own meagre wardrobe would need more than this one suitcase. She smiled at the bright purple colour before wheeling the case into the office where she left it inside the door to be collected on her way out.

Nerves tightened when she tugged out the top drawer of the filing cabinet. A quick scan through the few files indicated they were everyday receipts for tax purposes and Kyle's work related papers, much like the files in the office at her place of work. When none held her interest she went to the second drawer. This was far more interesting, especially the bank statements. She lifted out the file and opened it out on the desk. The bundle at the back was stapled together and had Angel's name on a sticky note on the front. Thank goodness the man was over the top pernickety with orderliness. When Rachel flicked through she realised they were photocopies and wondered if Angel knew. There were ticks against several debit amounts and big red question marks against others. Nasty. Had he given Angel grief about buying lunch, snacks with coffee and several items of pharmacy products? A big dark asterisk featured next to a shoe shop purchase. The pile was put aside before she lifted the next, much larger pile of stapled statements. Mrs Elise Jacobs.

'Wow.' Rachel plonked into the office chair and flicked through the photocopied statements. They had been gone through and marked much the same as the previous lot. Despite these not on the list, surely Dylan would let them leave. She had to ask so picked up both piles. First, she needed to inform Angel since the statements belonged to her and they might help convince the woman the depth of Kyle's skulduggery.

When racking sobs met her at the door to the main bedroom, she paused with indecision but finally knocked. There wasn't time to take care of what ifs or be over-sensitive to the woman's trauma.

'Yes?' was followed by a loud sniff.

Rachel opened the door. 'Can I come in? There's something I need to show you.'

Angel rubbed an already sodden tissue against wet, red eyes. 'Can't be any worse than what you've already told me.'

An open packing carton stood on the floor at the end of the bed. Clothes reached three quarters of the way to the top. A large assortment of make-up and hair products were piled on the end of the bed. Innumerable shoes had been thrown in an untidy heap on the floor. How can anyone need so many shoes? No wonder Kyle questioned the purchase.

'It might be worse. It depends on whether you knew.' Rachel held out the statements. 'Did you know

Kyle made copies of your bank statements to keep a record of what you spent and where?'

'He what?' screeched out as Angel grabbed the papers and studied them. A string of unladylike epithets followed as Angel fell to her knees and leant over the edge of the bed with the papers in front of her. 'The bastard. Look how he underlined the final balance each month. No wonder he wanted me to transfer my money into a joint account, but how did he get them? Bloody lowlife.'

'You might be giving him credit. I found a similar pile of statements for his wife. She didn't know about...'

Shouted words cut Rachel off.

Angel shot to her feet, stared at the door and back at Rachel. 'Kyle's back. What do I do?'

'How angry are you with him?'

'Beyond angry. There isn't a word in the English language to describe how angry.'

'Confront him but be careful. Stand in the front doorway but if he comes toward you, get back inside and slam the door. Don't let him get near you. Dylan will protect you. Tell Kyle you know about the wedding, you know his wife is still alive but don't mention the money. Dylan can't know I gave it back to you. Tell Kyle you know he's a liar.' Rachel turned and ran with her hands searching her pockets for Kyle's car keys and wallet.

In her haste, she fumbled the removal of all other keys from the keyring and dropped two. With no time to pick them up she hurtled towards Dylan who neared the front door at the same time. 'Key.' She held it out.

'Wallet?' Dylan asked.

'Give me a sec.' She opened it out, removed all bank cards and cash and checked there was nothing else he could use to get money. It was a shock to find a card from a different financial institution than the one she knew about.

'What the hell are you doing?' bellowed from outside. 'That's my furniture. Take it back inside. Who the hell are you? Angel?'

As if obeying an order, Angel arrived with a file stuffed with hastily put in papers, most with edges hanging out in a higgledy-piggledy mess. She flung the door open. 'Liar,' she screeched. 'Liar, liar, liar.'

'What the hell? What are you talking about and why have you got removalists here?'

Rachel stepped backwards and placed her back against the wall two metres from the front door. She handed the wallet to Dylan. 'I found a pile of papers to prove his lies. Gave them to Angel,' she whispered. 'They all have her name on them so they belong to her.'

'You should have checked with me.'

'No time but you'll understand.'

'Angel, what the hell is going on?' yelled Kyle.

'Bastard, you lied to me.'

'Never, about what?'

'Your wife isn't dead, you can't marry me because you're still married, you stole my money and you never booked a wedding or posted the invitations. You're nothing but a snivelling lying bastard.'

'I can explain.' The voice had developed a whine.

'Go ahead and explain.' Angel stepped outside. 'Explain why all of the invitations I wrote are here.' She waved the file in the air. 'Explain why the hotel said there is no booking for a wedding.'

'You've been in my private files?' Kyle roared.

'No the police officer found them.'

Rachel gulped at Dylan's stare and she shooed him outside with one hand. 'Go.' Thank goodness he shuffled Angel aside and stepped onto the landing.

'Calm down,' Dylan yelled.

'What the hell are you doing here?' Kyle yelled louder.

'I'm here to supervise the removal of the furniture and personal items that belong to your wife.'

'You have no right.' It sounded as if Kyle had come closer but his voice had dropped and Rachel was certain she detected a quiver of fear.

'I have a court order.'

'You can't. How can there be if I wasn't there to defend the ludicrous claims?'

'You chose not to attend after you were subpoenaed, which is an order to attend. The judge was more than happy with the evidence your wife gave and the proof she and her witnesses provided. Your non-attendance didn't mean there would be no judgement. It was your choice. You chose. This was pointed out to you both by me when I served you the papers and in the subpoena. Speaking of your wife. She asked me to give you a present.'

Rachel heard the tinkle of key and soft thud of the wallet.

'What the hell?' There was a long pause and a muffled curse.

'Get in your car and go,' said Dylan.

'What the hell? This is my house. I need to shower and change. I can't go to work dressed like this?'

'Only half the house is yours and from what I heard in court, you never gave your wife a chance to shower and change after you dragged her by the hair through the house, taking all the skin off her arm, or when you kicked her down those steps and broke her arm in two places. You left her there without offering any assistance. This was after you broke the nose, cheekbone and three ribs of your best friend after he came to her aid when she fainted on the front doorstep.'

'Is this true?' whispered Angel with open hands gripping her cheeks.

'Yes. He has a foul temper when he loses control and doesn't get his way.' Rachel moved so she caught sight of Kyle through a gap. He looked ridiculous in the garish outfit, especially since the rolled sock had moved to a position across the crease between torso and leg. It now looked like he had two of everything and one was growing from the crease above his thigh. It was difficult to stifle her giggle.

'She's a lying bitch. They slept together, cheated on me.'

'No, she was smart enough to go to all of the neighbours and collect their home security data. They all showed how your friend arrived at the house a mere five minutes before you. The house directly opposite here showed how your wife dropped to the ground and your friend did what any friend would do. He lifted her from the ground and carried her inside. They also show him stagger out a few minutes after you arrived, all bloodied and showed in minute detail how you treated your wife. You threw her car key and empty purse at her after you'd removed all means of access to money. She had to drive away in bloodied pyjamas and a badly broken arm. The E.D. doctor wrote a detailed report of her condition and took photos of her injuries. I suggest you leave now or I will arrest you for domestic violence, stealing, false pretences, forgery and I'm sure I can find a heap of other transgressions before I get you to the station.'

'You can't, I…'

Dylan stalked across the landing.

'All right, I'm going.'

Footsteps were heavy and rapid. A car door slammed, an engine came to life and revved. There was a screech of tyres, a slam of brakes and more squeals. Rachel moved along the wall so she could catch sight of Kyle through the open doorway. The car lurched over the kerb at speed. It veered to one side when Kyle turned onto the road too hard and fast. It fishtailed before he gained control and sped away.

'Are you okay?' Dylan asked Angel before he turned to Rachel. 'A word, please.'

'I'm half okay. Did he really do those things to his friend and wife? I can't believe it. He's never shown an ounce of aggression towards me.' Angel stood with her arms wrapped around her torso, the file gripped in one hand so tight, it shook.

'Yes, and I need to look at this file.' Dylan tugged it from gripped fingers. 'Rachel, come with me.'

With her top teeth biting into her bottom lip, Rachel nodded to Angel and followed Dylan to the kitchen, scooping up the dropped keys on her way. Not sure what to do with them, she shoved them into a pocket of her jeans. By the time she reached the granite-topped island, the file was already open with the contents spread out.

'You should have shown this to me first,' he said without catching her eye. Long fingers slowly slid pages from one side to the other as he read.

'I know, but there wasn't any time with Kyle's arrival. All of these are Angel's private paperwork. She wrote the invitations. The Hilton Hotel forgeries are about her non-existent wedding, so they can be used as evidence but the statements are her personal bank details. The only person who has a right to those is

Angel. There's nothing in the court order to say other people's possessions can't be given to those people. It only states Elise's items can be taken. If we have to leave all of Kyle's things here, we also have to leave all of Angel's things, therefore she can take them.'

With eyes shut, Dylan blew out a long sigh. 'Okay but I'll photograph them and write down details.'

'I could print copies. I made copies of the two birth certificates and passports. It's more accurate. Although Angel has the originals.'

'Yes, but not with these markings.'

'True, and there's a much bigger surprise.'

'I fail to be shocked any more at anything this geezer has done. What is it?'

'The house is in only one name – and it's not Kyle's. His name isn't on the document.'

'If it's not Kyle, who owns it?'

'The title deeds have only Elise Esquilante as the owner.'

'Are you certain?'

'I was as shocked as you so I read every word to double check.'

'Why would he not include his name and why the maiden name?'

'The house was purchased before the marriage but as to why his name isn't on it, how do you expect me to know? What if… what checks do they do on proof of who you are when you buy a house. What if he does have an alias and couldn't prove he was who he says he is?' Rachel brushed a hand through her hair. 'There could be other reasons. Only he can tell us. But this means he has no legal right to this property, which means it can be sold without any hassle.'

'Apart from getting him to move out.'

'With this proof, the court could order his eviction.'

'True, it will take a while.'

'Which would be too long. Oh, and here's another item for you to check.' Rachel took two phones from the back waistband of her jeans. 'The new model is Kyle's. It was on his bedside cupboard. Angel had this other one: said Kyle gave it to her. I'm sure it's the same phone. It has the tracking APP – connected to Kyle's phone.'

'You tried it?'

'Yes, I showed Angel what he had been doing.'

'I bet she was overjoyed.'

'About as pissed as she is with everything else she's learned today. Poor woman.'

Dylan shoved all the papers together and bundled them into the file. 'Copy the Hilton paperwork and these statements, give them all to Angel but make sure you run by me anything else you find. Before you leave, what in this kitchen goes and what other furniture?'

'Main bedroom – the bed but leave the mattress and bedding. They aren't wanted because of the connotation and reminder. Laundry – both washing machine and drier. If I remember correctly, outside is the wooden table with four matching chairs and the gas barbecue. Give me half an hour to sort kitchen stuff. I'll put what needs to be taken on this island. If you give me the list, I'll tick each off as I go. I've created a pile of items from the office. I'll stack them on the desk in there for you to check. It will take a while. Oh, and I found a suitcase of clothes. Not all of them but there could be another stash hidden in another room. There are four bedrooms.'

'Let's get the furniture loaded so the removalists can leave. We've got the entire day for the rest. What about Angel? What is she going to do?'

'She's packing. Took the day off. Kyle knows where she lives and works.'

'She doesn't live here?'

'Not on a permanent basis. She still has her home. I don't know whether she owns her place or rents. There hasn't been time to discuss it. I mean, we didn't know about her.'

'True. You sort this lot. I'll go and supervise the men.'

After she'd put the file to one side, Rachel opened cupboards and spent the next forty minutes sorting, leaving most of the bench full of kitchenware and left the paperwork next to them. Dylan could check and would. He was as pernickety as Kyle in some respects. With a job at the law courts, he ensured the law was carried out with every T crossed with a perfect straight line and every I dotted with each dot exactly the same length away from the stem. But underneath he was a great guy – the opposite to Kyle.

It took a lot longer to copy all of Angel's paperwork than she had time for. She'd almost finished when Angel walked in with a ragged face now cleaned of ruined make-up. She'd changed into slim fitting black slacks and a top Rachel figured must have cost more than her week's wages. It had a certain look of expensive quality but wasn't gaudy. On Angel's feet were smart pink canvas flats. A simple style but she bet they weren't supermarket cheap like those on her own feet. The clothes gave Angel elegance and suited her.

'I love your clothes. You have style.'

'Thank you. I like to dress well. Not so much for looks but how they make me feel. Today I needed the best because I feel like crap. I've packed but don't have a clue what to do.'

'Sit and talk to me. Oh, and jot down your contact details. Better make them your work number and email. If I need any more information I'll be able to reach you.' She passed over a blank sheet of paper and one of the pens from the desk. 'Dylan wanted all of your statements copied so he can report back to court.'

'Why?'

'Evidence to prove how underhand Kyle is. The marks Kyle made could help for they indicate a form of control and you didn't give him permission to photocopy your private bank statements.' Rachel gathered together the originals and handed them to Angel. The copied pile went on the far end of the desk. 'Legally, all of these papers belong to you so you are free to take them. Do you own your house?'

'No, I rent. My lease is up in four weeks.'

'Oh, when you were to marry?'

Angel winced. 'I would have been homeless.'

'Sorry, but this could be a good thing. You can find another home without breaking a lease and Kyle won't know where you live. Were you going to move in here permanently?'

'No. Kyle wanted to sell this place and we were going to buy another house together. We've looked at a few, put in an offer but haven't heard back.' She snorted. 'Or, I haven't heard back, which is for the best now.'

Rachel didn't like where her thoughts immediately took her. It was exactly what he'd done when he married. Had he done this before to other people? The names on the DVDs flicked through her mind. Or was the sale of this house an opportunity to disappear when he didn't turn up for the wedding? 'Surely four weeks isn't long enough to sell one place and buy another. Settlement can take months.'

'Kyle began the process ages ago. He's had several estate agents come in to value this property but…'

'But what?'

'Last week… I wasn't supposed to hear this but one agent was here when I arrived home from the local shop. I figured he was here to sign up to sell this place but there were heated words. I couldn't make out much of what was said. The agent left in a hurry and Kyle was furious. I'm pretty sure it was about getting signatures but I wasn't game to ask. I did hear the word illegal.'

'I understand. He can't sell without his wife's signature.'

'But if she was supposed to be dead... I mean, I now know she's not... wouldn't the house have belonged to him?'

'He would have to produce a death certificate, which he can't. And the title deed has her name on it. An estate agent can't sign up to sell a property without all legal signatures on the agreement. Kyle couldn't get the title deed changed without her signature or a death certificate.'

'Oh, true. I hadn't thought about those details.'

'There's something else you must do as soon as possible. Today.'

'What?'

'Contact your bank and inform them there is a possibility you are being scammed.'

'Huh, but I'm not.'

Rachel pointed to the statements. 'Kyle has every detail of your account. It's possible he'll try to remove as much cash as he can. He tried with the wife. More than once. He may already be at an ATM. Close your accounts and move to another bank.'

'But why would he? He's got his own bank accounts if he needs money.'

Rachel slid Kyle's bank cards from her pocket. 'I took these out of his wallet, and all of his cash. Dylan and I planned it because it's what he did to his wife. He stole her cards and money and threw an empty purse at her so she had no access to money. Within an hour, he made an attempt to clean out her bank account but fortunately she had a daily limit and he only got away with two thousand.'

'Holy sh... sorry. I'd better ring now.' She turned away with her hand patting her back pocket. 'Oh, can I have my phone?'

'Dylan has it for it was the wife's. Use the landline. There should be a contact number on the statements.'

'Oh, God, oh God,' Angel mumbled as she fled with the pile of papers and left the sheet with her details, which Rachel scooped up, folded into eight and pocketed.

With so much time wasted, she returned to the statements and began to copy those belonging to Elise until she figured they didn't matter because the account had been closed. She kept the couple she'd copied to show as evidence if needed. Kyle's were far more interesting. Those for the account she knew about were scanned over. They appeared to be normal with his pay deposited each fortnight, and everyday debits for everyday costs. There were no unusual debits or deposits. A regular monthly amount went to the bank as a loan repayment - one she knew about: one to which Angel contributed half. It was possible she would never be able to retrieve the amount owed to her but Rachel vowed she would do her best.

The other pile for the card she hadn't known about gained a much slower and more intense study until she spied the final amount at the bottom of the last sheet when a string of four letter words echoed around the room. The number contained seven figures. She searched for dates for the pile was thickish. Four years of statements. Lord, she had to copy these. Dylan would be interested and possibly the court for there was no way Kyle could have amassed this fortune in four years on the wage he earned. As she lay each sheet on the copier, she read the next sheet, stunned at the number of huge deposits when there were few debits. What was the man into? Drugs? Scams? Surely this didn't all come from scamming women? A picture of the wad of cash with Adam's name on it centred in her brain. Not only women. In only four years? Didn't banks query deposits over ten thousand? So far she'd spied more than three.

When the printer flashed a warning light she had to search for more paper, which she found stacked in a pile in the next door bedroom wardrobe, along with several ink cartridges. Since she would need a new cartridge, she shoved the corner of the packet in her mouth so she could carry several reams of paper. The printer didn't print fast enough so she went back to the filing cabinet and took out a file at a time to go through while she stood next to the printer to take off and put on pages.

'No,' echoed from the kitchen. 'No, no, no, no, no.'

Rachel winced. It sounded like Kyle had already succeeded. It was another two minutes before Angel barrelled in. 'The bastard,' she yelled.

'He got to your account? How much?'

'The daily maximum. Two thousand. They said he had a card and used the correct pin number. How?'

'It's not hard to peek over a person's shoulder when they use their card. If he was always with you, it would have been easy.'

'But my card? How?'

'There are a couple of ways. First, check you still have your card. He copied your statements so knew all of your details. How hard would it be for him to impersonate you and apply for a new card because you lost yours. Especially on-line. Is it a credit card?'

'No, only debit, thank goodness. I've got a separate credit card.'

'He could have a duplicate credit card as well.'

'Dear, God. Thank goodness I've stopped any more transactions on both. I can't believe he would be so... so... sneaky and underhand. What are you doing?'

'Copying Kyle's bank statements for Dylan.' With a second copy for her to keep. 'We can't take the originals but there's nothing in the order to say we can't take a copy. How and when did you meet Kyle?'

'About eighteen months ago. I work for a public relations company. We assist companies and individuals to improve their public relations.'

'He wanted his PR improved?'

'No, his company had received a bundle of bad reviews. I was sent to figure out why and make suggestions on how to overcome them. I met him at the general staff meetings. We chatted, became friendly and after a couple of months, went out for coffee. It turned into Saturdays spent together and once his wife... err...'

'Supposedly died?'

'Yes, well he... I don't know how to explain but he urged me to turn it into something more. One thing led to another.'

'So you get a fairly good annual salary.' Rachel kept feeding the machine new pages while she spoke.

'I suppose but what difference would it make?'

'To him, a lot. I noticed your fortnightly pay deposit when I copied your statements. Sorry, I know it's none of my business and promise it stays with me. It's about a thousand more than his. He's not high up on his company's echelon. He's a relative newcomer although no doubt he spouts a different story. He told his wife he was at management level.' And now, she had learned, he'd only been at the company for around four years. This time period now had significance.

'With me working for the company I knew the truth.'

'I'm surprised you didn't figure out what he was up to. Like his wife, you are a nothing more than a source of income. Well, you were. Not any longer but you need to keep looking over your shoulder. He's not a man to give up, especially when he's been caught out and you now know far more about his underhand activities than he would like or want. Revenge could be on the cards.'

'How safe am I?'

'I don't know. His wife changed her name and image, moved away, found an entirely different job. I suggest you pay outright for an untraceable phone. Not the fancy latest model with a monthly contract. Pay as you go is best as it has no contract he can search for. And get a VPN so he can't locate you. With more research I hope I can find enough evidence to have him put away, which is why I need to go through all of his files. And I've only got today to do it. What are you going to do now?'

'I called a taxi. I'll drop into work to give them the heads up. There's a friend I can stay with until I find a new rental.'

'Male?'

'No but she's got a big fiancé.' Her hands went high and wide.

'Smart. Make sure he's with you when you return to your current home to pack.'

'Do you think Kyle will turn up?'

'He'll be surreptitious in following you. You know his car. When the taxi leaves here today search in all directions. If you spot it, ask the driver to take you to the nearest police station.'

'Now I'm scared.' When she shuddered, Angel wrapped her arms around her torso and stalked across the room. She paused at the desk on the return journey. 'What's this money?'

'Money he stole from his wife. Dylan needs to count it.'

'And this?' Angel lifted the calico bag from the top.

'The missing jewellery, the wife's laptop and her personal papers.' Rachel grabbed the papers when Angel went to read them. 'Sorry, they are private.' A second after she put them under the laptop her phone rang. Her nerves twitched as she slid her mobile phone from the back pocket of her jeans and tapped the green button for there was only one person who would call.

'Is everything okay?' she asked.

'I can't settle Madeleine and she won't take the bottle. Can I bring her around?'

'Yes, of course.' Her womb contracted at the sound of the wails.

E ars alert for the approaching car, Rachel continued to plough through the statements. As soon as wheels rumbled over the brick paving outside, she placed another sheet on the glass and pressed copy. In case Dylan came in, she bundled up the copies she intended to keep and stashed them in the suitcase. It was a disappointment to spot a taxi draw up at the bottom of the steps but dismay turned to elation when a familiar car turned into the drive behind the taxi.

'Excuse me, coming through.' Angel was bent at the waist pushing the cardboard box along the tiles with outstretched arms.

Rachel stepped aside to let her through at the same time Dylan appeared from the other side.

'What's going on?' he asked.

'My taxi.' Angel rolled her shoulders as she straightened.

'Let me take your box.' Dylan lifted the box and shuffled through the doorway but paused when he noticed the other car. 'Why is Olivia here?'

'Madeleine.' Wails were heard when the car door opened and a woman alighted. Brown curls bobbed when the woman waved with a grimace and opened the rear car door. Rachel's breasts became heavy in anticipation, a sensation she loved but she waited inside for her baby to arrive.

'Ooh, so gorgeous,' Angel crooned when Olivia reached her. 'How old?'

'Six weeks.' Olivia brushed past and stepped inside.

She was about to hand Madeleine over when Rachel shook her head and took a couple of steps back in case Angel came back inside. It was hard to do when she was desperate to feel Madeleine suckle. Anxiety tensed her nerve endings while she watched Angel and Dylan wrestle the box onto the back seat of the taxi. It took forever before Angel got in, shut the door and the taxi did a three point turn before it left.

At last Dylan came inside and shut the door. Rachel grasped Madeleine and rocked her in her arms. 'Oh, precious girl,' she sang. The tiny head turned and rooted around until Rachel lifted the corner of her top and released one breast which was latched onto immediately.

'Who is the other woman?' Olivia asked.

'Kyle's fiancée.' An overwhelming sensation swept over Rachel as her milk let down.

'Excuse me?'

'The wedding was planned for a month's time.'

'But, but…'

'It has been a huge learning curve for Angel over the past couple of hours.'

'Angel? Surely not her real name.'

'I thought the same but it's the name on her bank statements and her reaction when I asked the same question indicated the poor woman is used to people questioning the validity of her name. Some parent's need to be shot before they name their children. It might sound cute when they are tiny but it can sure give grief when they grow up.'

'How's it going?'

Dylan brushed past and headed for the kitchen. 'The van is packed with the inside items. The guys are about to load the outside stuff. Let's have a break. I'm desperate for a coffee. What would you two like?'

'Coffee, white, no sugar,' said Olivia at the same time Rachel said, 'Black tea. I'll sit in the lounge. It's more comfortable.'

She couldn't help but smile at the tiny face streaked with drying tears as she rocked her way into the lounge and settled onto the only seat left in the room, a black sofa of dubious age. She never tired of studying this gorgeous miracle. Babies had to be the biggest ever wasters of time. She wished she had a whole heap more time to sit, stare and appreciate but her job kept her busy. The good side was how she could have Madeleine with her while she worked – until today, which was the first time she'd had to leave her with a babysitter and it had been an enormous wrench. Her brother and sister-in-law were the only people she would trust to babysit. It shamed her now how she had toyed with the idea of having an abortion until it was too late. After the three-month mark, adoption ideas came and went when there was no other option until she trusted her heart and vowed to be the best single mother ever. How could she have considered giving away her own flesh and blood? How could anyone? Despite circumstances, there is always a way and she had worked hard to find a way.

When the other two joined her, Dylan sat on the floor with his back leant up against the end wall while

Olivia settled next to Rachel. 'Sorry I had to bring her over but she was hungry and refused the bottle.'

'It's too new. I should have tried it before but deciding to come here at the last minute threw us off kilter.'

'Angel might be glad we came today.' Dylan sent her a wry twist of his lips.

'Not at the time but now she knows about Kyle, she might wish we came months ago.' Rachel related what she'd learned about the woman while holding Madeleine over her shoulder until a quiet burp was followed by a spurt of excess milk on her shoulder. She settled her miracle on the other breast.

'Have you found anything else of interest in the filing cabinet?' asked Dylan.

'I was in the process of copying four years of statements for a secret bank account.' She turned to Dylan. 'It needs to be investigated.'

'Why?'

'The account was opened four years ago; around the same time he began to work with his company. There is no way Kyle could have amassed over a million dollars in four years on the wage he earns.'

'Over a million?' Dylan placed his mug on the floor and straightened.

'A number of deposits have been huge: so huge, I can't believe the bank didn't flag the account.'

'Where is it?' Dylan stood.

'On the printer. I've copied most,' she called after Dylan's retreating body while Olivia sent her a questioning frown.

'How are you holding up?' Olivia placed a hand on Rachel's lower arm and gave a gentle squeeze.

'Not so bad. There have been a few shocks. I'll tell you later,' she whispered at the sound of footsteps.

Dylan was so intent on studying the pages, he sat on the floor without lifting his eyes. A few frowns, gasps and whistles came from him while Madeleine slowed and fell asleep. Olivia took her so Rachel could adjust her clothes.

It wasn't until he flipped over the last page, Dylan lifted his head and eyeballed Rachel. 'I'll have to get the detectives onto this. Do you have any idea what he was up to?'

'Apart from scamming women? No but it has to be huge.'

'Have you found any evidence of investments? He could be into stocks and shares.'

'Not so far. I'll search. It wasn't something I considered. But surely the deposits would come from a trading company whose name would appear on the statement.'

'True. Search in any case. I notice you found the missing laptop.'

'And the jewellery. All locked away in the bottom desk drawer with the missing cash, which I haven't had time to count yet. Can Olivia take the suitcase of clothes with her? You can check it if you like. It's not all the clothes, although no more would fit in the one case. I haven't searched for the rest yet.'

'Sure.' Dylan waved his hand as if the clothes held no importance.

Rachel's innards did jiggles of joy. She figured as much and was glad when they were interrupted by the arrival of the two removalists to take Dylan's mind away from the clothes.

'All done?' asked Dylan as he stood.

'All packed away. Is there anything else?'

'Show me the checklist.' Dylan scanned the list and handed it to Rachel. 'You check as well.'

Rachel read slowly, noted the ticks and satisfied, nodded and handed the papers back to Dylan. The items were going into storage for six months. Long enough for the dust to settle and get enough dirt on Kyle Jacobs, he could be put away for a long time. They had bits of information, much of it classed as hearsay but not a trail of proof. Today's discoveries might hurry things along but to gather indisputable proof was a long, slow process of leads, red herrings and dead ends.

It twisted her heart to let Madeleine go home with Olivia but there was no choice if they wanted to get all the research done in the time allotted. What eased the ache was the certainty her precious princess would be back when the next feed was due.

When all the statements had been copied, she ensured the originals went back where she found them, with pages in precise alignment with the edges of the files. To leave them skewed would give Kyle immediate proof they had been gone through, although he already knew about the wedding folder. After a good search there was no evidence of stocks or shares but her nerves tweaked when she found the up-to-date insurance for the house. She copied it, kept the original and had replaced the copy when a thought came about whose name the insurance policy was in. A sigh whooshed out when the insurance document had Elise on the form, which made sense because the property was in the same name.

'How's it going?'

Rachel jumped and put a hand over her heart. 'Don't scare me.'

'Sorry, didn't mean to.' A wry quirk spread on Dylan's face as he crossed the floor and took in the room. 'It's bleak in here. Good grief!' He came to a sudden halt in front of the huge picture.

'Not your cup of tea?' Rachel asked with a grin.

'No way.' With a shudder, he turned towards her. 'What have you found?'

She pointed to the separate piles on the desk. 'Jewellery, laptop, passport, birth and wedding certificates and copies of relevant paperwork you asked for. No sign of stocks and shares. I'm not sure what else to look for. You read while I scout around in the other bedrooms for more clothes.'

'Since these are copies, I'll take them with me to read later. You've done a lot in a short time. I'll come with you.'

'Fair enough.' She led the way. The fourth bedroom didn't contain much – an unmade single bed and mattress the only furniture. The built-in robe was empty apart from two boxes of books. Dylan drew them out and leafed through. At the bottom of the first box were two photo albums. Rachel reached over, lifted them out and opened the top one. 'These aren't listed but should have been. She pointed to the name inside the front cover and turned a few pages. Old photos featuring the Esquilante family. 'If we don't take them he'll destroy them.'

Dylan swore. 'Legally, I can't. Sorry.'

'Surely…'

'No, but I can ask for a new court order for anything we find not listed.'

'But…'

'Sorry. Put them back under all the books. Let's hope Kyle doesn't know they are there.' He took them from her, wriggled them into the bottom of the box and shuffled the other books over the top.

The second box contained D.I.Y. manuals and a host of pamphlets on cars and motor cycles. They gave the appearance of being well-read but the dates indicated most were years out of date. These items were unusual for from what she'd learned, Kyle wasn't a hoarder but more of a minimalist who tossed out any item once it had been used and was no longer needed. Before they left the room, she bent to check there was nothing hidden under the bed. The layer of dust indicated it hadn't been cleaned since the drama nine months previous. It surprised her Angel hadn't been ordered to keep the place spotless. Could be because she hadn't yet moved in. Now she never would, and it will never happen with the wedding a non-event. A warm fuzzy swept through her at saving one woman from Kyle's evil ways.

The next bedroom had a similar naked bed and mattress but at least there were two bedside tables, each with a reading lamp, although they didn't match. Dylan opened the small drawers and found them empty.

'There are extra office supplies in the wardrobe. I found paper and ink in the end.' Rachel opened the door to show him.

He opened the next door and bent to heft out a cardboard box, which he dropped onto the bed, sending up a whoof of dust. Rachel clapped her hands over her eyes and sneezed. By the time she rubbed the dust from her face, Dylan had the box open. A pile of well-fingered ledgers sat in one end with cardboard files stacked in the other. Her heart rate increased. Their hands brushed together when they both reached in. Rachel yanked her hand back and waited for Dylan to take out one of the ledgers before she lifted the top file. Photos fell out and scattered over the floor and bed.

'Holy...' Dylan bit off the words when he lifted the first photo and stared at the naked woman lying asleep on a bed with a sheet barely covering the lower part of her body. 'Do you recognise her?' he asked.

'How would I recognise her?' She lifted other photos from the bed and sifted through them. The shock sent waves of horror through her innards. All were of the same woman, some with welts and bruises as though she'd been beaten or viciously raped. And was the red curved line a bite mark? The photos weren't taken on the same day for the bedding changed, nor did it look like the main bedroom of this house. It was a different bedhead and the walls a pale yellow. She didn't know what made her do it, but she turned the photo over to find a date and name: a name she recalled. Laura – the name on one of the DVDs. The date was fairly recent if you counted two years as recent. Horrified, she knelt on the floor, lifted the other photos and dropped them on the bed. When Dylan took out another file and opened it a different woman featured in another set of photos.

'Not all the same woman,' she whispered. It didn't take genius status to figure out what Kyle had been up to. She turned over one of the second lot of photos. Madison. The date was more recent and the same bedroom as the previous woman. She stared at Dylan whose eyes were wide as he took his time to study each photo. 'There are names and dates on the back,' she added.

Dylan turned a photo over and when she saw it, a gasp shot out. It was a man in handcuffs and a long thin trickle of blood down his chest. 'Adam,' said

Dylan. 'Early last year.' He stared at Rachel. 'What the hell does this mean?'

A single word shot into her brain. 'Blackmail?' She had to turn it into a question but she knew.

Dylan's mouth gaped. 'Blackmail?'

'It would explain the other bank account - the money, or most of it. There aren't any photos of Angel or...' she scrabbled through the photos in search of any with Elise on the back.

Dylan must have read her mind for he went through the photos in the files. 'No, there are none.'

'The other files?' Rachel shot up but Dylan beat her to the pile. He brushed her hands away and lifted out the top one.

'No photos but... damn.' He held up a piece of paper.

It only took one glance to know what it was. A threat demanding money. A copy of the original for Kyle to keep as insurance?

'You can't leave these here, Dylan.'

'I can't take them.'

'Call it in. You're still an officer of the law despite working for the courts. Call another officer who can take them. If you don't I will. This has to stop. It's a serious crime and this box is definite evidence. If we leave it here, it will disappear. Kyle knows you've been here. He'll know you found this. Even if he's not sure, he'll get rid of it. He might move it to another place to hide. You can't let him get away with this.'

Dylan grubbed fingers through his hair and sighed long and deep. 'You're right.' He searched his pockets for his phone. 'I put my phone on the kitchen bench. Give me five.'

While he was gone, Rachel shuffled through the photos, horrified by what they depicted, especially those where Kyle was having sex with what appeared to be comatose women. The one of him on Adam, turned her stomach. Was he into men as well? Despite it being wrong to do, she selected two photos of each victim, checked the name was on each and slid them under the elastic of her knickers, glad she'd worn a longish, loose top. What little time she had left, she filtered through the files searching for surnames, contact details, email addresses – anything. Laura Jones – easy to remember until she figured there might be hundreds or thousands with the same name. But at least she had a starting point. Madison Hart. Less of them, so easier to track. 'Adam, Adam, Adam,' she murmured while scanning sheets. Hinkson. Much easier to locate. There can't be hundreds. When another paper had Kelly Barker, she searched through the photos again but couldn't find one. So what did Kelly Barker have to do with this? With the files back in the box, she took out a ledger, opened it when Dylan returned.

'They're sending around a couple of detectives now.' He eyed her. 'What have you found?'

'There's a ledger for each victim. This one has Kelly Barker inside the cover but I couldn't find any photos of her. So I'm not sure what hold Kyle had over her but he's got monthly amounts of $2,000 for two years. Dates indicate it began four years ago.'

'Might have been similar to Angel. A girlfriend who could have lived in.'

'Or wife. Was the recent marriage legitimate?'

'Why wouldn't it be?'

'Well, with the dual passports and birth certificates in different names – is Kyle a genuine name? God, I hope it's not legit.'

'The name or the marriage?'

'The marriage. Or both if it means the same thing.' She indicated the photos. 'There are a lot of disgusting images there. Kyle is one sick maniac. And I thought his only sin was being a serious coercive controller but this… this…' she didn't know what to call it. 'This goes beyond simple coercive control. He has to be a money hungry psychopath.'

'And a narcissist, if I take into account the way he was dressed this morning. Did you notice the sock when he got back?'

'You noticed.' Rachel struggled to prevent a burst of laughter.

'Impossible not to. I was so tempted to point it out to him.'

'I wish you had.'

He put everything back in the box. 'Let's get this packed away. Have you checked the other cupboard for any more shocking revelations?'

'I'm not game to.' But she opened the final wardrobe door and blew out a long breath when it was empty. 'No more clothes. I need to get out of here. I can't get those images out of my head. I'll let you pack this box up.' She took off and hurried to the lounge where she removed the photos from her knickers and slid them in a side pocket of her bag, glad it was huge. Never again would she complain about the amount of gear one had to cart around for a tiny human. Overcome, she dropped onto the divan and closed her eyes, desperate for relief from a churning brain.

Images flashed, brain cells quivered and shook, desperate to get a message out; one she couldn't put her finger on. She was missing something important. Fingers massaged her temples while her breathing eased. When it came to her, she bolted upright. Printed photos had to have a source. 'Dylan,' she yelled as she jogged to the office and began another search of the desk drawers. There had to be a camera.

'What is it?' The voice arrived before the body.

'Photos, camera. There has to be a camera. Check his mobile for the images. Although he'd be stupid to leave them so exposed. She turned to the top drawer, pulled it open, scanned the contents – no. Second drawer – no – but. Her fingers hovered over a bundle of flash drives she'd dismissed before because they were normal office supplies. She stilled while Dylan leant against the desk with his back to her. As surreptitious as she could, she turned over the top flash drive in case there were any words on the tiny label. This made more sense than old-fashioned DVDs. The words were small but she made out a capital A. Making out she was searching she bent lower and read Angel. Dear God. Eyes closed; she forced her lungs to work. Even though she didn't want to know what was written on the next one, she flipped it over, bent low and read – Elise. Damn, damn, damn. A quick glance at Dylan. He was immersed in the phone. With one hand, she used two fingers to scoop the two drives into her palm and used the other to pick up the rest. Side on to Dylan, she slipped the two she wanted into her jeans' pocket and made sure her top hung over the slight bulge before pushing the drawer shut and turning to Dylan.

'This might be what we need.' She flung the other drives onto the desk. They skidded across and scattered in an arc in front of him as he straightened and turned around. 'You could try them in the computer but there still has to be either a camera or a sim card for him to have printed the photos.' Overcome, she flopped to the floor and sat with her knees drawn up and wrapped her arms around them. Head down, she heard the creak of the chair, the press of a button, the hiss of the computer and click of a flash drive being slid into place. She could visualise Dylan's actions while he logged on and opened files. The swear word wasn't unexpected.

'I assume it's the photos,' she said without lifting her head.

'Yes. More than what has been printed. The first ones seem to be normal everyday shots of the same person in various locations. The type you take of your family and friends.' There was silence apart from barely there taps of a key. 'The later photos are similar to the printed copies. It doesn't make sense.'

'How many people?'

Flash drives were turned over. 'Six.'

'Laura, Madison, Adam, Kelly,' she reeled off. 'Angel and Elise,' she added despite knowing they weren't there.

'No, not the last two. Ethan and Jordan.'

'Two more with no printed photos, or at least, none we found.' She sighed and lifted her head. 'I don't want to know any more details but the flash drives can't stay here. This is real evidence, although it's not what we were looking for. This is worse, much, much worse.'

'Did you know about any of this? I mean, you know more than me. You have been researching this guy.'

'No way. All I've researched are the features of coercive and abusive control and how the traits fit him and are related to what happened nine months ago. The thirst for money fits but with him, it could be the reason behind the control. I had no idea about any of this... this... I don't know what to call it apart from sick.

'Sergeant,' a loud voice yelled.

Rachel waved Dylan away. 'Your friends are here. I'll look for more clothes.'

After a thorough hunt, Rachel couldn't find any more clothes in the house so went downstairs to the underground garage and stood in front of the workbench that ran all the way along the rear wall. She shook her head at the grease-laden pink cotton blouse. Obviously one of the items he complained about. Three more women's garments, now filthy, were piled at the end of the bench and an oily pair of women's jeans was draped over the oxy-acetylene gas bottles. It appeared Kyle figured they were so unappealing he used them as oil rags. The message received meant there was no point to continue the hunt for more clothes. With a shrug, she took her time to turn in a circle to study the walls, benches and shelves in the search for any item listed. A few cobwebs crept from tiny dark crevices, which seemed odd for the office had been overly neat. Satisfied there were no more items, or at least, none of importance, she climbed the internal steps to the small landing between kitchen and laundry.

Voices drew her to the study where three men were bent over the desk with photographs spread over the surface. Reluctant to join the quiet mumbles or set her eyes on the sick pictures again, she stood inside the doorway. Dylan must have noticed for he glanced up.

'Come in. This is Detective Sergeant Justin Smith and Detective Constable Rick Thomas.'

Both men nodded. Rachel stepped closer, peered at the desk and turned her head. The photos were too gross.

'Has he penetrated this guy or is it a staged act?' asked one voice.

Shocked, Rachel turned back. 'Could these be pretend acts?'

Dylan frowned. 'Not sure, it's hard to tell but there's something not right about the set-up. About Kyle's face and position. They give the impression of being staged.'

The constable picked up one of the photos and studied it closer. There was a frown on his face. 'I've figured it out.'

'What?' the other two men said at the same time.

'If he's in the photos – who took the pictures?'

'Oh, God.' Rachel stepped back. 'Surely there weren't two people involved. How sick can they be?'

'I don't think there were two.' The constable lifted a few more photos and lined them up next to each other. 'Look at the angle.'

Four heads bent over. The bed was in the exact same place in each shot. The linen was different to indicate they were taken at different times. And the bed was different in a couple, which made sense because there had been a different bed in a different house before the marriage and the bed was changed in this house after the marriage. Dylan turned his head and focussed on the ceiling. 'There had to be a hidden camera in the ceiling.' He eyed Rachel and left the room.

They all followed to the main bedroom and studied the pendulous three-globe light fitting hanging from an ornate ceiling rose. Rachel's gut heaved at the sight of the spaces in the carved plasterwork. She had to gulp down rising bile when nausea rose at the same speed her brow became covered in a cold sweat. Surely not. There couldn't be.

'I'll get a ladder,' she heard Dylan say through a wave of mist in her brain.

Unable to move, she sank to the floor and leant against the wall next to the door. There was a hubbub while the men searched for a manhole, set a ladder underneath and the constable disappeared into the ceiling space. Scrapes and thumps echoed in the room.

'Found it. It's a sophisticated set-up. Could be remote controlled or attached to an electrical controller. I'll take photos before we touch it.'

The muffled comments didn't ease her tension but increased it.

'Hand me gloves,' she heard when she was game to lift her eyes and shuffled on her backside to the door. The other two men stood either side of the ladder, both with a hand on the aluminium uprights. Their eyes were honed onto the small square hole in the passage ceiling. It amazed her how something so insignificant your never took notice of it, now loomed with dread.

It took ages of footsteps, muffled comments and yelled orders before the officer emerged, handed down a camera into another pair of latex covered hands and his feet descended to the ground where he shook off dust and cobwebs.

The men left everything there, stepped past her and entered the office, which, she now noted, had a similar ceiling rose. Dylan fiddled with the camera, removed the sim card and slid it into a slot on the side of the computer. Buttons were pressed, the mouse moved and the three men crowded behind the screen.

Rachel wanted to look but couldn't. She caught Dylan's eye.

He mouthed, 'Angel.'

'Are they as bad as the others?' she dared ask.

'Yes. I'm pretty sure she is comatose. She wouldn't have known.'

'Doesn't make it any better. In fact it's worse.'

'In one sense, yes but since we found this before he could blackmail her, it makes it a heap better,' said the sergeant.

Dylan's finger kept pressing on a key. Rachel bet it was an arrow key, bringing up photo after photo. All of a sudden he stopped, swore and slammed down the computer lid.

'Hey, we haven't finished.' The constable went to lift the lid.

Dylan stopped him. 'Yes we have for now. I know both of these women. The first one is Angel, the woman who was here this morning. At the moment, I'd say she is in a world of pain after finding out the truth about this piece of scum. The other one is Elise, his wife. I know her well from her court appearance. Since I know her, I want to be the one who informs her about this. Both women have been through hell, especially Elise. This will devastate both women so let me break it to them.' He eyed Rachel. 'There is an upside. Since we found this before any photos could be printed, they can't be used for blackmail and will never get printed.'

Rachel scrambled up and stood on rubbery legs determined to not hold her upright. The two flash drives she'd filched told her a different story. It was more than possible the photos had been downloaded. Will I or won't I, yo-yoed in her head. But so far there were no photos so it was possible they hadn't been printed. No, she'd keep the flash drives secret until she'd had a chance to study them. 'Are you sure there aren't any prints?'

'We've been through all of those files and haven't found any, so I'm pretty certain. The fact Elise disappeared and he hasn't been able to find her could mean he didn't make any prints until he could blackmail her. I'm surprised he didn't turn up in court because he would have been able to pinpoint her location.'

'From what I heard him say this morning, he figured the case wouldn't go ahead if he wasn't there,' said Rachel.

'True, but he could still have hidden outside in the hope he could follow her.'

'Do you think he did?'

'I can't say for certain but he hasn't turned up at her place and she was well disguised when she left the courthouse. As for Angel, we caught him before his relationship with her ended. Another four weeks and it would have been too late.' Dylan stood with his hand still on the closed lid. 'There is enough evidence here to arrest the man.' He twisted to face the other two officers. 'I suggest we freeze the million dollar bank account as it's obvious the money in it is ill-gotten gains. At least it can be frozen until we have evidence to the contrary but I doubt we'll find any.'

'What about his other account?' asked Sergeant Smith.

Dylan screwed his mouth. 'Too me, it looks like a normal account. His pay goes in, everyday amounts come out. Let's keep it active so we can trace where he goes. It will make it easier to catch him. He'll need money to live. If we freeze it, he might resort to more blackmail or other criminal activity to get cash. I doubt he'll return here tonight. He might but would be insane if he did. It depends on how desperate he is to get his hands on this camera. He might figure it's his best hope of extortion since he must know we would find evidence in the filing cabinet and he knows we've searched it. None of it was well hidden – well, except for the camera.'

'We need this sim card for evidence.' The constable tapped the computer.

'Not yet. Let me speak with the women first. There is more than enough evidence with everything else to get an arrest warrant. This man has to be stopped – now. You guys take all of these photos, copied paperwork and flash drives. I'll take the items under the court order. I suggest you get an arrest warrant ASAP. Jacobs knows where Angel lives and works. She might need protection. And Jacobs is in this area at the moment. Or he was earlier.'

An idea flashed into Rachel's head. 'The detectives can take the two passports and birth certificates as well.'

When two frowned faces eyed her, Rachel gave all the details. 'They are in the bottom drawer of the desk.'

'What about the wife?' asked the constable on the way to the door to retrieve the documents.

'She's safe for the moment. Jacobs doesn't know what she looks like now nor where she lives. I'll deal with her. The fewer people who know any details, the better.'

He took the sim card from the computer and dropped it into the top pocket of his shirt. 'Okay, I'm done here.' He turned to Rachel. 'Ring Olivia. I'll drop you off at the hotel in…' he glanced at his watch. 'Forty minutes.'

'I know you aren't asleep so it's no good pretending.' Dylan placed his hand over the lower part of Rachel's arm and gave a gentle squeeze. 'We need to talk.'

At the touch, her heart hammered against her ribs and she yanked her arm away. 'No we don't.' It was true they did but too difficult – too embarrassing. She kept her head turned towards the side window with her eyes shut. Outside, the breeze whooshed, the tyres hummed, passing engines whirred and revved but she couldn't look.

'Yes, we do. Before we get to the hotel.' He shook her arm.

The sudden touch sent her heart rate into the stratosphere. With a long sigh of regret about how sudden touches scared her, she straightened in the passenger seat but couldn't face him. 'Thank you,' she said when she couldn't think of any other way to begin a conversation.

'For what?'

'For hiding the other pictures from the guys. Was it as bad as the others?'

'No, but I only saw one and you are welcome.'

'Kyle drugged them all?'

'I'm certain, yes. And I asked the D's to search for a stash.'

'What sort?'

'Not sure. Could be Rohypnol or a simple sedative. There are others. A sedative would leave residual after-effects. Rohypnol causes the victim to not remember. The guys will do a more thorough search of the filing cabinet, office, house and the garage in particular. They will take every scrap of evidence. With a woman in the house, it's unlikely the hiding place will be in any of the cupboards used for everyday living. But there has to be drugs hidden close enough for him to get his hands on it at a moment's notice.'

'Could be hidden at his place of work or his car.'

'True. I'll suggest it to them.'

'Anything else?'

'They put a stop on the hidden account before we left and there's now an arrest warrant. I wish I'd arrested him this morning when I had a chance.'

'At the time we didn't know the extent of his evil.'

'No.'

'What are you going to do with the sim card?'

'I will keep hold of it for as long as I can. There should be more than enough evidence without it. Only if it becomes essential will I use it.'

'Please don't. You're going to look at the rest aren't you?'

'No, I promise.'

'Then let me have it.'

'I can't. You'll have to trust me.'

Rachel snorted. 'My ability to trust was stolen from me months ago. I trust no one apart from myself.'

'I understand but when I make a promise I do my utmost to keep it and I promise. You trusted me today.'

'I didn't have a lot of choice but I trust you more than anyone else at the moment, well, apart from family. And since I do trust you, I need to own up to something. I kept the original Title Deed and house insurance papers. Those in the filing cabinet are the copies. You can tell because the image is slightly skewed.' She winced at Dylan's curse. 'I took them on the spur of the moment because the house isn't in his name and it was the only redeeming feature of this entire ordeal. I knew you wouldn't let me take them but to me, it was the right thing to do because it could be while before this mess is cleared up. There are bound to be more long-winded court cases. The research needed will take months. With the Title not in his name the house can be sold straight away, the money used as part restitution. Angel has paid half the loan repayments for several months. She's entitled to get her money back. No amount of money will make up for the trauma he's caused.'

'He could argue the point how he's paid the mortgage for the past two years.'

'With whose money? I can prove it wasn't all his and there's the initial deposit with paperwork to prove the bank cheque didn't come from his account.'

'I thought all the paperwork would have been in the filing cabinet.'

'His, yes. Mine, no. Do you honestly think he'll take it to court when there's an arrest warrant for him? Although he doesn't know about it yet does he?'

'No.'

'Which means he's still likely to be drifting around town. He might have gone to work but I doubt it. At a guess, I'd say he kept an eye on the comings and goings of the house. He might go back there tonight.'

'He'd be an idiot if he does. The D's are going to have a patrol car checking it out overnight.'

'Yes, well he is an idiot, although a fairly smart one if you take into account how long he's got away with these ghastly crimes. With what we discovered today, he might chance it to retrieve all the evidence of his criminal life because he doesn't know what we found. He has to know we searched the filing cabinet because Angel had the wedding folder but he can't possibly know we found the other items. He'll want the camera for sure. And the flash drives. Definitely the photos. The passport would be handy to leave the country and there are his clothes. The furniture left was crap so I doubt he would care about it, especially if he's got well over a million dollars to start up again. Which reminds me…' Rachel lifted her hips and wriggled her fingers into the left hand side pocket of her jeans. She held up the two bankcards and paused before she checked them. 'I've still got his cards but I'm sure he has a credit card as well. It wasn't in his wallet. Both of these are debit cards from savings accounts.' And she had the house keys but wasn't going to mention them. Nor the five one-hundred-dollar bills she'd removed from his wallet. The bastard owed her more than a measly five hundred.

Dylan took the cards. 'I'm not sure what to do with these. I'll give them to the D's.'

'What happens with the stuff we took today? I know about the furniture.'

'I take it to court to finalise the paperwork and after the judge okays it, all the items will be released. It will be a private meeting between the judge and me. There's no court time involved so it should be cleared by the end of next week.

'At last. It's been a long traumatic haul.'

'The D's will want to contact you. Can I give them your email and phone number? I said I would ask.'

'Can I trust them? I hate to say this but not all cops are as honest as you. They dismissed me nine months ago. Weren't concerned. As far as I know, they didn't interview Kyle about my injuries or the events. They spoke to him about Chris's injuries, which got swept under the carpet with nothing more than a slap on the wrist and a warning to not ever do it again. Which is why I did my own research.'

'You sound bitter.'

'Hell, yes but more furious than bitter. So you can understand why I don't trust cops, especially of the male variety. Therefore, no phone number and nor my address. If they want to make an appointment, they can email me. An email won't lead to my whereabouts. If it is urgent, they can phone you and you can ring me – but no-one else.'

'Fair enough. I understand. Where do you want me to drop you off?'

'Drive into the underground carpark. I can take the lift to my floor without entering through the front. He could have followed Olivia.'

'Why would he?'

'Because she's my sister-in-law and he would want to find out where I am. She has spotted him lurking near their house over the past few months.'

'Have you visited your brother since leaving town?' Dylan turned on the indicator, paused to wait for a car and turned onto the hotel drive.

'Are you kidding? Of course not. I've only been back for the court hearing and today. I learned my lesson. Isn't there an old saying about fool me once? I was fooled – in the worst way and the lesson I learnt was harsh. It won't happen again.' Rachel had to blink at the sudden darkness when they went underground. The car swept around a wide curve and slowed.

'Where's your car?' Dylan drew to a stop as close to the elevator door as he could get.

'I borrowed a different car.'

'Why?' The word echoed in the sudden silence when the motor ceased running.

'None of the licence plates here can be linked to me.'

Dylan twisted around to face her with raised eyebrows. 'You're terrified, aren't you?'

'Wouldn't you be? I can't take any chances he'll find me, especially now I've got Madeleine.'

'Does he know about her?'

'What do you mean?'

'He's the father.'

Rachel squirmed. 'Says who?'

'I'm good at maths.'

Rachel didn't like the wry twist of his mouth. 'The father was listed as unknown on the birth certificate despite the arguments on how I couldn't do it.'

'He could demand a DNA test. A judge would order it.'

'Only if he's told about the possibility otherwise he'll never know Madeleine exists.'

'What about Madeleine? She has a right to know who her father is.'

'When she's an adult I might tell her. It depends.'

'On what?'

'The list is long. How mature she is, what happens to him - criminal-wise, whether he's still alive at the time. If he's not, it will be easier. If he's alive, I don't want her to ever seek him out. She doesn't deserve such evil. And if I had listed his name – who is he? There are two birth certificates and two passports. Which one is true? Are either of them true? If he's changed his identity once, who's to say he hasn't done it before? We may never know his true identity. Fate has dealt me a plus by not naming him because any name I wrote could have been false.'

'You've thought hard about this.'

'My brain hasn't had any rest for over nine months.' Her phone dinged. 'I have to go. Olivia's here.' She opened the door, reached over the back to get her bag. 'Thank you for today and for believing in me.' She wriggled out.

'I always believed you and thank you for trusting me. I won't let you down. Keep in touch and remember, if you ever need me, you have my private number.' He nodded and turned on the engine.

As Rachel waved, the scratch of tears swept over her eyes. To make sure they hadn't been followed, she searched the area but spied nothing other than parked cars and none of them were bright yellow. A quick stab on the elevator button and she stood facing the cars until the doors swished open. While the doors swept shut, she kept her eyes on the car park.

On the fifth floor, the elevator doors opened to reveal Olivia leant against the wall opposite, Madeleine asleep in her arms. Rachel's heart and innards hitched when she spotted her precious daughter. The baby capsule, purple suitcase and huge bag of baby necessities sat on the floor at Olivia's feet. Eager for a cuddle, Rachel hoisted her bag over one shoulder and reached out for her princess. It was impossible to describe the sensation that swept over her every time she held her baby. Every atom in her body heated up and exploded with a tingling warmth. 'How has she been? She must be hungry again.'

'After I got home, we played for a while, she slept and woke with a choice nappy after which we played for another ten minutes. When she became grumpy I tried the bottle again. She drank half a bottle and fell asleep. She's such a good baby. You're lucky. My Jess suffered with gripe for months.' Olivia picked up the things from the floor. 'How did it go today?'

With one hand, Rachel searched for the hotel keycard and opened the door with the help of a shove from Olivia's backside. 'Better in one sense, much worse in another.' It was impossible an intruder would be in the room but an ingrained habit meant she searched the interior with her eyes to ensure no one else was there before game to step inside. Happy, she dropped her bag on the bed and settled into the only armchair in the basic single hotel room although it was larger than what she had become used to.

'What do you mean?' Olivia followed and placed all the baby gear on the floor by the door before wheeling in the suitcase. She filled the electric jug with water, turned it on, tore a coffee satchel apart and popped a tea bag into the other mug for Rachel.

'Drinks first,' said Rachel as she dropped her eyes to see two blue eyes stare back. 'Hello, precious girl.' Two tiny arms jerked around at the same time Madeleine turned her head in search of food. It was as though she was saying *at last, where have you been*. A wave of guilt swept over Rachel but she laughed to dispel it, lifted the hem of her top and opened her bra. A satisfied sigh escaped at the tug on her breast with the sensation shooting to her inner core.

Refreshments made, Rachel related the day's discoveries while they sipped and Madeleine filled her tiny tummy. After a change of nappy, Rachel asked if Olivia would help her carry all the belongings to her car.

'Are you going home today? I thought you were staying overnight.'

'I was but we finished early. It's a four hour drive. If I leave now I'll be home not long after dark. To be honest, I don't want to hang around when I don't have to.'

'I hate how you have to hide so far away but understand.' Olivia reached out. 'Here, let me cuddle my gorgeous niece while you get your things together.

Soon, I hope, you can return to the city to live so we can catch up more often.'

'Now there's an arrest warrant out for the slimy bastard, it might not be long.' With few items to pack, it took mere minutes before Rachel settled a now sleeping baby in the capsule, shoved all of her gear in her capacious bag and hooked it over her shoulder. Olivia grabbed Madeleine's larger bag of gear and wheeled the suitcase into the passage.

Rachel handed Olivia the door keycard. 'I've paid up. Can you drop the key off and let them know I've gone? I don't want to go anywhere near the entry.'

'Sure, but why would he be hanging around? He doesn't know you're here and wouldn't recognise you in any case with your wig and different coloured lenses. I barely recognise you.'

Rachel flicked the shoulder-length dark brown waves. 'I can't take any chances, especially after what we discovered today.' After a good search of the area, she pressed the elevator button. It took too long to arrive. Once inside and the doors were shut, her nerves relaxed until they reached the carpark when they twanged tight again while the door swished open. It was always the same no matter where she was: the fear of Kyle being there when she opened a door or went around a corner. Despite Olivia's presence, the entire time it took to buckle in the capsule and load the car, her head jerked around in every direction. Ready to go, she relished in the long hug with Olivia before she folded into the driver's seat and double-checked the doors were locked before turning on the engine. Olivia waved and went through the door to the reception area while Rachel took her time to reverse out and swing around.

Before driving off, she blew out her cheeks and studied every car for signs of human presence as she crawled past each vehicle. Before driving out in the open, she paused and studied the opening. Two people walked past, a man and a child of about six. Not Kyle. Another hauled in lungful of air. She drove to the entry, out onto the wide hotel driveway where she had to wait for the traffic before edging onto the road. A glance right – clear. A glance left – she swore. Kyle had Olivia bailed up. A car beeped from behind. God, what could she do? With no choice but to leave, she drove out, turned right onto the road and went around the next corner where she pulled onto the verge and rang Olivia.

'Are you okay?' she asked when Olivia answered.

'Yes.'

'Has he gone?'

'No.'

'Does he want to know where I am?'

'Yes.'

'I'm going to give you words to say. You repeat them aloud. Do you understand?'

'Yes.'

'Here goes. Repeat exactly. Hi, Sergeant.'

'Hi, Sergeant.'

'Is there anything else you want me to confirm?'

'Is there anything else you want me to confirm?'

'Oh, there's an arrest warrant for him. Well, Sergeant, he's right here in front of the City Park Hotel.' Rachel stilled while Olivia repeated the last sentence.

'He's running across the road. Thank you. It worked. Go, go, go,' Olivia yelled.

With her heart like a yoyo, Rachel dropped the phone in the console and planted her foot, too scared to linger, desperate to get clear of the city centre. Both side mirrors and the rear-vision mirror were scanned on a continuous roundabout while she took back streets until she reached the main highway south, umpteen suburbs from the hotel. Her nerves didn't ease off and the tension in her stomach remained taut to the extent nausea became a concern, which was ridiculous because she hadn't eaten any solid food since the early breakfast before sun-up.

After an hour she turned on the radio and searched for a station with classical music to help ease strung-out nerves. Another thirty minutes and the tension returned when a thick dark band of leaden clouds appeared from where she wanted to be and were headed her way. Within mere minutes the first spatters hit the windshield. The further she drove, the more insistent the downpour with the wipers soon unable to cope. It became impossible to see the side of the road or more than a few metres ahead for the next thirty minutes. Madeleine must have sensed the tension for she woke with a squeal and let loose with a continuous wail. Nerves stretched tight enough to snap, Rachel slowed to half the regulated speed for the next fifty kilometres and huffed out a sigh of relief when she spied the lights of a service station through the sheet of water. Since it was a suicide mission to keep driving, she turned onto the drive of the station and hunted for a vacant parking bay near the entry. The nearest was so far away they would both be drenched by the time she got them inside.

Instead, she unbuckled her seatbelt, twisted around on her knees and eased the screaming, red-faced baby from the safety capsule. Baby and blanket in hand, she twisted back around and put Madeleine over her shoulder to calm her. It took several minutes before a loud belch erupted in Rachel's ear and Madeleine gradually quietened to gulps and sniffles. It took another thirty minutes of play before the downpour eased off enough, Rachel was game to go inside. She not only needed food but a full bladder kept pressing the message it had to be emptied. The only way she could manage was with Madeleine back in the capsule, which she could unbuckle and carry.

Inside was brightly lit with strong whiffs of coffee, fried food and wet clothes. It appeared she wasn't the only one to seek safety from the deluge. At least she was a lot drier than many of the crowd although her cheap canvas shoes squelched at each step. There had been so much water on the ground in the carpark, it had been impossible to avoid it. Her empty stomach rumbled with pleasure at the aromas but a visit to the conveniences was first on the agenda.

She stayed only long enough to buy a steakburger with the lot and a cardboard mug of black tea. The entire time she was inside, she searched the crowd for any sign of a person she never wanted to lay eyes on again. Now he knew there was an arrest warrant for him, he wouldn't hang around the city. But would he go south? Or would he hide away long enough to go back to the house and remove the incriminating evidence? She bet on him staying for the night. What he'd hidden in the house was way too damning. For sure, he'd want to get the camera and flash drives.

Back in the car, she settled Madeleine to her breast for a top-up while she wolfed the steakburger and listened to the music she'd turned low to barely there in the hope it would lull Madeleine to sleep. The burger was so darn good she fingered up the escapee strands of lettuce, carrot and grated cheese. It wasn't until Madeleine slept, Rachel buckled her into the capsule and reversed from her parking spot. The sight of the petrol pumps reminded her to glance at the fuel gauge where the red arrow was too close to the empty mark to take the risk of not getting fuel. It took several manoeuvring tactics to park next to a pump in the direction the arrows indicated before she could get out and unhitch the hose. The reek of fumes tickled her sinuses while she studied the rainbow colours of oil spreading on the water of the saturated concrete. It was pleasant to relive the aromas of coffee and food while she was inside again to pay.

Music accompanied her while she continued the journey, taking sips of the hot tea as she drove along still wet roads, strewn with an extraordinary amount of debris but at least the rain had stopped. Too scared to speed on the slippery bitumen, cars passed her in both directions, their lights reflecting in a shimmer from the black surface. The trees turned pitch black against the setting sun but dusk brought the danger of kangaroos so she slowed more, glad she did when a mob of five bounded across the road less than ten metres in front of her. Her heart beat like bongo drums as she veered onto the verge and came to a standstill to prevent any following cars from ramming up her backside. With her head resting on the steering wheel, she studied the bush and yes, there it was, another roo bounded across the road in a frantic race to catch the others. Most Aussies who lived in the bush, had experienced this tailender enough times to be cautious. Emus were worse. After the roo had disappeared into the dark underbrush, she gave her racing heart a chance to calm before she dared to ease back onto the road and continue south.

Instead of the four hours it usually took for the journey, she pulled in front of her motel unit at the five hour mark. Storm detritus was strewn over the entire area in front of the all the buildings, puddles abounded and water dripped from overhanging branches of the line of mature trees across the front of the car park. There would be a major cleanup in the morning.

The relief was intense while she unpacked the car, fed Madeleine and settled her in the cot. Despite exhaustion, a shower was needed. In the bathroom, she took out the coloured lenses, yanked off the wig and shook her short mousy hair in a frenzy to rid it of the constraint of being plastered to her head all day. Though she was desperate to hunt for details of the other victims, after a long warm shower, she fell into bed, pulled the covers around her shoulders and begged for oblivion but it was a long time coming for she was nervous and edgy, with a cacophony of ideas racing through her mind so fast they became all jumbled up and made no sense. There was one thing she was determined to see through. She would do everything in her power to ensure all the victims were paid back the money they were owed as some form of redemption. Money didn't ease the mental trauma but it was one tiny spark of relief.

First on the agenda after the early morning baby rituals of a fun bath and feed, was to drive the car she'd borrowed around the back and park it in front of the owner's residence. In the light of day, the mess outside was a lot worse than she'd envisioned the night before. The storm had been, caused chaos and gone, leaving behind torn branches from tiny to humungous, scattered everywhere, thousands of mushy leaves, huge puddles, piles of mud and now a clear sky made a mockery of the mess. Her own car could stay where it was, parked behind the main motel building and now in need of a good clean. It gave the impression of being an abandoned vehicle that had been sitting there for years, there was so much crap covering it. Even if Kyle did come, he wouldn't recognise the car as hers and it wasn't registered in her name.

Since she had the day off from work, she unpacked the suitcase and sorted all the snaffled items, lining them up on the bed to study and figure out which to research first. The clothes held no interest for, now she had them, she wasn't sure if she ever wanted to wear any of the garments again. In a few months' time she might consider it but not while Kyle was on the prowl for he would recognise most since they were the garments he urged her to buy and wear – idiot she had been to succumb to his bullyboy tactics. She sure knew better now: knew the signs to look for and avoid in the future. As if she ever wanted to get close to a man again.

A good pair of sneakers caught her eye. She could sure use them since her soggy canvas shoes were dripping upside down in the shower cubicle, and the underwear would come in handy now her tummy had shrunk to her pre-pregnancy shape. Having to work within days of the birth had ensured she got the exercise needed to work off baby excess. The rest of the clothes got zipped back into the case, which she stood on its end in the narrow wardrobe of her single room. Soon, she prayed, she would be able to rent a decent home. Joy swept through her innards at the idea. Even better was the thought that when the house she now knew belonged to her, was sold and the small loan paid out, she could buy a new home. Nothing large: two bedrooms would be enough although a third to use as an office and store room would be better. A back yard was essential. One big enough for a vegetable patch, and shady lawn for Madeleine to play on. Visions of pretty properties swept through her mind until a knock on the door brought her back to the here and now.

'Rachel, are you there?'

It was a pleasure to hear the voice of her boss; the woman who had taken Rachel under her wing, given her a job and a place to stay all those months ago after she'd been released from hospital and climbed aboard the first bus out of the city. At the time she didn't much care where she ended up as long as it was at the end of the line for the city to country bus. It had pulled up in front of the tourist bureau in the strip mall across the road. All the passengers alighted, collected their luggage and dispersed, leaving Rachel under the portico with the small bag of essentials Olivia had gathered for her in a hurry, at her feet. At the time she felt like a lone survivor marooned on an uninhabited island without a clue as to what she was supposed to do. With hunger pangs etching at her stomach, she had crossed the road at the invitation of the lit up café sign over the door of the eatery attached to the motel.

Knock, knock. 'Rachel.'

'Coming.' Even though she knew it was Ella, Rachel peeked through a crack in the always drawn curtain at the small front window. It was a habit she was too scared to break. Ella was the only person who knew Rachel's real identity, a necessity for the legalities of her pay and taxes. Certain it was only Ella outside Rachel opened the door. 'Hi.'

'You're back early. You said you wouldn't be home until tonight.'

Home, Rachel's mind shot back to the pretty property. Who calls a motel room home? A sigh escaped before she could come up with an answer for Ella. 'We didn't take as long as I predicted. Thank you for your car. It was a brilliant idea of yours.'

'How did it go?'

'I'll tell you later. During lunch if you have the time.'

'I won't have time to breathe today, which is one of the reasons I'm here now. Do you want a shift in the kitchen today? Nate's house received storm damage last night so he won't be in.'

'I need a moment. I've got a lot to process and with what we found…'

'I wouldn't ask if I wasn't desperate. How about half a shift? Four hours to get us through the lunch rush.'

'Only in the kitchen? No serving?'

'You're still scared?'

'More so after what we discovered. Kyle is one sick maniac and he's on the loose although there is now an arrest warrant for him.'

'I wish I had time to talk. Will you do eleven to three?'

Rachel owed this woman more than she could ever repay. 'Okay, as long as I can park Madeleine in the kitchen.'

Ella surged forward and gave Rachel a tight hug. 'Of course. Thank you. I owe you one. Now I have to hurry to get the clean-up crew to work.' She turned and half-walked, half-ran towards the motel reception where she usually sat in an office.

Rachel sighed again and closed the door. Until now, the day had been a perfect opportunity to research. And poor Madeleine deserved one-on-one time. A quick glance at the clock told her it was only eight. Three hours to fill. Her eyes travelled over the piles of evidence before landing on the cot where a swaddled Madeleine lay on her back, pink-cheeked and eyes closed. A warm fuzzy enveloped Rachel at the sight. She crept over, tugged up the soft blanket and pressed a light kiss on Madeleine's brow. 'You're seven weeks old today, precious girl. The only good thing in my life for close on two years.'

Back at the bed, Rachel dismissed the DVD's because she would have to hunt for a player to look at them. Instead, she picked up the two flash drives she'd stolen and played Eenie, Meanie, Miney Mo between left hand and right; even though the outcome was obvious. At her new laptop on the bench under the window, she sat, closed her eyes, blew all the air from her lungs and slid the flash drive into its slot. Her thumbs twiddled while she waited for the system to warm up and open. The arrow appeared. She clicked on USB Drive (D:) and sent a prayer skywards asking if the over-confident Kyle was so arrogant, he never password protected any files the same way they were unprotected on his home computer. The Elise flash drive opened to a page of yellow folders. There had to be twenty of them. Nerves twitched and her pointer finger shook as it hovered over the first folder.

A wail filled the air. Rachel swore before a nervous laugh shuddered out as she went to retrieve Madeleine, who must sense a bad vibe.

'What is it, precious girl? You can't be hungry.' She lifted the squirming bundle from the cot and held Madeleine against her shoulder with one hand gently rubbing the tiny back. When the warm head snuffled into Rachel's neck, every atom in her body jiggled in pleasure. If only she could spend every minute of each day, holding this precious gift. The cries slowed; the body relaxed. Rachel eased her baby into her arms and was rewarded with a smile. 'Cheeky girl, all you want is attention. Okay, play time.' Relieved to be doing anything other than open the folder, she spread out a thick rug on the floor, gently unwrapped the baby blanket, placed Madeleine in the middle and used her foot to drag over a plastic box of toys. With so little space in the room, no item was far away.

'Who wants to look at creepy flash drives in any case?' she added as she shook a multi-coloured caterpillar in front of Madeleine who kicked her legs, waved her arms and gave another smile to the fabric creature.

It was thirty minutes of pure delight before Madeleine's eyes drooped and Rachel could put her back into the cot.

Back at the bench, she tapped the mouse to open the page and stared at the computer for a minute or two, too scared to open a folder. A snack and drink sounded a far better option so she made a mug of black tea and tore open a muesli bar. Back in the chair, she chewed and sipped until both drink and food were gone.

'Stop procrastinating. Get it over with,' she ordered and grabbed the mouse. In one swift movement, she clicked on the first folder and gasped when a photo was revealed.

Elbows on the bench she dropped her chin into her hands and stared. The photo was of her and Olivia at a swanky dinner. 'But this was over three years ago,' she said in shock. She hadn't even met Kyle. So how? Why? Memories surged. She had accompanied Olivia to the function because her brother, Pierre, had been called to the south of France to finalise the sale of their father's property. Rachel had agreed to go as Olivia's partner because the tickets had been pricey – too expensive to forfeit the function. So how did Kyle get a photo of the two of them and why? They'd both hired swish evening gowns for the night since neither possessed such formal wear. She peered at the photo and noticed the jewellery they both wore. The necklaces and bracelets looked expensive but were of the fake variety since neither woman wanted to spend umpteen thousands of dollars on items they'd never wear again. Sure, they both had a few precious mementos, like the pieces Kyle stole, but none were worth more than a few hundred dollars. Well, her engagement ring might be worth more, and she'd never wear it again. Especially after it had also been given to Angel. Second-hand goods now. More like third-hand. There was a type of creepy vibe about it. Who would wear such an item again? Not her. A wave of shivers swept across her shoulders. Since the price of gold had gone up so much, it might be a good idea to have the ring pulled apart and the gold, along with her wedding ring, could be sold to the mint. The money would come in handy. Her heart hummed in pleasure at the idea and pressed on the next photo in the file.

The same night. They were about to get into Olivia's car to drive home. Puzzled, Rachel clicked again and swore. There she was in front of her unit, waving to Olivia after she'd been dropped off. There was only one person who could have taken these photos because they weren't taken by the function photographer.

Click. This time it was Olivia getting out of her car after she'd arrived home. Rachel sat back and trolled through her grey matter in an effort to make head or tail of why Kyle had followed them. A picture flashed. The DVD with Olivia's name. Still unable to figure it out, she clicked through all the photos in the file. An inkling came when there was a photo of Olivia with Pierre after he'd arrived home from France and there were no more of Olivia. But there were plenty of Rachel near her workplace, at the shops, in front of her unit and in various eateries. And she had a suspicion they were all taken within weeks of each other. She opened the second file and clicked through the photos. More of her outside her home, workplace, the library and various eateries and shops. All before she'd met the man. It took a bit of shuffling through her brain until she figured these were taken during the week after the first lot. She scanned the third file. Definitely the following week. She counted back months and counted the files. There was a file for each week up until they married, when they stopped.

She shuddered for she knew what type of photos had been taken after, not that she'd seen them and never wanted to.

'The bastard had been stalking us as targets,' she yelled. 'Oh wow, talk about creepy! Unbelievable.'

So many scenarios tumbled through her brain. Had he done this to all the people in the photos? Had he stalked them all to find out if they were worth targeting? How many other people had he followed before deciding if they were... what? The right words deserted her. Money had to be the answer. At the time, her car was new and quality because both she and Pierre had inherited a reasonable sum from their father when he passed away the year before. It wasn't a fortune but had been enough for her to upgrade a second-hand bomb to a brand new latest model with enough left over to make her bank balance appear healthy. Her job had been well-paid and she received half the proceeds from the sale of her dad's property. But how did Kyle know? Had he gone inside her place of work and asked questions? And their first meeting? He must have finagled the meeting between them. At the coffee shop. He'd stumbled and dropped a small pile of papers, spilling her coffee as he hit the table. On a snort of derision at her stupidity, she rolled her eyes. Now, it was so darn obvious. One of the oldest tricks and she'd fallen for it. Oh how sweet he'd apologised and bought her another coffee to make up for his carelessness. He'd sat opposite mumbling words of a huge humble pie. And stupid naïve Elise had fallen for it.

Too overcome, she turned off the computer to get ready for a shift in the kitchen. After a long shower to wash away regret, she fed and changed Madeleine, dressed in jeans and T-shirt and pulled on an oversize hoodie to hide her hair, features and body shape the same she did every time she left the unit. Normally she donned a wig but not when in the kitchen for it became way too hot.

It took swipes of the bottom of the apron to rid her brow of sweat. The majority of the meals Rachel cooked over the past few hours had been burgers, toasties or sandwiches for the clean-up crew. Few of the regular locals had ventured out. Most would be cleaning up their own properties for she'd heard from those few who had come in, tales of missing roofs, fallen trees, along with flooded backyards and streets. There had been only about a dozen travellers game enough to battle with the storm debris on the roads, who stopped by for a meal, snack or plain coffee. Glad for the reprieve of no customers for a while, she put the last few clean dishes away and scooped Madeleine from her pram for a feed.

'You have been such a good princess,' she said to a smiling face as she settled them both into a chair she'd snaffled from the restaurant and placed in the far corner near the huge walk-in pantry. It was out of harm's way from food preparation at the hot plates, frier and benches. After Madeleine was settled at her breast and covered with a gauze cloth, she leant her head back against the wall and closed her eyes. A weird lethargy rolled through her. The tiredness from waking every four hours to feed Madeleine had become the norm she was now accustomed to. This was different. It could be stress related for yesterday had been full of stress, from discovering the gross activities of the man she'd so stupidly let sucker her in and married, to the ordeal of driving through the storm of the decade. Or it could be the knowledge she'd gained and how lucky she was to escape from his clutches. God, she'd been a first class idiot. And she was supposed to be an intelligent woman. Well, there was one adage she could now live by: Fool me once, shame on you. Fool me twice, shame on me. It will never happen again. Although a sense of shame had become a part of her psyche and she couldn't shake it off, even when her gut insisted she had nothing to be ashamed about. The shame lived with Kyle. Her shame was more about letting him inveigle his evil into her life.

'Are you okay, Rachel?'

She jerked upright at the voice and tap on her shoulder. The bongo drums returned to her heart and a swear word slipped out. Darn it, how could she not stay alert? A soft squeal came from Madeleine about being dislodged from her food source.

'Sorry, I didn't mean to scare you.' Ella squatted in front of her and placed a hand on Rachel's arm to give it a squeeze. 'There's a man in the office asking for you.'

Rachel jolted again and put Madeleine over her shoulder when she screwed up her face in protest. 'Who?'

'He showed me his I.D. card. Sergeant Dylan Marshall.'

'Huh, what's he doing here?'

'Do I tell him you're not here or let him come through?'

'Dylan's fine. He's the officer who was with me yesterday.' Rachel waved her hand towards the restaurant. 'I don't want to go out there.'

'It's fine if you speak in here. No need to worry. I'll take over if any orders come in but it's close to three so I doubt there'll be any more meals until tonight. Take your time.' Ella stood. 'I'll show him in.'

Rachel quickly pulled her clothes into place although Dylan had watched her nurse Madeleine several times before, especially when he was her body guard to protect her from Kyle whilst waiting interminable hours in the court house and he stood at the back of the court room while in front of the judge. Kyle not showing up had been utter relief. She turned at the scuffle of footprints.

'What are you doing here? Shouldn't you be at work?'

Dylan neared with another chair in one hand and a cardboard carton balanced on his hip. 'It's Saturday and a long weekend.' The legs screeched when he set the chair opposite her, sat and placed the box on the floor between them. 'I figured I could do with a few days by the beach and bring you this.' He tapped the box with the toe of his leather sneaker.

'It might be a bit wild at the beach. What's in there?'

'I called into the courthouse on my way home yesterday. Judge Anderson had a free hour. We discussed what you and I found and he released your belongings. The furniture as well, so you are free to take them out of storage whenever you want. Your case has been finalised. You will receive official paperwork in the mail. But essentially, this case has been dealt with and closed.'

Rachel used her foot to drag the carton closer. It was difficult to bend low with Madeleine in her arms but she was able to lift the folded lids and peer in. Shocked, she stared before lifting her eyes to Dylan. 'You took the photo albums as well? Thank you.'

'Well, it's the other reason I came.' He leant over, took out the two albums and waved them in front of her nose. 'Sniff.'

She sniffed and stared. 'Smoke?'

'I'm sorry.'

'Sorry? What do you mean?'

Dylan replaced the albums and took his mobile phone from the pocket of his collared T-shirt. He pressed a button and swept his finger across several times. When he turned the phone around to her, his face held a grim message.

Rachel glanced at the picture, jolted and stared. Her mouth gaped as she leant forward to get a better view. 'Is…?'

'Yes.'

'He destroyed my house?'

'Most of it, yes. The fire began in the underground garage. Your neighbours called the brigade after hearing an explosion around two last night. The oxy-welding tanks. It would have taken a fair bit of heat for them to blow so the fire had to have been burning a while. In fact, they are sure the fire was set around the tanks. It's possible he turned the gas on to ignite the fire. By the time the fire trucks arrived, the flames had spread to the rooms above the garage. The explosion would have weakened the wooden structure. The fireys and rain arrived at a convenient time, saved the structure of the end three rooms, hence the albums they let me retrieve from the singed wardrobe after things cooled. The rooms over the garage collapsed to the ground. I spoke with the inspector early this morning. It was definitely arson.'

'Holy, Moley. Why? Why would he do this?'

'Why does he do any of the evil things he does? In this case, to get rid of evidence.'

'Would he have searched inside before setting it alight? Would he have looked for the camera and money and all the other things we found?'

'I can't say one way or the other. The D's from yesterday were there when I left, along with the arson investigator. They will make a thorough search and write a report.'

With her mind in a whirl, Rachel plonked back in the chair and closed her eyes. 'I don't know what to say. This is unbelievable. All his stuff was in there too. Do you think he took anything?'

'I can't say but when I walked through the ruins with the investigator, there was an awful lot of rubble left. All the furniture, and he wouldn't have had time to take much. The D's had patrol cars drive by and officers check the premises at irregular times from the time they left yesterday. There had been no sign of him up until 1:00 a.m. So there was little time for him to have broken in. At a guess, I'd say he wanted to burn all the evidence, although there wasn't any left to burn but he couldn't have known what was found and taken. I doubt he would suspect we found the camera. But now we know he was in the city last night. The D's have promised to keep me in the loop. I'll pass on any info to you. They may want to check where you were as well.'

Rachel straightened. 'Why me?'

'Routine investigation. Pure protocol. Everything has to be done by the book.' He sent her a questioning quirk of one eyebrow. 'Where were you last night?'

'Driving through the storm from hell until eight. Took refuge in the servo a hundred kilometres north. They might have security films of me buying a hamburger and going to the loo. I had Madeleine with me. I stayed in the car to feed Madeleine until the worst of the rain passed, filled with fuel at the bowser. I paid with cash but I might have the receipts in my bag if needed. I'll find them and keep them. There could be security film of me arriving here in Ella's car. After nine, I was in bed asleep but was up twice to feed a hungry baby. I drove Ella's car around the back to her residence around seven this morning and she can vouch for me since.' She eyed Dylan. 'Why would I set fire to the house the same day I discovered I owned it?'

'Might be why he set it alight. Revenge.'

'More than likely. When these abuser's lose control they can often seek revenge. Especially if their abuse is exposed and Angel confronted him yesterday, exposed his crime in front of you. Kyle would want revenge on her. He could have thought Angel was still in there or her belongings were. He didn't spot me and had no idea I was there. But he did see Olivia and must have followed her for a while because he confronted her in front of the hotel after you left.'

'You should have let me know. What happened?'

While she related the incident, Rachel put a now sleeping baby back into the pram, tugged the blanket up and bent to press a kiss on the sweet brow.

'So he didn't spot you at the hotel?'

'No, I'm certain. I never went outside or to the lobby and he wouldn't have recognised me or the car. He ran when Olivia mentioned the arrest warrant. He still could have followed her home. He knew where she and Pierre live. He's always known.'

'I'll contact them and give their details to the D's. They must let us know if Kyle hangs around. Is he likely to?'

'He's been seen many times over the past nine months. Not to harm them but to find out where I am. As if I would be stupid enough to go visit them. It won't happen until he's locked in a cell. They understand. We do face time on a regular basis.' She should let Dylan know of her earlier discovery about being targeted. Hmm, not a good idea yet. More research was needed without the authorities knowing and he wouldn't be happy about her filching the items she'd taken. He might even charge her.

'Is my money in there?' she asked with a toe point to the box, as a way of changing the subject.

'Yes, $27,485 dollars. I sealed it in a large brown envelope. Is it the right amount?'

'Close enough. I wasn't a hundred percent certain.' The amount sent a shimmy of pleasure through her. 'I can afford a decent rental now.'

'Not happy with your digs?'

'It's been fine but has become a bit too cosy with Madeleine and her bits and pieces. A motel room was a godsend nine months ago and Ella has been more than kind to let me stay at a reduced rent but a place of my own with a separate bedroom for Madeleine sounds like heaven.'

Dylan leant forward. 'There's something I want to ask you.'

Rachel frowned. 'This sounds serious.'

'When this is all over… when Kyle is no longer a threat, would you let me take you out to dinner?'

Stunned, Rachel rocked back and thumped her head on the wall. 'Why?'

'I'd like to get to know you better and why not?'

'I figured a guy like you would be married.'

'A guy like me? What do you mean?'

Heat infused Rachel's neck. 'Well you're better looking than most. You're tall and fit and…'

'And?' Darn man grinned.

'You're a nice guy.'

'No I'm not married and there's no significant other. I came close to walking down the aisle two years back.'

'Close? What happened? You get cold feet?'

'No. I caught her cheating on me three weeks before the big day. I wasn't with the court system at the time. I fished a young lad who resisted arrest, from the river. I needed a clean, dry uniform so went home. Her car was in the drive along with another: one I recognised as a male work colleague of my fiancée. She was supposed to be at work. My gut told me to beware so I snuck in the back door and caught them in my bed: the same bed she and I had made love only a few hours before.'

'Wow, nasty. What did you do?'

'Threw both of them out, packed up the fiancée's belongings and left them on the front lawn. Left a message for her to pick them up and took a few hours off to change the locks on my house. She begged forgiveness: begged for the marriage to go ahead but cheating is one thing I can't abide. To cheat on your partner signifies total disrespect. When I arrived home from work in the evening, her father was waiting on the front porch. The moment I got out of my car he shirt-fronted me, furious I'd cancelled the wedding. He had paid a lot in deposits for the whole shebang.'

'I guess he would be furious but it wasn't your fault.'

'It wasn't the story he was told. Apparently I rang her at work to say I no longer wanted to marry her.'

'What did you do?'

'Took out my mobile phone and logged onto the video I took. Held it in front of his face and informed him it was taken around 10.30 that morning. It was easy to make out both her and a man who wasn't me. I informed her father I could never trust her and a marriage is based on a lot of things, trust being high on the list.'

'You videoed it?'

'What can I say? I'm trained to take photos of evidence and glad I did.'

'How did her father react?'

'His fury was no longer directed at me. Told me he didn't blame me and gave me a pat on the shoulder before he drove away. I sold the house because of the bad vibes and bought a town house in a secure building. It took me while to get over it, hence no significant other.'

'And you want to take me out to dinner?'

'Yes, why not?'

'I'm a frumpy nobody. Take a look, I service rooms and do the laundry for a motel…' she waved a hand around to indicate the kitchen. 'And the occasional cook.'

'You're a beautiful woman who works hard to keep a roof over her head and provide all she can for her child. What you do to earn a crust has no bearing on who you are as a person. And you didn't always work in a motel. You still have the skills to return to your old industry.'

'I'm not beautiful.'

'When did you last look in a mirror?'

'I try not to.'

When he took her hands in his, she flinched and tried to yank them back. He frowned. 'He did a real number on you didn't he? I will never hurt you. It's not my scene to physically harm a woman.'

'I know, it's…'

'You find it hard to trust a man. I understand and don't blame you. Especially after seeing those disgusting photographs.' He rubbed his thumbs across the back of her wrists, released her hands and sat back. 'You've lost your self-confidence but in front of me is a woman who is strong. You were brave enough to walk away from an abuser the very first time he caused physical harm. Not enough partners do. I figure the emotional blackmail had been there a while but emotional abuse is insidious and often not recognised until it becomes entrenched. You ended up recognising it. You've been strong enough to keep yourself hidden and safe, while at the same time, you have kept tabs on him, done research and been brave enough to take him to court to regain all of your possessions. To appear in court was heroic. He was the one who didn't have the guts to face you in court. Abusers are cowards and he's a prime example of a coward.'

'He's still roaming around out there.'

'Not for long. His mug shot and details, along with a warrant, have been issued state wide. We will catch him.' Dylan leant forwards again. 'So how about it? Let me take you to enjoy a meal out because I like the woman you are and would like to get to know you better.'

Rachel pointed to the pram. 'I've got a seven-week-old breast fed baby.'

'So? We'll take her with us. There are plenty of family friendly eateries.'

Her jaw dropped in disbelief. 'I... you don't mind?'

'Madeleine is a part of the woman you are and I like the woman. You come as a package deal.' He indicated the pram. 'I like the entire package, so how about it?'

'But I live here and you live in the city.'

'When Kyle is tucked away in a nice sparse gaol cell, will you stay here or move closer to your brother?'

Rachel paused to consider. 'Move back. He's the only family I've got left.'

'So what will it be? Dinner for three?'

Excited butterflies danced through her stomach at the notion of dinner out with a guy. 'Okay and thank you but I doubt Madeleine will need any solid food for a while, so make it dinner for two.'

Dylan stood. 'I'm delighted and can't wait. Now, I'm off to the coast. I've got two nights booked in a hotel overlooking the wild Southern Ocean. I'll call in on my way back to the big smoke. You've got my private number if you need me but I figure you're pretty safe here. Ella gave me a thorough inquisition without letting on you were here. Ella won't let anything happen to you.'

'I owe her a lot.' She indicated the box. 'Let me put all of these things in the pram carrier. I don't have enough space in my room for a cardboard carton.' When she took out the two albums it was hard to fight back a rush of tears, not only because she had the albums but because Dylan was kind enough to get them for her. To hide her emotions, she took her time to shuffle baby requirements in the tray under the pram and stacked the albums on top of each other in the space she'd made. Dylan handed her a clear plastic file containing all the certificates, printed copies and passport. The bag of jewellery came next and brought on a fresh rush of moisture because most had belonged to her mother. When he handed her the old laptop, she wondered if she would be game to even open it for Kyle had been able to log onto it before. Was he still able to? She didn't have enough knowhow to be certain and wasn't about to take the chance. The last item was a large brown envelope with three thick bundles. Her cash: the means to find a decent place to live without eating into her savings. A few tears escaped. Embarrassed, she used the bottom of her T-shirt to wipe them away before she was game to lift her head.

'Hey, are you okay?' A large hand gripped her forearm.

Too choked up to speak, she nodded, stood and forced her lips to widen. 'Yes, I'm overwhelmed. I can't believe I have any of these things. It's been…'

'A tough journey. But the end is near.'

'Thanks to you. You went out of your way to help me and were about the only person who… I don't know what, but it was difficult to get anyone other than Pierre and Olivia to believe in me.'

'The judge did. He had no doubts at all. You could have brought it to court sooner.'

'Not until Madeleine was born. I couldn't risk Kyle seeing me pregnant. And now I'm glad because after those photographs, can you imagine how he would treat a child he swore he never wanted?'

'He told you he never wanted children?'

'Not until after we married. He insisted I take a pill every night to the extent he took the pill out of the packet and handed it to me.'

'How did you fall pregnant?'

'By accident. I caught a bug and spent a couple of days throwing up. When I discovered I might be pregnant, I asked the doctor how. She said the contraceptive wouldn't have had time to get into my system if I was throwing up so much. The news was when I made a more concerted effort to get out.'

'You planned to leave before the day he threw you out?'

Rachel wiped her face again. 'From the day after we married, yes, but only in my head. I didn't dare write anything on paper or send messages although I did speak with Pierre from my office, using my burner phone. We were working out a plan to get me away but...'

'Kyle beat you to a pulp before you could execute those plans. I'm sorry.'

'Pretty well and you've got nothing to be sorry about, but I appreciate everything you've done for me, especially coming all this way to bring me my gear – and the albums.'

'Hey, I wanted to and it was a good excuse to leave the city for a couple of days break. Now let's get you back to your room. Or are you still working?'

'No my shift has finished.' She grabbed the hoodie she'd piled over the pram handle, and tugged it over her head, ensuring the hood hung low over her brow and the hem was tugged halfway down her thighs. 'If you could check in the diner for me to make sure Kyle isn't there, I'll come as far as the door with you. It might be better if you went out alone and I'll give you a few minutes before I go outside.'

Dylan frowned and pointed to her hoodie. 'Do you take these precautions every time you go outside?'

'Sure. I don't dare take any chances and I can't wear a wig in the kitchen. It gets too hot.'

'I had no idea you were still this scared. Let me check.' He moved to the swing door and poked his head out. 'There's only one woman in there, apart from your boss who gave a nod. Does she know what Kyle looks like?'

A laugh slipped out of Rachel's mouth. 'All the staff do. Over the past nine months there have been a couple of guys who've been overtly checked out because they had similar features. There's a picture of him under the counter in both the reception area and restaurant. They all know the basics of the story but not my real name. Only Ella knows I was his wife. For my own safety, there wasn't much choice. You go and thank you again. You have no idea how much I appreciate all you've done for me.'

'My pleasure. I'll catch you Monday. Around noon.' He grabbed the empty carton and left.

Rachel watched from the door until Dylan was outside. She turned back, swung the pram around and went into the restaurant after another quick glance to ensure the coast was clear. From inside, she watched Dylan get into his car and drive off. 'I'll catch you later,' she said to Ella as she wheeled the pram across the floor and paused in front of the window. A yellow car pulled out of the parking lot in front of the strip mall across the road and went in the same direction as Dylan.

After her scare a couple of hours ago, when adrenalin shot through her body like a lightning bolt at the sight of a yellow car, Rachel had been too scared to be alone. It took a quick glimpse of the car's rear end to realise the number plate was not Kyle's. It took a lot longer for her heart to cease thumping at a rate she was certain wasn't healthy. Would she ever get over this fear?

It wasn't a surprise when Ella figured something was wrong the very second Rachel had scampered back to the kitchen, shoving the pram at such a rate it tipped on an angle when it caught the edge of the counter. So here she is, eating pizza with Ella, who hadn't left her alone for even a second.

'You still look pale.' Ella reached over and grasped Rachel's hand.

'I'm sorry I scared you.' With her free hand, Rachel dropped the end crust of the pizza they'd shared, onto her plate. Madeleine snuffled at the movement but remained asleep.

With a full complement of cooks and servers now ensconced in the restaurant, Ella insisted Rachel join her for dinner in the office so she could be on hand if any travellers arrived in search of a motel room although neither expected any. She folded the paper plate into quarters and stashed it on the empty pizza carton.

Ella patted Rachel's hand. 'You were the one who received the scare. Are you sure it wasn't his car?'

'Different number plate. Even the colour was different than our normal plates. This was one of those older blue personal plates. It stood out.'

'Do you want to come over to the house for the night?'

Yes, yes, yes, demanded her fear. 'No. I'll be fine. Too much hassle with all the baby gear and you must be exhausted. It's been a long day for you.'

'It's been a long day for everyone but I am tired, which is why I needed this time to relax over dinner with orders to not interrupt me bar a raging fire. Your company made it a whole lot more pleasant.'

A warm fuzzy centred around her heart at the compliment. 'It wasn't much of what I would call a healthy dinner but it sure was yum.' Rachel gathered all the other bits, shoved them on the box and folded the lid over. 'And much appreciated.'

'Takeaways have their uses when one is too damn exhausted to cook.'

'We could have brought a meal over from the restaurant.'

Ella laughed. 'I won't tell anyone if you don't. All restaurant owners eat at other establishments so they can have a break. I'm no different.' Her face altered in an instant to one of alarm. 'Quick, pull your hood over your head and don't speak or turn around. Kyle is about to come inside.'

Ella shot from her office seat and barrelled out to the motel reception area while everything inside Rachel stalled as though she'd been hit with a stun gun before she had the nous to do as she was told and yank the hood over her head a split second before the front door creaked open with a swish and whine. It had to have been Kyle's car. But how? Did he have another set of number plates? She searched amongst the scrambled brain cells for the name on the personalised plate but could only remember the colour and there were two words on the plate. No way could she recall the words and they couldn't have been long words.

'Good evening, can I help you?' she heard Ella say in a strained voice.

'I'm looking for my wife.' The voice she never wanted to hear again still held the officious tone that hadn't surfaced until after a ring was placed on her finger. Never once beforehand. If it had she wouldn't have been such an idiot.

'Oh, when did you lose her?'

Rachel choked at the sarcasm, then followed with a snigger, even though her heart was determined to beat the world speed record and her stomach was so tense it hurt. She huddled over Madeleine in protective mode. Please, baby girl, don't wake now.

'No need for the smart arse comments. I know she's here. Who's in there? I bet it's her.'

Rachel's heart stalled and her heart replicated a big bass drum.

'My daughter is feeding her baby so please drop your voice and give me your lost wife's name. And who are you?'

'Kyle Jacobs, not that you need to know.'

'If I don't know your name how can I match it to the names of all the people here?'

Rachel gulped and quietly chortled at Ella's quick thinking.

'And your wife's name?'

'Elise.'

'There's nobody here called Elise. The only two people registered in the motel are an elderly married couple and none of my staff are called Elise. What makes you think your lost wife is here?'

'The copper came in here earlier today.'

'Copper? The only police uniform I've seen today was on my daughter's husband who is the local constable.'

Wow, Ella is prepared to lie and what a whopper.

'He wasn't in uniform. He wore plain clothes.'

'Well if an officer dressed in ordinary, everyday clothes came into our premises today, how am I supposed to know he's a police officer. We don't make it a habit of asking our customers what they do to earn a living. How about you come with me to the restaurant to check out all of my customers? If you are certain she's here, she could be in there having a meal.'

'The officer carried in a cardboard carton and came out with it twenty minutes later. Why else would he do such a crazy thing unless he wanted to give what was inside to someone?'

'And why would the someone be your missing wife?'

'Because he knows her.'

'What makes you think this particular officer knows your... umm... Elise was it?'

'Because he was at my house yesterday.'

'Your house? And your wife was with him was she?'

Oh, wow, Ella was getting too close to the truth. Rachel shut her eyes and didn't dare move.

'No.'

'No? I don't see the relationship but I do remember the carton. The owner had a pastie and coffee, went to the men's room and left. Could be he had valuable items in the box he didn't want to leave in the car while he took a break from driving. The same way women carry their handbags and guys with their wallets and phones. Who knows? It's not my place to ask such questions.'

'I know the bitch is here,' Kyle yelled.

'Okay, let's go and search if you are so sure.'

Footsteps moved around the bench, Kyle grunted and added his clomps before the door screeched and whooshed again. Heart in her mouth, Rachel waited, waited, waited and dared to turn her head far enough to ensure they'd gone. In an instant she stood and raced with Madeleine in her arms, along the short passage to the wooden door which took her outside behind the building. Keeping to the shadows, she sidled with her back to the wall so she could keep an eye on any movement, until she reached the end of the motel units. Around the corner she paused to catch her breath and search the area. Where could she hide? It was impossible to get to her room without passing the end of the restaurant.

The glint of water from the lake caught her eye. Spring fed, it ran about a hundred metres behind the playground and park along one end of the motel. She'd only walked around it twice, at sun-up, too scared to be out in the open any longer or later in the day. Thankful for so many trees, she scooted from shadow to shadow with Madeleine clutched against her chest until she reached the childproof gate, where she pulled up the latch on top of the head-high post. She winced at the screech when it opened, edged through and took more care to shut it slowly to prevent more give-away noise. The entire area was still strewn with detritus from the storm. The council hadn't got this far yet which might be a good thing. To prevent obvious footprints in the damp soil, she kept to the line of bushes along the edge of the playground, stepped over and around fallen branches and rocks. Even with her hood, the cold snuck into tiny gaps to find her skin with prickles of cold.

In the dim light the lake gave off a spooky vibe but this kind of spooky was way less scary than what waited for her at the motel. With no wind there were no ripples and no sound. Her presence had hushed the night life. As long as it was only her presence. Ahead was a large splodge of wet darkness surrounded by blurry shapes of boulders, bushes and tall shadowy trees. During the day, it was a popular place for the locals to walk their dogs or jog for fitness. At night it was unusual for anyone to frequent the park or track. To wade through was impossible for the water became deep and beneath it was thick mud. The noise would be horrendous, let alone the stench of rotting flora. The lack of background noise tightened already fraught nerves for any sound she made would give away her position. It was impossible to make out a clear pathway through the storm strewn detritus to get around the lake for the moon was yet to show its face which was good, for moonlight would have picked out her movement.

Above the trees stars twinkled, giving life to the black void. In one sense the darkness was a comfort and the reflection of stars on the water gave a sensation of peace. Her innards told the exact opposite. Now, she wished she'd explored the surrounds over the past few months so she would know where to hide. But when had there been time and when had she dared?

When Madeleine snuffled, Rachel glanced down and gripped the bundle tighter. Please, please, please, don't wake now. With utmost care she turned left, away from the buildings, and peered at the ground, desperate to spot any object she might trip over, or loose stick ready to snap and echo. The ends of bushes reached out, determined to grab a hold of her jeans and drag her back. Sticks stabbed, prickles scratched but she ignored them all and kept on, step-by-step-by-careful step.

One step at a time, her mind chanted: every step is a step towards safety. The nasty side of her brain didn't believe it. She hadn't been safe for too long, less so since she'd been stupid enough to go back to the house to retrieve her belongings. At the time, she was certain he hadn't spotted her, didn't know of her presence with all the hoo-ha and carry-on. But somehow, he had now found her. Had he caught up with Angel? Surely not. The woman had been furious with him and scared enough to take utmost care. But he knew where Angel worked. It was possible he'd hunted for her, demanded the details on how she found out the truth. Although today was Saturday so she wouldn't have gone to work and she didn't go to work yesterday. Poor woman if he had found her. But Angel had no idea who Rachel was or where she lived and she didn't want to believe Angel had figured it out for at the time, neither she nor Dylan had divulged exactly who she was. Angel thought she was a cop. A more probable answer meant he followed Dylan for they'd confronted each other and Kyle knew who Dylan was. He must have followed him yesterday and he sure knew how to keep tabs on people, if what had been on the flash drive was any indication.

A car engine revved. Rachel paused, spotted a log a few metres off the track, shoved a way through low shrubs and settled her backside on the rough bark. It was difficult to make out objects through the underbrush but she spotted her room and ran her eyes along the back of the building. Lights flared from the occupied room two doors along, which should make it easy to spot a figure passing it. Thank goodness her room lay in darkness, especially since there was no car in front of it.

Now her panic reflex had settled, logic returned to scrambled brain cells. Ella would have returned to the office. She would never reveal Rachel's whereabouts. If anyone, especially a man, asked, no-one called Elise was either staying there or worked there. But none of the others knew her real name – only Ella. Lord, but her mind was a mess.

Bright headlights startled her when they lit up the area in a straight line towards the bush along the edge of the road – away from her. In the silence, the crunch of tyres echoed from the far end of the property. Not fast but too slow. Ever so slow, the beam of light reached further into the bush, lit up the side of the road and about five metres along the edge of the bush. There was no doubt it searched for her. The car stopped, turned, the light beam swung around to seek her out amongst the few buildings across the road. It swung her way.

She slid off the log and crouched low with her head over Madeleine. When she noticed the paleness of the blanket, she tucked Madeleine further under her arms and turned her back to the light. Her dark hoodie should blend with the shadows of the shrubs. She prayed it would. Through half-closed eyes, she sought out the light beam. It passed over her, searched the pathway from the park to the lake, and glinted off the still water. So close. If she'd lingered on the log any longer she would have been caught.

Madeleine whimpered: a whimper Rachel knew well. The first sign of wakening from hunger or discomfort. A snort, a yawn, a snuffle. Rachel lifted one side of her top and shirt, freed one breast and a hungry mouth nuzzled, found its target and latched on. The sensation always overwhelmed her. Tonight was no different despite the ridiculous situation. When knees and ankles ached from the crouched position, she unfolded and sat on the ground with her back to the headlights. Dampness seeped through her jeans and a rock protruded. She shuffled away from the rock and ignored the icy moisture. Jeans would dry. Madeleine's safety was her only concern. If he ever found out… she didn't want to think about the consequences.

When the light moved, Rachel followed the beam with her eyes. It swung away from the lake, towards the back sheds lined up behind the motel complex. A six foot high fence ran all the way along the back and far end of the property to keep out intruders on foot. It didn't keep out intruders in cars for it must be at the end of the row, around the other side of the café section. The light brightened to indicate the car had turned into the backyard. The beam swung over her. She ducked despite it not being low enough.

Madeleine whimpered at being dislodged, snuffled and latched on again. Thank goodness she was way too young to understand or ever remember.

The lights swung around, vanished and returned to show up the other side of the highway. Tyres crunched and the engine revved. It wasn't until the yellow car tore along the road, Rachel knew he had gone, but where and for how long? Was he satisfied she wasn't there or would he hide further along the road and come back? What the hell was she supposed to do?

Head down, she leant against the log while Madeleine sucked. Unstoppable tears streamed as hopelessness overwhelmed her.

'Rachel, Rachel, are you okay? He's gone.'

Awareness came when arms swept around Rachel's shoulders. She lifted her head. Three people with torches crouched around her. One had Madeleine in his arms. She had to shake her head to gain clarity to make sure she was seeing right because he was dressed in a blue uniform.

'Come on, Rach, everything's fine. He's gone. We've been searching for you.'

'Huh?' Rachel sniffed an awful sound and winced in embarrassment.

Ella swiped a cloth over Rachel's face.

'I'm okay,' Rachel managed to get out through a thick throat.

'No you're not. Let's get you up.' Both Ella and the third person placed hands under Rachel's armpits and hoisted her upright.

Through bleary eyes, she made out the features of Caro, the regular server for the restaurant. 'Thank you,' she said through stiff lips. God, she was cold. 'How long have I been here?'

'You don't know? We've been searching for almost an hour.' Ella rubbed her hands up and down Rachel's arms. 'Good grief, girl, you are frozen. Let's get you inside to warm up.'

'I… I can't…' She wavered a hand in the direction of the motel. 'I can't go back there. He'll come back.'

'We've come up with a plan for the night.' Ella used her arm to urge Rachel forward. 'Pete, here, is going to sleep in the unit next to you with his squad car parked outside. We'll park your car in front of your room. Kyle doesn't know the car belongs to you. It will look as though we have another customer for the night and my white lie about my daughter's husband being an officer means it makes sense for a police vehicle to be here. The night shift will keep an eye from the office for any sign of a yellow car. Pete already has the details of make and model and all the local police stations within cooee are on the lookout for Kyle. They know there's an arrest warrant.

Rachel was having trouble keeping up with all the information. Her head still hadn't cleared and she was worried about how she had blacked out for so long. It had happened before when stress overwhelmed her. 'Madeleine.' She reached out for her baby. 'Is she okay?'

'She's fine. She'd fallen asleep at your breast. She's warm as toast for you had her wrapped up in your hoodie. But you're damp in the rear end. You need a hot shower and warm clothes.'

Rachel's legs didn't want to work properly. She stumbled over the first lot of shrubs then plopped each step along the path and through the playground. She figured she wouldn't be able to walk without two people holding her up and pressuring her forward. God, she had to get with it. To make it happen she forced her body to straighten, concentrated on every step and drew air into her lungs.

Everyone crowded into her unit.

'I'll catch you later.' Caro waved and left while Ella shoved Rachel towards the bathroom.

'Madeleine.' Rachel stopped and reached for her daughter.

'I'll put her in the cot and watch her while you shower.' Pete leant over the cot, laid Madeleine on the mattress and tucked a blanket around her.

Ella shoved. 'If you don't get in the shower right now, I'll strip you off myself. Now get.'

Rachel forced her lips to turn up, took the final two steps into the tiny room and shut the door. With her back towards the small mirror over the equally small vanity so she didn't catch a sight of her image, she hoisted the hoodie over her head and tossed it into the corner. Her bra and baggy top followed. It was a struggle to peel wet jeans and briefs down her legs but they finally settled around her ankles where sodden canvas shoes prevented them from going further. After a struggle to toe off the shoes, it took two kicks for them to join the mounting pile of damp clothes and another four kicks to get rid of the jeans. It was as though she had no strength left when the tap took an extra heave to turn. At least her brain had cleared enough to wait the few seconds for the cold water to run out before the hot came. Pure pleasure erupted when she stood under the stream of hot water and let it course over the top of her head and trail down frozen skin which prickled at first. She stilled, eyes shut and one hand against the tiles to keep her upright. Slowly, slowly, the heat penetrated to melt away the ice and warm her blood. A long sigh of pleasure blew out. Her one free hand reached for the shampoo and squirted a large dollop into the hand she'd held against the wall. She not only rubbed the shampoo through her hair but massaged as well, the pressure easing the tension. After another dose of shampoo and a good rinse out, she soaped her body and rubbed with a flannel, twice. By the time she was ready to turn the water off, the pads of her fingertips replicated dried sultanas but she didn't much care.

A rap on the door while using the towel, sent a wave of shivers across her shoulders. 'Who is it?'

'I've got a set of clothes for you. Open the door a fraction,' came Ella's voice.

Rachel couldn't hold back the whimper of relief. She stood a moment with the towel pressed into her eyes while she convinced her brain she was safe. Kyle had gone. One of the local police officers was right next door. She had known Pete Simpson ever since she arrived. He was one of the good guys. She could trust him. Not every man was an abusive bastard.

At another soft knock she opened the door and gulped at the clothes. Her turquoise fleecy pyjamas covered in pink pigs. Terrific. Now everyone knew what she'd worn to bed for the past nine months. Please, Pete, don't be there. The warm, soft fabric was pure bliss against her skin, which was why she loved wearing them. After setting the room to rights, she picked up the laundry and opened the door.

A single bedside light glowed to break the gloom. Ella sat on the end of the bed with a mug in her hand. A coil of steam rose and a pleasant aroma swirled. Hot chocolate.

'Pete's next door. See that shoe?' Ella pointed to one of the new sneakers on the bedside table. 'You are to belt it on the wall if you need him. His orders. Now, you need to get into your bed and sleep. We'll discuss everything in the morning. The night staff are alert and will phone Pete if there is any sign of unwelcome visitors. All of us will do everything in our power to keep you and Madeleine safe. You are a treasured part of our collective family. Here,' she lifted the mug, 'real hot chocolate with all the trimmings. It will help you sleep.'

Tears threatened to escape Rachel's eyes again when a warm fuzzy enveloped every cell in her body. She took the mug to hide her reaction. 'I can't thank you enough. All of you.' With the mug held out to the side, she gave a one-armed bear hug to Ella when she stood.

'Rest well,' Ella opened the door, studied the outside and stepped out. 'All clear.' The door closed on what appeared to be a scene of calm serenity, the exact opposite to what was happening in the depths of her mind and soul.

Perched on the side of the bed, Rachel took sips of the amazing drink. She had no idea how Ella had produced such a luxurious, rich version of hot chocolate in so short a time but didn't much care how, for it was downright delicious and warmed her from the inside out. When she glanced around what had been her tiny home for so long, her eyes settled on her phone, which someone had plugged into the charger. She also noticed the room had been tidied. Ella's work, she guessed.

Dylan came to mind when her eyes studied the phone. He needed to know what had happened. With the drink on the table and phone in her hand, she bunched up the pillow, settled against the bedhead and pressed Dylan's number in her sparse list. It only rang twice.

'Rachel, is everything okay?'

'How did... never mind, you've got one of those fancy new-fangled phones.'

His laugh didn't lighten her tension. 'You didn't answer my question. Are you okay?'

How was she supposed to answer? 'Kyle came.' Nothing like straight to the point.

'Huh? How? What happened?'

'He must have followed you.' She winced at the string of swear words.

'Tell me everything.'

'I spied a yellow car pull out of the car park opposite the motel within seconds after you left. It followed you. It was the same model as Kyle's car but there was a personal number plate on it. You know, one of those older blue ones, so I figured it wasn't Kyle. Not long after six tonight, he came into the motel reception demanding where I was. To really turn my innards inside out, I was in the office eating pizza with Ella. Luckily, she saw him arrive and ordered me to pull the hood over my head and thank goodness I had my back to him. I heard him say he had watched you come in earlier with a cardboard box and walk out twenty minutes later and insisted it was because I was here. He was aggressive with Ella but she was able to calm him and took him to the restaurant to check out all the customers. It gave me a chance to escape. You can't come back here on your way home. I'm certain he'll be tailing you again. He might even be watching you now or he could be parked near here waiting to come back in the early hours.'

'Hell, I'm sorry. I didn't spot him following me. I did catch sight of one yellow car on my way here but it was a yellow Beetle and I did keep a watch the entire journey. I need to call this in to the local stations.'

'Already done. The local constable, Pete, is sleeping in the room next door. I'm to belt my shoe on the wall if Kyle returns.'

'Damn it. I want to be there for you.'

Her heart thrummed at the idea. 'No way. You can't come. If you come back he will know for sure.'

'I understand. I'll drive home another way. Go west along the coast and take the coastal highway home. You still haven't told me how you are.'

She sniggered. No way could she mention how she'd had a total melt down to the extent she'd been lost in the ether for almost an hour. 'I'm fine. The guys here have been amazing. If Kyle does turn up again there might be a public lynching. I have to remember my car can't be traced to me and he doesn't know it's mine. The only way he will ever recognise me is if he's up close and studies my face.' And it sure came close tonight. What if he'd insisted on me turning around? Lord, but it was too damn close.

'So, you're okay?'

'I'm fine. Madeleine is safe, which is my only concern.'

'It's going to eat at me how I brought him to your door. I'm sorry.'

'It's not your fault and he can't know for certain I'm here. Ella told him I was her daughter and my husband was the local police constable who is asleep next door and his car is parked outside. So it gives credence to her little white fib.'

'Yeah, it is my fault, although I can't figure out why he would choose to follow me or how.'

'You need to have a look at those flash drives.' Rachel slammed her mouth shut. Sweet mercy, she shouldn't have mentioned them. Now he'll want to know why and how she knew.

'What do you mean? And the D's have them.'

'Forget it. I have to go. Madeleine needs a feed. Bye.' And damn me for lying. She switched the phone off. 'Big mouth,' she muttered to herself before picking up the mug. A soothing drink was needed.

And a new brain. Along with a huge dose of serenity and a far off country would go down well. Maybe a tiny Greek island.

While her mind raced, she sipped. As if she would be able to sleep now. To stop the rabid cyclone of ideas, she moved to the computer to search for names on the internet. Names of those in the photographs. They had to be city locals, or at least close by the city. No, go through the notebooks. No, search for Kyle's other name. Keith, Keith, Keith... Jackson.' On a loud groan of frustration she stood, spun around and plopped onto the mattress again. Bed sounds a darn sight better but with this amount of angst there was no way she would be able to drift into la-la land.

Instead, she removed the pile of stolen items from where she'd hidden them under the bed and spread them along the front of the bench under the window. If car lights shone in this direction she would notice, despite the drawn drapes. They were thickish but not of the blackout variety. When she first arrived, the constant night-time flashes annoyed her, now they were barely noticed. Until tonight. Let's hope, if he does comes back the police car will deter him from further investigation.

She pulled out the chair, sat and ran one hand along the items. The pile of black notebooks caused her hand to pause and linger. She drew out the bottom one, opened the cover. Olivia Esquilante, in neat capital letters stared back at her boggled eyes. 'Hooley, Dooley,' whistled out, followed by a string of unladylike words.

She turned the page. The first date was the night of the dinner: the night of the first photos. Dot pointed notes gave brief details.

- *Expensive dress.*
- *Good jewellery.*
- *Slender.*
- *Good looking.*
- *Expensive car.*
- *Nice home – worth a bit.*
- *No sign of a partner.*

The following pages were dated three or four days apart. It was of major concern when she reached a page with full address, phone numbers and email address. How the hell did he find out such details? It couldn't have been a legal method. There was a big black Asterix next to the words - Bloody kids. Yes, well, she now understood the sentiment after his tirade about never wanting children and the extent he went to, to avoid them. On the last entry came the word – husband, three days after Pierre returned from his trip to France. All the entries confirmed her suspicion how they had been targeted for months before he set things in motion.

It was a relief when Madeleine stirred but difficult to force her brain to switch off so she could soften her tone and facial features in the half hour of feed, change and play. When Madeleine closed her eyes and sent out a soft snuffle of contentment, Rachel decided it would be best if she did the same.

A soft tap at the door sent Rachel's heart to race full pelt. Pete had left around six with little noise apart from footsteps and an engine coming to life. It was likely the poor guy was due back on duty and would need to go home to shower, change and eat. Since then, anxiety had been her partner while she fed, bathed and changed Madeleine, who was now absorbed in the mechanical toy slowly moving five glittering space objects around in a circle. Now Madeleine could focus, she became intrigued by anything that moved. What brought joy to Rachel's heart was how Madeleine smiled at whatever moved. Her hands and legs waved as if trying to catch the items. It wouldn't be long before she could. It amazed her how fast these tiny creatures developed and learned. Only seven weeks old and already Madeleine could follow objects, could almost reach out and grab, smiled at things which gave her pleasure, knew where her food came from with unerring accuracy and had developed different whines and noises to indicate different discomforts and needs. Truly amazing.

'Rachel, are you awake?'

Her heart slowed at the familiar voice. She dropped the spoon in her almost empty bowl of muesli and yoghurt, got up from the floor and opened the door. 'I'm always awake at this hour. A certain someone makes sure I'm up before six.'

'With the happy look on your face, I guess you don't mind.'

Rachel laughed, which was so darn good. 'As long as I get a decent number of hours of sleep, I don't mind and she now gives me five hours at a stretch.'

'Are you up to doing the rooms this morning? It doesn't matter if you're not. I can call in Mags. There are only two so not a big pile of laundry.'

'I'm fit and able and Mags filled in for me on Friday.'

'And you filled in for Nate yesterday. Dylan rang me last night, after he'd spoken to you.'

Rachel straightened when her heart did some extra pitter pats. 'Why?'

Ella raised her eyebrows. 'He wanted to know what it was you didn't tell him about Kyle's arrival. You didn't mention how frightened you were, or how you hid in the bush and blanked out. He's a nice guy – and single.'

'Jeeze, Ella, yes, he's nice but so was Kyle until he put a ring on my finger. I doubt I could ever trust a man again.'

'You trust Pete, and my hubby and the guys on the staff.'

'Not enough to ever marry any of them. I can do Pete's room now. I heard him leave.' To stop the conversation about men she turned back inside, grabbed her hoodie and yanked it over her head. Ella left and laughed all the way along the veranda. It took a few more minutes to settle a still playful Madeleine in her pram and fix the space toy onto the hood. Since she needed the cleaning trolley she pushed the pram outside, to find Ella had brought the trolley with her and parked it in front of Pete's room with the master key dangling on a wire from the handle. A shake of her head at Ella's cunning, she took her time to search the surroundings before she stepped from her room. Even at this early hour there were cars galore in the parking spaces across the road but without a hint of yellow on any vehicle, she scampered next door, grabbed the key and shoved the pram in first before another search of the environs, after which, she hauled in the cart and slammed the door to keep out the world.

There was little to do apart from change linen for the only item in the room Pete had touched was the bed. While she tucked in sheet corners, Rachel's mind kept flinging different ideas until a single one settled and stewed. Insurance. She needed to contact the insurance company. But it was Sunday. And Monday was a public holiday, or at least, it was in this state. Who knew what state the insurance company had its headquarters? Not her. She hadn't even known about the policy until two days ago. Well, it wasn't quite true for there was a policy but she hadn't known it had only her name on it, which led her crazy mixed up brain to ask why? Was the name Kyle Jacobs only a pseudonym with no legal status? But he had a passport with the name. What about his driver's licence? She didn't know because she'd never seen it. Oh, wow, how weird to have never seen your husband's licence. She snorted. There were a lot of items she'd had no idea about. And what about the marriage certificate? Surely the celebrant had to have had legal names.

The jumbled questions refused to move until she trundled the trolley in front of the still occupied room on the other side of hers and left it there against the wall until after ten when the couple were required to vacate. Back in her room with a now sleeping baby, she flicked through the papers she'd copied and picked out the insurance policy, which consisted of umpteen pages of do's, don'ts, what was covered and not covered and oodles of miniscule fine print, which she took her time to read through in the search of the word arson. As far as she could figure out, she couldn't be accused of setting light to her own house since she wasn't there at the time and hadn't been resident for months. Her innards jiggled in delight to find a twenty-four hour contact number, which she immediately dialled to follow innumerable computer generated directions, press countless numbers and wait and wait forever until she heard an actual human voice.

'How can I help?' The female voice asked.

'My house burnt down. What do I need to do?'

'Do you have your insurance policy number?'

'Yes, I have the policy here. Give me a sec.' Rachel searched, stabbed a finger and read out the ridiculously long line of letters and numbers, moving her finger under each to ensure she read them right.

'And you are?'

'Elise Esquilante.'

'Are you sure?'

'What do you mean, am I sure? I know who I am. Why would you ask such a stupid question?'

'No need to get antsy. I ask because Mrs Esquilante has already put in a claim on this property.'

'Huh? No I didn't.' Rachel closed her eyes and did her best to steady the sudden increase in heart rate to calm nerves which had taken on a challenge to stretch so tight they wanted to snap and ping apart. What had Kyle done now? And Mrs Esquilante? 'I can assure you I am the owner of this property and the insurance policy has only my name on it and it is Miss Esquilante. If anyone else claims to be the owner, they are lying.'

'Or maybe it is you who is being less than honest.'

This conversation was so darn ridiculous but she understood. 'Could this other person prove who they were, for I can? I have my passport, birth certificate, marriage certificate, bank cards and driver's licence to show you. I also have in front of me, the registered Title Deed to the property, which is in my name and the insurance policy open at page two.'

'But all the paperwork was destroyed in the fire.'

'Is that what this imposter told you? What a handy excuse to carry out a fraudulent claim. For none of the important paperwork was in the house when it burnt down. I have it in front of me and I can give you the name of a police officer and the Family Court judge who can verify both who I am and how the paperwork I have is the legitimate paperwork.'

'I need to discuss this with my boss.'

'Please do but before you hang up, if required, I can scan relevant papers to send to you, although you need to see the real copies. Are you able to get back to me today? And what happens next, once I have proved who I am?'

'Our assessor needs to meet you on site. We have already set a time for nine o'clock Tuesday morning with… um…'

'The imposter, I get it. I'll be there. With the papers and a police officer.' She hoped but how she was going to wangle an officer to be with her, she would figure out. Maybe Dylan could help. One of the detectives? 'By the way, I know why this other woman has made a claim and who set her up. It would be wise to not let her know there is a change of plan. This is a serious legal matter. There is an arrest warrant for the man who set her up. I can give you the details of the police officer so you can discuss it with him. This might be an opportunity to nab this person. Sorry, I'm rambling but you have no idea how important this is.'

'Oh, err... I'm not sure. Can I get back to you after I've spoken with my boss. He can listen to this recording and make a decision.'

'Sure. I'll give you my number and also Sgt Dylan Marshall's number. This is so weird.'

'About the weirdest thing I've come across for several weeks and I get some weird claims and excuses. I'll get back to you.'

After giving the numbers, Rachel sat back, eyes closed and a mind in turmoil. How did Kyle organise this when he was here in the south? Who has he coerced into pretending to be me? One of his victims? And now she had to return to the city. With Madeleine. She dropped her head on the desk and thumped twice.

Outside there was a scuffle of feet, voices and the slam of a door. Rachel lifted the corner of a curtain and peeked. It was cute the way the elderly gent held the door open for his wife and gripped her hand to assist her. Something Kyle never did. More like the other way around. He would prefer the woman open the door for him, although Rachel had never stooped so low. Oh, and the gent kissed his wife before shuffling around to the driver's seat. So sweet.

This was a timely intervention. She waited until the rumble of the engine vanished before she opened the door, searched the area and wheeled Madeleine out. It was amazing how quick one could change from one room to another when you were petrified of being caught. This room had a tidy mess in need of a complete clean, which would take a while and give her brain plenty of time to create chaos in her mind.

With so few sheets and towels to wash, Rachel had shoved them all in the one industrial washing machine, the café laundry in the second and her own laundry in the third, all at the same time while she handwashed Madeleine's tiny clothes in her special laundry soap. The three huge driers now hummed and tumbled while she fed Madeleine. It wasn't often she could do her own laundry at the same time, which would now free up a couple of hours: time she needed to figure out the details of another trip to the city and she was desperate to read more notebooks.

When the door opened at the same time there was a knock, Rachel shot from the chair and turned her back. Madeleine's whimper of protest didn't help ease off the sudden tension in her nerves.

'How's it going?' Ella poked her head in.

'Far out, you scared me.' Rachel yanked her top down and placed Madeleine over her shoulder.

'Oops, sorry. I didn't mean to frighten you. Laundry almost done?'

Rachel glanced at the timers. 'Another ten minutes before I can fold.'

'Do you need anything?'

'How about a new life?' She sat and sent a supercilious grin to Ella.

'Can't help you there. What about a coffee and something to eat?'

'Thank you but no. You have enough to do without waiting on me as well. But there is one thing I need to discuss.'

Ella came right in and shut the door. 'Tell me.'

'I have to go back to the city to meet the insurance assessor nine a.m. Tuesday morning.' She related the story as she placed Madeleine on her back on the small thick rug she'd laid out on the floor in the far corner. 'I'm not sure how long I will need to stay or what will happen.'

'Do you want to borrow my car?'

'No. I'll be safe in my car since Kyle doesn't know it belongs to me. I could have taken my car last time. I don't relish the drive not knowing where he is…' She paused when Ella waved a hand at her and pointed to the floor. 'Oh, my.' Rachel flew across the room and knelt beside her daughter who had rolled over onto her tummy. 'What a clever girl you are. But you are naughty to roll over when I wasn't watching. How dare you let Ella see it first.'

With a hearty laugh, Ella joined her on the floor and knelt right down so she could look Madeleine in the face. 'You are brilliant. You make sure you say Ella before you say Mama.' She placed the small soft dragon in front of the baby who slammed a hand on the toy and kicked her legs as though she thought it was the greatest fun. Ella sat and crossed her legs. 'She is such a good baby and you are a brilliant mother.'

Embarrassed, Rachel dropped her eyes. 'It's a case of muddling along and learning as I go.'

'The same as it is for all first time mothers. And you haven't got a partner to share the load.'

'I couldn't have coped without you and all the staff here.'

One after the other, the tumblers stopped to leave them in silence apart from gurgles from Madeleine who gripped the dragon tight and belted it on the floor.

Ella stood. 'It looks like Madeleine has a new game. Let me know your plans. I'll give the heads up to Mags.'

She opened the door and left while Rachel took a few minutes to play with her daughter before she opened the door to the first drier and folded each item as she drew them out. Still warm, the soft sheets folded with ease and didn't need an iron, especially when they were placed with precision on the shelves in the linen cupboard and weighted down with the previous day's pile. The tea towels and cloths for the restaurant were folded and left in a pile on the end of the bench for the staff to collect later. Her own laundry was folded and stacked into two piles, hers and Madeleines. She picked up Madeleine and put her in the pram, the backrest up a shade so the still alert little girl could watch the action. She was about to pile the clothes on the end of the pram when her phone rang, which meant a mad scramble to find it.

'Hello,' she huffed out after fishing the phone from the carrier under the pram.

'I don't dare ask how you are because you will say, fine, which is such an inane word with many meanings and none of them mean you are well and happy and aren't hidden away in some dark, dank place, terrified.'

Dylan's voice brought warmth to her heart. 'Hello to you as well and at the moment I am well and happy.

Madeleine turned over onto her tummy, my work for the day is completed, I'm about to go to my room to have lunch and have the rest of the day to myself. So, I'm fine.'

Deep laughter tingled her eardrum. 'I could come and pay you a visit.'

'Don't you dare.'

'Why not?'

'You know why not.'

'Kyle is back in the city.'

'How can you possibly know that?'

'He went back last night through back roads.'

'How…'

'He used his credit card to buy fuel in one place and food in another. His credit card was used in the city this morning.'

'How on earth… but you have his card. Oh, no you don't. His credit card wasn't in his wallet.'

'It's possible he had it tucked in his clothes with him or it could have been in his car. The detectives have the two cards you gave me and are tracing his movements through the credit card usage. He has a second card attached to his credit account – in your name.'

'Excuse me. I never had a card to his account. Or he never gave me one. Don't the banks only give a second card if it is a joint account?'

'His credit card account is a joint account. You never knew?'

'No way. Does it mean I'm liable for any debts he has on the credit card?'

'I'm not sure.'

'If they are tracing his movements, how come they haven't caught him?'

'They know where he's been but he's never there when they turn up. Do you know if he has any relatives he could hole up with?'

'He always told me he had none in this country. He said his parents lived in the U.K. although he doesn't have an English accent and now I doubt it's true since everything else he told me was a big fat porky pie. For all I know he could have another wife stashed away somewhere. And who's to say his parents have the surname of Jacobs. It could be Jackson or even some other name. I need a favour.'

'Now I'm worried. You added on your favour comment after a tirade as though you are too scared to ask.'

'I have to meet the insurance assessor on Tuesday. At the property.' With her feet beginning to hurt, she sat on the chair, rocked the pram with her foot because Madeleine had become restless, and related her tale about the insurance.

'I'll call Justin. I'm certain he will want to be with you in case Kyle turns up. If I didn't have to work I'd go and since we both have to return to the city tomorrow, I'll follow you to ensure you are safe. What time do you want to leave? I'll be there.'

'You don't have to.'

'Yes, I do. It was due to my slip up he came knocking on your door. Allow me to go some way to atone for my huge blunder. And I have to go back in any case so it's no big deal.'

'I'm… thank you.'

'Time? Is ten too late?'

'Ten is good.'

'See you in the morning.' The call ended.

Eager to do more research, Rachel changed Madeleine and settled her in the cot for a nap. She made a cheese and tomato sandwich with a grate of carrot and fresh beetroot to give it a bit more healthy substance and filled a large glass with water. There was no hesitation in what she wanted to examine this time. She tugged out the bottom notebook from the pile, opened the front cover and read Adam Hinkler. The name sounded familiar but she couldn't figure out why. It wasn't one of her associates nor a past work mate.

Over the page there was a date of over three years ago with another dot-pointed list. Kyle sure was a creature of habit.

> · *Maserati.* Well a flash car would attract Kyle.
> · *Mansion on the water.* So would a mansion.
> · *Separated.*
> · *No kids.* Rachel scoffed.
> · *Father – senator.* Now Rachel knew where she'd heard the name.
> · *Millionaire.* Bullseye as far as Rachel figured. A prime candidate for blackmail.

While she mulled, she could picture the senator. A tall man with a full head of hair, grey at the temples.

He often featured in newscasts but she couldn't remember why. It had been a while since she'd bothered with the political scene. They didn't matter much in this part of the world. It wasn't often she watched any news broadcasts either – all doom and gloom as far as she was concerned. Reading books was a far better use of the little free time she had nowadays.

She turned the page and was delighted to find all the contact details, although she doubted Adam Hinkler would be as delighted. Did she or didn't she? There was a pile of cash tucked under her mattress which belonged to this man. Unsure how much cash there was she retrieved it and snapped off the elastic band. Wow, they were all one hundred dollar bills and looked to be brand new. Maybe they came from a bank. It took a while to count, especially when she lost count and had to count again, this time putting each one thousand pile crossways. When she was sure she'd counted right, she sat back in stunned awe. So much. This man needed to get it back but was it the only amount for which he'd been blackmailed? Or was it a recent payment Kyle hadn't had a chance to bank. Or had he kept it as a cash reserve? But it wouldn't explain her money nor Angel's, although Angel's could be still have been there because it was recent. But her own pile wasn't recent.

One way to find out. She fetched her mobile phone from under the pram and dialled the number with her nerves doing little jigs while her heart rate increased.

'Who is this?' barked a male voice at the click.

'Are you Adam Hinkler?'

'Who's asking?'

Wow, this guy is as angry as a nest of bull ants. 'You don't know me but I am another of Kyle Jacob's victims.'

The hiss was long. 'What do you want?' There was definitely tension in the voice.

'I don't want anything but to give you some information.'

There was a long pause after another hiss as though the man was drawing in a breath through clenched teeth. 'Go on but first tell me who you are or I'm hanging up.'

Decisions, decisions. Does she give her real name or her present name? Best not to mention Jacobs. 'My name is Rachel Scott. There is an arrest warrant out for Kyle Jacobs. The police raided his home on Friday. They have all of the photographs.'

Adam swore, hissed again and paused so long, Rachel thought he was about to hang up. 'I was there with the police to collect a few of my items including a pile of cash which had my name on it. I also have in front of me, a pile of cash with your name on it. I counted it. There's fifty thousand dollars in what appear to be new one-hundred dollar bills. I want to return it to you. I don't know if this amount was the only money you gave him but there was a bank account with a lot of deposits the police are sure came from the victims. They froze the account so if you are owed more, there is a chance you could get it back. You will need proof. I had proof so the court granted me the cash with my name.'

'How come the cops didn't get my money if they raided the place?'

'Because they didn't know I took it and I don't want them to know. I'd appreciate it if you didn't tell them. My life has been a misery for fifteen months. I don't need any more. Look, it is obvious Kyle blackmailed you and you aren't the only person. I don't want to know why or how but I did see the photos of you – with him. It wasn't hard to figure out you, along with all the other victims, including me, were drugged and had no idea we were being photographed in compromising poses. The police found his hidden camera set-up. They know your name and should contact you. They will need all the victims to testify.'

'How did you get my number?'

'You ask a lot of questions I don't want to answer.' She had to be careful how she explained so she didn't incriminate herself. 'I found a few notebooks in the lining of a suitcase after I took out a pile of my clothes that had been stored in it. There is a separate notebook for each victim. Kyle noted down every detail about each person. As far as I can figure out we were both stalked as prospective targets for blackmail long before the blackmail began. The first entry in the notebook with your name is over three years ago.

'Three years?'

'I'm not sure how he went about it but in my case and in the case of another woman, his latest victim, I am sure he spotted his target and stalked them to figure out a way to hook them into his web.'

'How did he hook you in?'

'I'm not prepared to tell you. Maybe later down the track. My trust levels of anyone have been eroded to non-existent.'

'Join the club.'

'The club consists of eight members I know about and one potential he never went ahead with. There could be more. All I want is to warn you Kyle is on the run and to return this money to you. I presume it is yours.'

'Yes.'

'So how can I get it to you?'

'Where are you?'

'Not in the city. I escaped nine months ago. Changed everything about my life so he couldn't trace me. But I will be in the city on Tuesday and possibly a little longer. It depends on what happens on Tuesday as to how long I will stay. We can meet somewhere public if you want, although I have your address written in this notebook along with all of your contact details.'

'Holy hell.'

'Oh, and there's something else.'

'Am I going to like this?'

'It depends. I can't be certain this applies to you but it happened to me. Do you have a modern phone with a tracking app?'

'Huh, why?'

This time it was Rachel who paused and sighed. 'It's possible Kyle is able to track you with his phone. He tracked me. Knew where I was at all times. I'm not *au fait* with all these latest phone capabilities. I don't even know if he can track more than one phone. Although it's possible because parents can keep tabs on all of their kids and not only one.'

'Huh, how could he possibly link my phone with his?'

'He drugged you. How easy would it be for him to get into your phone while you were unconscious?'

'Damn it. It might answer a few questions. Oh, God. Give me your number, I'll get back to you with a time and place. Please don't come here.'

'I might add, the police have his mobile phone. Therefore, at the moment, Kyle won't be able to trace your phone. I bought a new one – without any modern tracking facilities. Mine is a pay-as-you-go version with no contract. It's an idea. Oh, and he put a magnetic tracking device under the driver's wheel hub on my car. You might want to check. When I escaped I attached the one I found to a road train headed for the eastern states.'

The string of swear words were colourful. 'Is there anything else I need to know?'

'I can't think of anything right now. If I do, I'll let you know when we meet. I'm sorry.'

'Why are you sorry?'

'I'm sorry for giving you bad news and more than sorry I ever met the bastard.'

'Make that two of us.'

'It might be an idea to be on the lookout until the police are able to arrest him. He's mighty angry at the moment and could seek revenge for losing his power and control. With a frozen account and loss of all this cash I found, it's possible he'll do the blackmail threat again to get more money. If he comes knocking, tell him the police know everything.'

'If he turns up here, he's in for a shock. I appreciate the call. I'll get back to you but you need to give me your contact number first.'

Number given, Rachel hung up and flopped over the desk, mentally exhausted. Two down, another seven to go, although she could cross Olivia off the list because Kyle gave up on her. And her own name was another to cross off. Four down and five to go sounded a heap better.

To let the last ten minutes cogitate, she hoed into the sandwich and washed it down with half a glass of water. Still antsy, she stood, jogged on the spot for the count of two hundred, checked on Madeleine and wished she was awake so they could play, and swept the floor. All because she needed hard activity to prevent what she'd learnt, taking up residence in an already overwhelmed brain.

Back at the desk, she decided to read more about Adam Hinkler and turned the page. As she read, she wished she had kept all of the flash drives for there would be photos to go with the details. Kyle had stalked the guy for months, to gather intimate details of his family, broken marriage and his life in general. It appeared he came from old money, had been wealthy from birth and become independently wealthy through property dealings. The guy never had to work but had a Master's degree from university in finance and business administration and worked for a big mining company at their city headquarters.

So how did such an intelligent man get involved with Kyle? She read on.

Oh, Kyle created some big business deal, which she bet was a complete sham. It would be one way to meet the man. A memory of a childhood poem surged. The Spider and the Fly. To check it out, she opened up her computer and searched for the poem. The seven verses caused her to laugh. 'How darn appropriate. You, Mary Hewitt, got it right way back in 1828 and it seems we haven't learnt from your lesson in almost 200 years. Kyle is the cunning spider who entrapped multiple flies into his web through the use of seduction and manipulation.' How many times had he used flattery, charm and the false offer of help or friendship, and marriage, to trap unsuspecting victims so he could blackmail them into giving him vast sums of money? He sure had mastered Manipulation 101.

And poor Adam, it seems, was threatened with exposure to his ex-wife when she went to court for settlement and to bring his father down by putting the photos he took in the public domain with explicit wording. Bastard. But why, oh, why didn't Adam report it to the police? A snort escaped. Who was she to question Adam? It took her months to take Kyle to court, although she had a specific reason but when she did find the guts, she got results.

The next notebook at the bottom of the pile belonged to Angel. Rachel couldn't figure out why she went to the bottom each time. Could be for the mystery of the unknown or how hers was on the top and she couldn't face reading about her own utter stupidity. She had to be the dumbest of the fly clan for she got hooked in so far she married the bastard.

"Alas, alas! How very soon this silly little fly,
Hearing his wily, flattering words, came slowly flitting by:
With buzzing wings she hung aloft, then near and nearer drew…"

She repeated the beginning of the sixth stanza several times for weren't they her to a T and she doubted the words would ever leave her brain.

Determined to put her own stupidity aside, she opened the book to the first page. Angel Lombardo. Well, she was right about the Mediterranean bit for Lombardo had to be an Italian surname. It would account for the gorgeous, tanned skin. She flipped the page over to find the same dot-pointed list. The first date was two years ago. Rachel searched her brain for when Angel had said she met Kyle. Yes, eighteen months ago so Kyle had to have had around six months to work out a plan. It was then she remembered she'd stolen Angel's flash drive. It took only a couple of minutes to set her laptop up, find the flash drive, shove it into the little slot and open up the un-protected files. Kyle's arrogance about no-one would dare enter his office or touch his computer, now paid dividends. She sure never entered the study, not even to clean the room. One scary scolding was more than enough.

She figured the folders were the same as in hers with photos in weekly lots so clicked on the first folder.

Angel sat in a coffee shop booth, her laptop open and a mug of some hot drink held between both hands. Her eyes were on the screen. The pale blue blouse and navy jacket were of the business dress variety. Nowhere near as vibrant as the red outfit Rachel had seen on Friday. The biggest shock was the hair for it was black, glossy and long, which made her look more beautiful. No wonder Kyle was attracted to her. It went with the first dot pointed comment – *Stunning.*

The second photo was of her leaving the shop, followed by her entering an older style office block, one Rachel recognised but had never had the need to enter. She presumed it was Angel's place of work. Thus began the stalking process for the rest of the photos in the first folder were of her leaving the same building, her car – with a separate shot of her number plate, the car parked in a carport and several shots of what Rachel guessed was her home – a red brick, semi-detached unit with a strip of a well-maintained garden in front, a concrete driveway into a carport and a narrow path down the side, blocked off by a tall, cream Colourbond gate.

Kyle had become daring in folder two for he had followed Angel inside the building where she worked, taken a photo of her pressing the number button inside the elevator. He had to have been using his phone to take these photos but they weren't on his current phone. Was there another phone hidden away somewhere or had Kyle downloaded the photos and deleted them from his phone? She paused. He had given her his old phone and bought a new one after they married. There were no photos on the old phone for he had cleared off all of his data. Which meant he must have downloaded these photos onto the flash drive. It still didn't make sense for some of these photos were taken after he'd given her the phone. Did he have two phones? She would have to suggest it to the detectives. In the meantime, the only way to find out was to ask Dylan if the photos were on Kyle's phone, if she was game. Dylan would want to know why.

Photos followed, including one of the front of the office of Angel's workplace with a close-up of the name, hours, contact email and phone number. With what she knew now, it didn't take genius status to figure out why he wanted those details. She laid a bet with herself. Kyle orchestrated the bad PR within his own company, offered to research a company to help solve the problem and recommended Angel, right down to her contact details.

The photos in the other folders ran along the same lines as those in her folders. It gave her a creepy sensation to see all were of Angel at various functions, eating places, coffee houses and weekend outings, giving him a detailed montage of her life.

With a sigh of derision she went back to the note book to find short jottings about each photo. The comments when Angel had been with someone else, a man in particular, were a shock for each ranged from nasty to vile. *Gotcha, baby* went with a shot of Angel about to get into Kyle's car. Another suckered in fly caught in the web. Her weekly wage was mentioned early on. How on earth did he find out such private information? The two big ticks next to the amount said a lot.

When she saw *Saturday* with a date after she'd married the bastard, she took a closer look. *Perfect afternoon. Hot, hot, hot. Best set of tits ever.* Well, hell, she didn't need to know those details. Nor the details on the following Saturday where there was a blow by blow description of their afternoon in bed. But whose bed? It wasn't the one in the house. Must have been Angel's bed. So much for golf. And he dared blow his stack and accuse Rachel of cheating. Bastard wasn't a good enough word to call him.

Despite the stabs of deep pain etching her innards: a pain she should be over; Rachel was intrigued to read on when money was mentioned. He knew down to the last cent how much Angel had in her bank account, what her car was worth, how much she spent each week on food, rent, entertainment and sundries. Wow, he had to be a master at snooping to find out all of those details. He'd also worked out how much he could get from her. *At least fifty grand,* was highlighted and circled. Well, he'd achieved over half the amount, add in the fortnightly amount she had been paying, most of which he would have got back when he sold the house – if he could have sold the house.

Rachel sat back in the chair to muse over how he thought he would achieve the fifty thousand mark in the last four weeks before the day he would have left her stranded at the hotel. What had he planned? It couldn't have been good and the only things she could think of sent a shudder down her spine. Would he have physically harmed her the same way he had with Rachel? Had he done this before? Was it his *modus operandi?* Was he a serial abuser? If so, why hadn't anyone reported his activities to the police before she did? Not that the police believed her at first. At the time they weren't interested in marital spats. They were sure interested now. Of course, he planned on emptying the joint bank account.

Overcome, she slammed the notebook shut, yanked out the flash drive and closed down her computer. This was too much. With a wave of nausea through her stomach she stood, gave her body a vigorous shake and jogged on the spot until sweat poured and her breaths became laboured. She wished she dared go for a long run around the lake but she would never leave Madeleine alone and there was no way she could run with her.

Instead she made plans for another trip to the city by jotting down what she needed to take and making a phone call to Pierre and Olivia to organise a few hours of baby-sitting. To chat with normal humans was a far better option.

It was after a two-hour session of a cleaning frenzy broken by a feed and extra-long play with Madeleine, Rachel was in the right frame of mind to go back to the notebooks. Even the thought of what she'd discovered so far, curdled her innards. Guilt raged for being a part of the obscene activities, mixed with a strong dose of shame. Logic told her there was no reason for either emotion to be attributed to her but logic couldn't convince her brain.

The bottom book belonged to Kelly Barker. This would be interesting for this was the one woman with no photos, or at least, no photos they'd found. With eyes closed. Rachel trolled through what she remembered about Kelly. For two years she'd paid $2,000.00 a month. The payments had ceased close on two years ago. Why?

She turned the page.

- *Daddy's girl*
- *No mother*
- *No boyfriend*
- *Nervy*
- *Okay looks – designer clothes – omega watch.*
- *Easy target*
- *Goes alone to bars and nightclubs looking for a guy*

· *Too scared to approach any lone men*

'Oh, you poor woman,' Rachel said to the page and muttered the first two lines of the poem.

'Will you walk into my parlour?' said a spider to a fly:
'tis the prettiest little parlour that ever you did spy.'

A picture of what happened next centred in her brain without turning the page to read what was written. Kyle made the move. Kelly was overjoyed a guy came up to her with sweet talk and bought her a drink. He invited her to dinner, or supper. Took her home. Gave her a farewell peck on the cheek and invited her to go on another date. He was the epitome of a gentleman – considerate, opened the door for her, didn't overdo the touches, showed restraint. And told her a lot of porky pies about himself while calculating his next move.

She put a finger on the corner of the page, blew out her cheeks with raised shoulders and flipped the page over. The date was on the top. She counted back the years and months. Four years and three months ago. Seems he didn't waste much time if the blackmail began after only three months of set-up.

Finnegan's Bar. She knew where it was, had gone in once with a friend. The name described it well. Typical Irish bar with good pub food, lots of Guinness and loud Irish folk music. It wasn't her favourite type of entertainment but she'd enjoyed the night. The beef and Guiness pie had been a stray from her normal healthy diet but was yummy. She'd tried a sip of Guiness from her friend's glass but didn't like it. She'd never been a beer drinker. Her glass of chilled white wine had been far better.

The next comments were as she'd predicted.

A walk-over. One drink was all it took. Ordered a meal, took her home. Next date in two days.

The following page had all the contact details and address but the details were scant in the next few pages apart from the date and places he took her. This might have been his first attempt after which, he'd learnt to keep a more detailed diary. Without hesitation, she dialled the phone number.

'H… h… hello.' The voice was soft and tremulous.

'Hello, my name is Rachel Scott. You don't know me but I'm another victim of Kyle Jacobs.'

'Oh, God, leave me alone. I don't want to speak to you. Go away. Dad?' The last word was yelled so loud, it hurt Rachel's eardrum.

The call ended. Rachel figured it wasn't wise to reconnect. Kelly sounded traumatised and made it obvious her father knew all about Kyle. She hoped Kelly had been wise enough to go to her father and he confronted Kyle. She flipped through the few pages. The last one told the story for in large thick letters were four words.

BITCH TOLD HER FATHER.

'Good on you, Kelly. You get a medal for being a brave woman.' But it had taken two years for her to find the courage. Rachel snorted and laid another bet. This was about the time Kyle bought a new phone. It had to be because the chicken had to change his number. And he'd moved house. Well, good and now he has to move house again, without any furniture. She high fived herself at the idea.

Before the next book, she checked on Madeleine and considered her own meal for the outside light had dimmed. A quick glance at the clock. The meal could wait. There was time to read one more notebook. She tugged out the bottom one, opened to the first page. Laura Jones. Her jaw gaped when she read the first dot point on the next page.

Assistant to the Premier.

Wow, wow, wow. Rachel plonked her hand over the other points so she could guess what they were. It had to be a super well-paid job, which would be the biggest attraction to Kyle. He wouldn't much care what she looked like if she had a lot of money. There would be either a decent car of her own or a government car. Laura would live in a fairly well to-do area and have the right contacts. The downside would be the long hours she would be required to work and maybe public appearances. Although those would appeal to Kyle because he was such a narcissist. Rachel snorted when she wondered how often he tried to be centre stage. Hmm, might be worth a search of old newspaper articles. It wouldn't be hard to work out dates.

She lifted her hand and grinned at how many she got right but her eyes boggled at the annual salary. Lucky for some and more than lucky for Kyle. On the next page she wavered on whether or not to contact the woman. Kelly was too traumatised, which was a pity for the knowledge how Kyle had been rumbled might go some way to ease the trauma. Another glance at the clock. Madeleine would wake soon. She could read the notes later so phone call it is.

She dialled the home number. It rang six times before she heard a click.

'Laura speaking.'

'Good evening. My name is Rachel Scott.'

'I'm not interested in whatever it is you're selling.'

'I'm not selling anything. This isn't one of those nuisance calls.

'Then who are you?'

'I'm another victim of Kyle Jacobs.'

'Oh, God, please no.'

'The police raided his home a couple of days ago. They know almost everything and have put out an arrest warrant for him.'

'Oh, thank God.'

'I might warn you; he still hasn't been caught so be careful.'

'How do you know?'

'I was there with the police when they raided his house. I had a court order to collect my belongings.'

'You were game to go to court?'

'Someone had to.'

'But what about…?'

'The photos?'

'Y… y… yes.'

'I've seen them and the police have them all, so Kyle doesn't have the ability to use them against you for any more blackmail threats. Plus they have his hidden camera, his computer, mobile phone and every other piece of evidence. They know you were drugged, along with at least seven others.'

'Seven? I thought I was the only one.'

'So did I, but there were nine I know about. He stalked them all for months before the initial contact. There are details in notebooks, which is how I found your contact number. There is a chance you could get your money back. Kyle had a separate account, which the police have frozen but it will mean you need to go to the police and tell them everything. Although they have your name so they might contact you first. Personally, I would contact them. I can give you the name of the two detectives in charge of this.'

'Oh, please, yes.'

She'd given the names when there was a kerfuffle outside. She lifted the corner of the curtain, peeked and reeled back at the shock. 'I'm sorry, I have to go. I'll be in the city Tuesday and will contact you again.' She slammed down the phone and made a mad scramble to collect all the evidence and shoved it in the bottom of the wardrobe. Why, why, why?

Rachel was about to open the door when there was a loud tattoo. She fought to calm shattered nerves and a good dose of anger. 'What are you doing here?' she said the second she opened the door.

'What a pleasant greeting.' Dylan smirked with a fist in the air ready to knock again.

Rachel planted her hands on her hips. 'You didn't answer.'

'Why am I here?' He lifted one finger. 'There's another storm due tomorrow so we need to get away early.'

'You could have rung me.'

A second finger rose. 'Kyle is in the city.'

Rachel shook her head at his persistence but his words gave her pause. 'How do you know Kyle is still in the city?'

'Recent credit card transactions – all in the city and I might add, all over the city and suburbs. The man must know he's being tracked for he's moving around – a lot. They are certain he has a different set of wheels because the yellow car hasn't been caught on any CCTV cameras where he's been but the bank ATM machines have caught his ugly mug each time he used one.'

The third finger rose before she could say a word. 'I can protect you better if I'm on the spot.' Fourth finger. 'It's the perfect chance for me to take you and your beautiful daughter for a nice meal.' The grin widened at the same time he nodded towards her room. 'Are you going to invite me in so we can discuss this in private?' His eyebrows rose in question.

She sighed, stood back and made a dramatic sweep of one arm out and towards the inside. His eyes crinkled in humour before he followed her in, studied the décor and perched his big frame on the end of the bed with his knees spread to keep his balance. Rachel sat as far away as she could - in the chair, which was in reaching distance.

'A bit cramped in here,' he said.

'It became cosier with the addition of Madeleine and her basic necessities but it's warm, dry, relatively safe and affordable. Why didn't you phone before coming?'

He sent her a half smile. 'Your answer would have been no. I have the room next door. Your boss was far more pleased about my presence. *Thank, God*, were her words when I rang to book the room. She also suggested the Thai restaurant in town, where we have a booking in…' he glanced at his watch, 'fifty-four minutes. According to her you love a couple of the dishes served there. And before you come up with a heap of excuses about safety, your Constable Pete and his fellow officers have assured me the yellow car in question hasn't been sighted in town since it left here the other night and they have searched every street, back road, back yard and known lover's hideaways. I have Pete's number on speed dial if I suspect Kyle is around. I get the impression the entire town like and respect you a great deal. *Part of the family*, I have been told by all. And they *look out for family*.

Rachel dropped her head when a rush of heated embarrassment hurtled up her neck to her face.

Dylan laughed. 'So how about it? Thai for dinner?'

She didn't get a chance to answer for Madeleine squawked.

Dylan laughed again as he stood and took the entire two steps to the cot where he lifted the baby and put her over his shoulder as if he'd done it a million times before. 'No need to answer for little Sweet Pea here has answered for you.' He eyed her and must have noticed her angst. 'I've got four older siblings, two brothers and two sisters. I'm an uncle to a small tribe and have done my share of babysitting. I know how to handle a baby, how to change them and clean their cute little backsides. The only thing I can't do is breastfeed them so here.' He came around the bed and handed her over. Another glance at his watch. 'I'll be back in fifty-two minutes. Will you have enough time to feed her and get ready?'

Miffed, Rachel sent him a glare. 'I haven't said I'd go.'

'Do I have to beg? I can guarantee I, along with every person in this town, will ensure you are safe. It's a meal and you have to eat. Hmm, maybe I should take Ella up on her suggestion.'

'What suggestion?'

'Call her if I need someone to shove you in the shower, throw some decent clothes on you and kick your butt out of this room, which I believe you have holed yourself in since lunchtime.' He raised his hands in submission. 'Not my words. Ella's words but I'm certain she will carry them out. She can be one bossy woman.'

Rachel couldn't hold back a laugh. 'When you run a place like this, you need to be a tad bossy to ensure it runs smoothly but Ella is one of the kindest people ever put on this earth.'

'No husband?'

'He works for the council and does the heavy lifting around here at weekends and after hours. He's a terrific guy.'

'You still haven't said yes to dinner.'

Dinner out sounded so darn good. 'Yes, thank you. I'll be ready.'

He opened the door. 'I'll knock in fifty minutes.'

When the door closed panic set in. Fifty minutes to shower, do magic with her hair, find something to wear and deal with Madeleine. Shower first. She set Madeleine on the floor with her space toy, stripped off as she walked to the bathroom, tossed her clothes in the hamper, swiped paste on her toothbrush and turned on the taps. She scrubbed teeth until the water ran hot, spat and rinsed when she moved under the water and had the fastest shampoo, rinse and body wash in her history. Delight shimmered through her while she towelled her body dry. Dinner. With a guy. An experience she figured would never happen again. A couple of guys in town had asked her but she'd been too scared to say yes for several reasons. Trust was the biggest issue. She plain didn't trust a guy's intention. Her personal safety came a close second for until now she could never be sure Kyle wasn't hiding somewhere close by waiting for her to show her face. PTSD came in third for hushed sounds, the sudden appearance of a human and several other triggers caused her body to react and shutdown through utter terror.

While she used a blow drier and rounded brush to give her hair a bit of life she tried to figure out why Dylan didn't scare her half as much. He never made demands. Well, not true because she'd agreed to dinner after clever manipulation but there had been no secrets or underhandedness and she bet if she'd said no, he would have backed off. He always took a step back if he got too close and she shrank away. She knew she did it, knew he had noticed but it was something she couldn't help even though she hated it when it happened.

Hair done, she searched her drawers and wardrobe for something other than old jeans and a baggy T-shirt to wear. She frowned at the open wardrobe full of clothes from the thrift shop. Not one item was suitable for dinner out with a guy despite it being at the local take-away or eat-in Thai restaurant. She'd never eaten in before. Never been game.

When the purple suitcase caught her eye she dragged it out, unzipped the zip and sorted through. A pair of silky black slacks caught her eye and delight rumbled through her. Let's hope they fit. The delight sparkled after she stepped into them and did up the zip. Now for a top. She held up several before a red knitted long-sleeved top with sparkles around the neckline said – pick me. Perfect. It would be easy to bunch up to breast feed if needed and the long sleeves suited the coolish weather. Dressed, she changed Madeleine, put her in a clean onesie and gave her a feed with her eye on the clock. She had hurried but time had hurried quicker. Shoes, she needed decent shoes. A pair of black shiny low-heeled sandals she'd taken from the case and dropped on the floor were perfect. While Madeleine sucked, she managed to bend to the side and get the sandals on. A warm fuzzy zipped through her innards. It had been so long since she'd worn anything so glamorous.

Footsteps outside neared her door. She unlatched Madeleine, pulled her clothes into place and settled her in the pram. *Knock, knock.*

Phew. 'Coming.' She wheeled the pram to the door, opened it and gasped. Dylan was dressed in dark grey trousers, a pale blue shirt and black leather jacket.

He stared. 'Wow, you look stunning.'

'Clothes from my old life. They were in the suitcase.'

'I don't care where they came from, they suit you. Can you walk in those shoes? We can drive if you want.'

Rachel scowled. 'It's a hundred metres at most. I'm sure I can manage.'

It was a surprise when Dylan took control of the pram and wheeled it while she kept pace beside him. Despite having to squint at the glare, the setting sun ahead of them gave a hint of what was to come for instead of orange and red hues, the bank of clouds on the horizon was dark purple. The stillness was kind of creepy and the warmth of the day wasn't able to escape but had become trapped under the dense clouds while the moisture in the air was dank. It all gave meaning to the adage of the calm before the storm.

'When is the storm due to hit?' she asked.

'Mid-morning, which is why it would be better if we left around eight and headed north to be ahead of it.'

'How was the beach?'

'Rough as guts.'

'Did you go swimming?'

'I got my feet wet. I didn't relish being shark bait in the murky undertow. Even when it's rough, I enjoy walking along the coast. There's a raw beauty about it. I'm glad I came despite the distance.' He paused and turned to her. 'When did you last go to the beach?'

'Too long ago for me to remember.'

'You didn't go to the coast from here? It's only forty kilometres away?'

Rachel dropped her head, didn't answer and kept walking. The pram raced up beside her.

'Can I ask why not?'

'You can ask but the answer should be obvious.' She had to stop for they had reached the doorway to the restaurant.

Dylan moved so he faced her. 'You were too scared to spend a day at the beach, too scared to relax and enjoy yourself despite the odds of him being there were remote to zero?'

'Remote odds were way too many. Can we go inside?' Rachel took the handle of the pram and edged around Dylan to nudge the door open. He reached behind her and pushed the door wide until she was inside.

Spices hit her nasal passages, while the warmth from heaters wrapped around her and the murmur of voices gave her a sense of serenity. She had only been game to come in here once with Ella and her husband to buy takeaway. At other times she phoned for a delivery or someone else picked her order up for her. Dylan went to the counter and returned with a server who held menus in one hand, a carafe of iced water in the other and led them to their booked table. She blew out a sigh of relief when it was a table tucked in the rear corner, away from the door.

Dylan pulled out a chair. 'I figured you would want your back to the door. I'll sit where I can see it.' He nodded towards the other side. 'Pete and his wife are also having dinner out tonight.'

'You arranged this?'

'It was his idea to give you a bit of confidence to know you will be safe while you enjoy a night out.'

When tears washed over her eyes at their kindness and consideration, she fought them back as she settled into the chair with her head down so Dylan wouldn't notice. He wriggled the pram so Madeleine faced them both. After he sat, he lifted the wide awake baby from the pram, wrapped the blanket loosely around her and settled her on his lap with her semi-upright in the crook of his elbow. When Rachel caught his eye he had a smug face.

'Sweet Pea is my guest as well so why shouldn't she join the party?'

'You don't have to.'

'I want to.' He leant forwards and opened out a menu. 'Do you want separate dishes or to share?'

'Share sounds good.'

'Let me see if I can work out what your favourites are.' He studied her face before running his eyes down the menu. 'I'd say you are a Thai beef salad person, maybe Massamam curry or Pad Thai.' The quiver of his lips told her he had cheated.

'Ella has a big mouth.'

He laughed. 'I'm good with those, what would you like to drink? I'm having a mid-strength beer since I'm not driving.'

'Water and green tea. No alcohol because of Bugalugs there and I'm not into sugary sodas.'

After he'd given the order to the server, Dylan settled back in his seat and gave his attention to Madeleine, who eyed him with curiosity before she reached out, grabbed a handful of his shirt and sent him a smile.

'She might remember me from the courthouse.'

'Possible but she wasn't so good at focussing back then.'

He caught her eye. 'Tell me a little about yourself. Why the French names?'

'Pierre and I were born in France. Dad was French, Mum an Aussie. They met in London where Dad was a pastrycook in a French patisserie and Mum was on a working holiday for a year. They met, fell in love and Mum followed Dad to Paris when he went back to the patisserie where he trained. They married, Pierre arrived on the scene and I arrived two years later. Dad opened his own patisserie near his parent's vineyard in the Dordogne region and did well. When I was seven they decided to come back here to the city where he opened a patisserie. He baked while Mum ran the shop. You might remember it - Armand's Patisserie.'

'I do. There was always a queue waiting for it to open at nine.'

They sat back while drinks were served along with a bowl of rice.

'Dad only baked enough to sell on the day, hence the queues. When he ran out they closed the doors. We lived behind the shop. Dad baked before dawn while Mum saw us off to school and was in the shop at nine to open the doors while Dad had a couple of hours' kip. When the doors shut, they cleaned up, prepared for the next day and were there to pick us up from school, when they both spent quality time with us until bed time. He never opened on the weekend because family time was important to him. When I was eighteen, Mum was killed in an accident. A drunk driver veered onto the sidewalk, rammed into Mum and a couple of other pedestrian. Mum died instantly. It destroyed Dad. He sold the shop and hence, our home, split the proceeds three ways and returned to his parents' vineyard in the south of France.'

'You didn't go with him?'

'We could have but Pierre was in the final year of his university degree and I was in my first year. We pooled our money and bought a two-bedroom unit near uni. When Pierre began work he met Olivia. They married in my final year. We sold the unit, split the proceeds and he bought the house where he still lives while I bought another unit, which I kept until…'

'I get the picture. Do you still see your dad?'

'He died two years ago.'

'I'm sorry. You were close weren't you?'

'Very. Every year in our spring he would come here and spend three or four weeks with us and every Northern spring we flew to France to spend time with him. I have dual citizenship, although Kyle never knew I had another passport.'

'Why didn't you use it to go back to France?'

'Several reasons. I didn't have enough money, was pregnant and needed to earn to save and also needed to get back our family furniture and my belongings. I couldn't let Kyle get away with his vindictiveness so I spent the time planning until after Madeleine was born. Madeleine was my French grandmother's name. She was an amazing woman with the softest of hearts. Now it's your turn.'

The food arrived, which halted conversation while they piled food onto their plates and began to eat, Dylan with one hand while he kept an arm around Madeleine who became engrossed in his every movement with the fork. She managed to grab the fork and cause the food to drop off.

Dylan raised his eyebrows. 'You aren't ready to eat spicy Thai, little Sweet Pea.' He plopped her back in the pram and lifted the back halfway up so she could still see what was going on.

Rachel was overcome at how good he was with Madeleine and how he understood the mind of a seven-week-old baby, who hadn't uttered a sound since he'd taken her from the pram.

Silence prevailed while they ate until the silence began to unnerve her.

'You were going to tell me about yourself,' she said to get the conversation going again.

'Was I?' His shoulders rose and fell. 'My life is nowhere near as interesting as yours. My parents are still with us, thank goodness. They raised five kids in a great family atmosphere. I joined the force at eighteen but studied part time. I'm interested in forensic science. I was on the beat for a few years, did two years in the bush, which I enjoyed even though it was hard at times. Studied to become a sergeant. I've been in the court system for eighteen months. I enjoy the regular daytime shifts, which gives me a chance to complete my forensics degree. I would like to become a detective. The court system is an eyeopener and family court kind of depressing. I spend part of my time in the courtrooms, guarding people, like you, who have been threatened, or being a deterrent against angry parties who can't, or don't want to be civil. Other times I protect people as they arrive or leave when their previous partner levels threats against them and it's not always the male partner who is the instigator. There have been more than a few females who are the violent partner. And I've had to protect judges and magistrates on occasion. But the hours are good with no overtime and no night duty. Never married but you already know about my disastrous engagement.'

'Has it put you off marriage?'

'No. I'd love to find the right woman and have a family. What about you? Are you up for marriage again?'

'I don't want to spend my life alone but don't know how I could ever allow myself to trust again. Men scare me.'

'Do I come under the same umbrella?'

Rachel quirked one eyebrow. 'I'm sitting in a restaurant opposite you and walked next to you to get here and let you into my place of abode without another person there.'

'Thank you, I'm honoured although Pete over there keeps one eye on me all the time so I don't have any choice but to behave.'

'And if he wasn't there?'

Dylan laughed, leant forwards and sobered. 'I've heard all the details of your story. You have every reason to be scared for the treatment you received was appalling but there is no way I would do anything to bring you more terror. You have all the control when it comes to us. You tell me to back off and I will but I hope you don't because I'm attracted to you and like you a lot. You are a gutsy woman with an inner strength. You could have gone back to France to escape this bastard but you stayed to ensure you received retribution. I see your fear all the time but guess once Jacobs is in gaol, you will be able to let go and begin to live again. We will catch him. At the moment he's living on borrowed time.' He relaxed back in the chair. 'So tell me, do you want me to back off?'

Rachel buried her head in her hands. It was such a difficult question. She liked him, even trusted him to a certain extent. And it sure was a change to be able to... she couldn't think of the word. Relate with someone? Socialise? She lifted her head. 'The short answer is no.'

'But?'

The word brought a grimace. 'I have reservations.'

'Understood. Tell me what they are although I've figured out some. You can't handle being touched. Triggers set you off. Trust is a big issue. Men scare you. You will do anything to protect your daughter to the extent you would walk away from a man who didn't accept her as a part of you. All of these, I understand and accept.'

Surprised by his perception, her mouth gaped. 'Wow.'

'Several units of victim and perpetrator psychology under my belt and you are an easy read. You don't try to hide your fear. You are upfront with your emotions but underneath all of your trauma you have a soft and generous heart.' He waved his hand over the remnants of their meal. 'Are we done here so I can get you home? We need an early start in the morning, which reminds me, where are you staying in the city? The same hotel?'

'I haven't made a reservation yet.'

Dylan stood and manoeuvred the pram around after tucking the blanket tighter around Madeleine. 'I do have a suggestion. I have a three bedroom townhouse...'

'No, no way.'

He held up one hand to stop her. 'Hear me out. I was not suggesting you stay with me, although you could if you wanted to. A fellow officer owns the townhouse next door. He and his wife are overseas for a few weeks. I messaged him, told him about you and how you might need somewhere secure to stay for a couple of days. And it is secure. You need a code to get in the front entry and another to get the elevator to work. I live on the second floor. He okayed it if you want. It's up to you. I won't be there during the day but can be on hand after hours. I won't pressure you. There is a hidden garage for your car and its free. I'm only giving you a safe option.'

'Thank you. I appreciate the trouble you've gone to. I'm overwhelmed and thank you for tonight.'

'My pleasure.' He wheeled Madeleine to the counter and paid while Rachel moved to Pete and his wife and gave them both a hug.

The moment they were outside, the chill of the evening cause her to shiver. As she pushed the pram, Dylan wriggled beside her.

'Don't be alarmed,' he said in her ear at the same time he draped his coat over her shoulders.

His kindness brought back a threat of tears which she blinked away while a warm fuzzy swept through her innards. 'Thank you.' She turned her head. 'Why are you so nice to me?'

His shoulders rose at the same time dark eyes swept over her. 'You shivered and I was raised to be a gentleman, although a lot of women these days don't appreciate old-fashioned values. I've been derided by a couple of females because of things I've done. One berated me on the sidewalk because I opened the car door for her. I didn't regard her as an equal or capable, according to her. Another made a scene because I moved to the outside of the footpath. Neither lasted beyond a single date.'

'Feminism gone too far. It's nice when a person cares enough to do those things for you. So thank you for caring. I know someone who never considered or practised old-fashioned values,' she added in an undertone.

'Let's not spoil a beautiful evening.'

Within minutes they arrived back at the motel and parted ways with a time set for the morning which meant she needed to pack before she went to bed.

While she drove, Rachel made lists in her mind to make sure she had packed every item she needed. It had been a mad rush earlier to bathe and feed Madeleine before she could pack her car. It still amazed her how much gear a tiny human needed for a couple of days. Her own gear fitted into a sports bag. Jeans, tops, hoodie, two different wigs, underwear, socks and a warm jacket, which she still wore for the morning had turned from the chill of last night to downright cold with a brisk wind straight from the South Pole. Add the basic toiletries in a smallish bag. She didn't need much; toothbrush and paste, brush, deodorant, soap, shampoo and hair elastics, whereas Madeleine's toiletries required a bag double the size. Her clothes, blankets, nappies, chuck-up cloths, wipes, along with amusement toys required a small suitcase. Money – yes, she'd packed Adam's money and most of her own to deposit into her bank account. Did she put in the list of contact details for the other victims? Lord, she had to delve deep to remember. Yes, they were in her handbag, tucked into the inside pocket. She'd put them there last night.

So far the drive had been steady. With a police officer not far behind, she wasn't game to let the speedometer needle climb over the regulated speed limit, but his presence sure made a difference to her nervous tension compared to last Friday. The storm was determined to catch up with them with a few spatters of rain every now and again but not yet heavy enough to set the wipers going. They'd not long passed the service station where she'd taken refuge – was it only three days ago? With the last day of a long weekend, traffic was much heavier than she'd like. Concentration was a must yet her brain cells kept wandering to every conceivable *what if* that could happen and *maybes* that were impossible, yet they still raged through her mind.

She straightened at the sight of a notorious wide bend ahead and slowed to leave more space between her car and the car in front. Stupid, for there was already at least ten car lengths between them. A stream of vehicles was coming the other way. The car in front vanished around the curve which delighted her for there was a long space between them.

'Oh hell!' she screamed when a large utility sped out from the opposite stream onto her side of the road and headed straight for her.

Horns blew.

A single finger shot high from the utility window a split second before the car wove from side-to-side in a desperate bid to get back into the stream.

With her heart lodged somewhere uncomfortable, she stared. The utility neared. Came close enough she could see the driver struggle with the steering wheel. With no hope of him righting his car, Rachel swung the steering wheel left and aimed for the clearest route through the bush. Hands gripped around the wheel, she jolted and bumped down the embankment, over shrubs and did her best to avoid a tree with a yank further left. She missed the tree, aimed for a large shrub but didn't see how it hid a huge boulder until the front wheel slammed into the corner of the rock and the car jerked and shuddered to a stop on an angle. Madeleine squealed at the same time all the air shot from Rachel's lungs at the impact when she jolted forward and the seatbelt yanked her back into the seat.

Stunned and breathless, she sat until Madeleine's cries brought her back to reality. When her door opened Rachel screamed.

'Are you okay? Are you hurt? Rachel, speak to me.' Dylan's head appeared. 'I'm going to unlatch your safety belt.' He leant over, the belt clicked, he eased it back and squatted at her side. 'Did your head hit anything?'

'Excuse me, I'm a nurse. Can I help?' A female voice penetrated Rachel's confusion.

'My baby,' came out a little too loud but she'd lost the ability to control anything. 'I have to check my baby.' Despite her heart making out it was a set of kettle drums booming full pelt one after the other, she tried to get out.

'Sit there a minute to catch your breath. I'll get her,' said Dylan.

'Leave her in the capsule. I'll check her over.' The nurse's voice faded.

Rachel tried to turn to make sure Madeleine hadn't been turfed out of the capsule and flung around the car but her chest hurt so she rested back and prodded around her ribs. Ribs seemed intact with no sharp pain. She pulled the top of her T-shirt away, peered down and noticed the red mark left by the pressure of the seat belt. Okay. A seat belt burn. She could live with a bruise so she leant back, closed her eyes and forced her lungs to even out her breathing. It felt as though a huge vacuum had sucked out any functioning brain cells.

'Pete, there's a white Ford Ranger utility headed your way.' Dylan squatted by her side. 'Personal plate Big Makk 007. M.A.K.K. Arrest the driver and charge him with dangerous driving causing an accident and failure to stop to render assistance. Lock him in a cell for the night. Do every substance test you know about and impound his car for the maximum length of time for hooning. You might want to see if he has a record and get his car insurance details for Rachel will need them. I also need a tow truck with a tilt-tray. Rachel's car is undrivable. Front wheels are out of alignment.'

'Dylan?' Rachel leant forwards when her brain cells aligned and she understood what Dylan had said.

He held up a hand to stop her. 'Rachel is in a state of shock but is okay and the baby is unharmed. Rachel did a spectacular drive off the road to save their lives.' Dylan eyed her. 'I'll pack all of her gear in my car and take her the rest of the way.' There was a long pause. 'We're about forty clicks north of the servo. Yes, the big bend. Okay. I'll leave her car key on top of the passenger rear wheel. I'll send you a police report tonight. I saw the entire incident and have it on dash-cam. You might want to inform the idiot next time he decides to hoon he shouldn't do it in front of a cop who has a dash-cam. Thanks Pete.'

Dylan switched off his phone and held out his hand for Rachel to take. 'Come on, let's get you in my car so you can cuddle your daughter and put your mind to rest. Those capsules do a good job. I'll empty your car. Pete will arrest the guy and throw the book at him with as many charges as he can. How do you feel? Any aches?'

'Seat belt burn.'

'Understood. A few bruises are better than the alternative. Your quick thinking and great driving skills saved your life.'

She wasn't so sure about great driving skills. It all happened so fast there wasn't time to consider driving safely. Still stunned, she took her time to step out. With legs determined to not hold her up she was glad of Dylan's support as she managed to straighten. Not too bad. A few twinges. Before she took a step she studied her car and winced. There was a big dent on the front fender and a skewed wheel. 'Can it be fixed?'

'I'm not sure. It depends on what broke. It could be the entire chassis. If repairs cost more than the car's value it might be a write-off.' With one hand held tight around hers and the other on her shoulder, he led her through the bush, which was easier to negotiate on the walk out than the drive in for she'd flattened and torn out many of the shrubs. She had to lean on him to get up the embankment to his car parked on the verge, a blue flashing light on the roof.'

'Where did the light come from?'

'I've always carried a portable blue bubble. This isn't the first time I've used it. Even when we are off duty, we are still cops under oath to up-hold and maintain the law.'

They reached the car where a middle-aged woman held a sobbing Madeleine in her arms. The nurse held her out. 'This little one needs her mama. I checked her over. There are no injuries, not even a bruise.'

Rachel reached out but Dylan beat her. 'Sit in the passenger seat, buckle up and I'll hand her over.'

Too overcome to argue, she did as asked. Tears she had no control over, rolled from her eyes as she kissed Madeleine's red face and gently held one ear against her heart. She couldn't help lifting clothes to touch each part of Madeleine's body to see for herself there were no injuries, or bruises, or red marks. Satisfied, she cuddled Madeleine closer and put her to her breast even though she wouldn't be hungry yet but the sensation eased her own angst and calmed her baby until Madeleine's eyes closed and she fell asleep. Still Rachel held her, too scared to let her go until all of her gear had been packed in Dylan's car and he sat in the seat next to her. Wet. She hadn't noticed the rain.

He handed over a bunch of keys. 'I left the car key and remote with the car. We can sit here as long as you need but Madeleine has to go back into the capsule before we leave. You can either stay in the front or sit next to her in the back. I understand this is a big ask for you to trust me but there is little choice.'

'Thank you but I trusted you when I went in your car last Friday. I trust you now.' She opened the door, got out and immediately got back in when the rain hit. 'Hold her a sec.' After handing Madeleine into Dylan's arms she climbed over the console, knelt on the seat and took Madeleine back. She hadn't noticed but Dylan had strapped the baby capsule into the seat behind her and draped an extra blanket over the top. Tears at his kindness fell while she wrapped her baby in a comfortable swaddle, clipped the harness into place and tucked the other blanket over the top.

Embarrassed at her loss of control, she wiped the tears away before getting back into the front seat.

'Are you okay,' Dylan asked with a held out small box of tissues.

'Thanks to you, yes.' She *whooped* two tissues from the box and swept them across her eyes with her head turned away, embarrassed to be caught with tears in her eyes. She didn't do tears. 'Oh, I forgot to thank the nurse.' She said over her shoulder as she searched for the woman.

'I thanked her on your behalf. Let's get you to the city. You are free to close your eyes and sleep.' He turned on the radio to a classical station, lowered the volume, started the car and drove off, the wipers in a furious effort to clear the downpour from the windscreen.

It wasn't until she figured Dylan was a careful driver and slowed his speed to suit the awful conditions, she eased tense innards to relax back and close still scratchy eyes. Sleep was impossible with her innards still humming and the gradual realisation of how close she'd come to losing both her life and Madeleine's. The burn across her sternum and chest eased to a dull twinge until she moved when it warned her to not move.

They drove in relative silence until Dylan turned into a service station about a hundred kilometres from the city. 'I need a bathroom break and coffee. How about it?'

'You go in while I stay with Madeleine. I'll go in when you get back. Never wake a sleeping baby because you will always regret it.'

Dylan laughed. 'True.'

He was back within minutes with a hot chocolate and blueberry muffin for her. His thoughtfulness almost brought back another round of tears but she fought them back because she could not show weakness. She was strong. She repeated the mantra while making as little movement as possible on the way to the rest rooms and while she waited in the inevitable queue at the ladies.

'Where am I taking you?' Dylan asked when they reached the outer suburbs and slowed to what felt like a crawl after the speed of the open road. 'The hotel or my neighbour?'

'I was going to the hotel but without a car I guess the townhouse is a better option. Is it close to the city?'

'It's in the city, close enough I can walk to work.' He pointed to the still wet sky. 'When it's a bit drier than today.'

'Your neighbour it is. Thank you. I appreciate you organising it. I need the address for Olivia because she's going to babysit tomorrow morning.'

'Which reminds me, Justin will pick you up in the morning and stay with you. If this other woman turns up, she had to have been in contact with Jacobs. It might be a good chance to find out where he's been holed up. And I have a cot for Sweet Pea.'

'You have a cot?'

'A semi-permanent loan from my sister. There are still two nephews at the toddler stage and it's too dangerous to let them loose in a bed.'

'Dangerous?'

'As in waking before sun-up to create chaos if they aren't hemmed in. Neither has yet figured out how to climb out of a cot.'

'Do you have any faults?'

Dylan's shout of laughter echoed. 'Plenty, ask my sisters. No, better not.'

'I'm intrigued.'

It took an hour before Rachel had settled into the unit, so spacious she was lost in it after the cramped motel room she'd become accustomed to. Dylan had asked if she wanted to spend time together, which would have been good in one sense for when she was with him her loneliness dissipated. She did agree to a shared take-out for the evening meal. Not having any food or a car to buy food made it an easy decision. And she sure wasn't about to walk to any shops.

She made the excuse how she and Madeleine needed together time, which was true to an extent. There were also a few phone calls she wanted to make without Dylan's knowledge. While she sat on the floor playing with Madeleine, who kicked and waved her hands around while Rachel wriggled toys, the first call went to Olivia to finalise babysitting. The half hour chat about anything apart from a certain bastard and her little car escapade, restored her equilibrium and lightened her mood. It was so good to laugh. It was even better to see Madeleine smile at her laughter.

The second phone call was to Adam since she hadn't heard from him. His hesitancy seemed odd but he finally agreed to meet in his lunch hour tomorrow. The meeting with the insurance assessor shouldn't take three and a half hours. All she had to do was talk Olivia into hanging around long enough and drive her to the meeting for she wasn't about to expose herself on the streets to get across the other side of the city. A taxi was an option but it meant dealing with the car seat and pram.

To avoid the other phone calls she eased onto her stomach with a few winces when bruises met the hard surface, to face Madeleine who had managed to roll over and was intent on bashing a fist on the caterpillar with a gurgle at each hit when it squeaked. Rachel copied, cooed and laughed. 'You are such a clever girl,' she said over and over. It was far more fun until Madeleine tired of the game and whimpered.

A feed and nappy change filled in the next thirty minutes until Madeleine fell asleep. With baby tucked up in the cot Dylan had wheeled in, Rachel sat at the dining table with her phone in her hand and the list of other victim's details open in front of her. Ethan Barnes and Jordan White's names stared back at her. Madison Hart was at the very bottom. She hadn't had time to go through their notebooks so had no idea what their relationship with Kyle was. If there was a relationship, it couldn't be good for there to be a notebook. And she didn't bring them with her. There was enough to bring as it was.

After the Eeny, Meanie, Miney, Moe between the three names she dialled Madison Hart's number but received the message to wait for the tone and leave a message. Instead, she hung up. Who would get the message? And what would happen if Rachel dropped Kyle's name? Madison might have a panic attack and Rachel understood from her own personal experience how bad panic attacks could be. Better to call later and speak in person.

Jordan White came second so she dialled his mobile number since it was a public holiday and it was likely he wouldn't be at work.

'Who is this?' came a deep voice.

'My name is Rachel Scott.'

'I'm not interested.'

'Please, this isn't a scam call.'

'It's always a scam call.'

'Scammers don't give their name.'

'They do if it's not their real name.'

This gave her food for thought for nor had she used her real name. 'I'm a victim of Kyle Jacobs and have some information for you.'

The hiss was long and so was the pause. 'I want nothing to do with that bastard.'

'Nor do I but please hear what I have to say.'

'Okay, go ahead but if I don't like it I will hang up.'

'I have no idea how he blackmailed you but the police raided his house and collected every scrap of evidence about his crimes and you aren't the only person he blackmailed. There are nine of us I know about.'

'Nine! Hell. Go ahead.'

'There is a warrant for his arrest but he's on the run. There's a chance he might try to blackmail you again because the police froze his account and I believe he's desperate. He doesn't have access to the pictures he took of all of us. The police have them.' It was then she remembered she hadn't seen any photos of the other two men.

'Shit. Err, sorry.'

'It's okay. No worse than some of the things I've said over the past fifteen months. They also have the flash drives on which he downloaded photos and detailed notes of how much he blackmailed from each person. If you go to the police and have proof, there's every chance you will get your money back. I don't know why nobody went to the police to report him.'

'Did you?'

'Yes.'

'So he didn't threaten the lives of people close to you?'

'Only my own and I'm still terrified he might find me but someone has to stop him.'

'How do you know all of this?'

'I was with the police when they raided his home.'

'How come?'

'I had a court order to get back all of my belongings, including the money he stole from me.'

'Your belongings?'

'You don't want to know.'

'Oh, I do want to know.'

'Tough. My personal pain isn't for public knowledge the same way yours isn't.'

'How did you get my number?'

'Ask no questions and I'll tell you no lies but the names are in notebooks where he wrote all the details about each victim. There were photos of a lot but I never saw any photos of you.'

'The one of me he uploaded to the internet was bad enough. I haven't seen any others. How many did he have?'

'He put a photo in the public domain?'

'Oh, yeah, with enough information to force the issue.'

'You need to inform the police. I can give you the name of the detective who is investigating this. And there were a lot of photos of most people, but I saw none of you. Some were downright disgusting. I didn't know he'd put photos on the web. Damn.'

'One of me, with threats of more intimate ones with all of my details if I didn't pay up.'

'You know he drugged you?'

'I figured it out pretty quick.'

'He drugged them all, including me and I didn't know about the drugs or the photos until last Friday.'

'He didn't blackmail you?'

'Bit hard to when he didn't know where I was and now he can't because the police have everything.'

'So Jacobs doesn't have access to the photos any longer?'

'I'm almost certain but can't be one hundred percent sure. The police took his computer, phones, photos, notebooks, papers from his filing cabinet - everything, and his hidden camera. They found it.'

'Thank God. Give me the name of the detective and your number.'

She gave both detective's names but not her number and hung up, worried. Kyle had put photos out to the world. Were any of them of her? If they were how would she ever find them? Where did these cranks send them to? She could handle computers to a certain extent but didn't have any social media accounts, which now had to be the best thing ever because nobody could search for her or log onto her social media and give her strife. And the dark web wasn't a place she would ever attempt to delve into – even if she knew how.

Too antsy to make the final call, she paced around the unit while muttering epithets, filled the electric jug and turned it on. Hunted the cupboards for a tea bag and shoved it in a mug she found in a drawer under the bench, which closed by itself. Such fancy storage. While she made another round of the unit, her innards did a great job of tying themselves into a tight tangle. When the kettle whistled she jerked around and swore at the sudden sound. Tea made she settled on the sofa with her feet tucked under her and her eyes on the narrow gap in the curtains.

Outside was the still wet street busy with a constant stream of vehicles on the road and pedestrians on both sides who strode in intermittent splashes of sunshine between greyness of scuttling clouds. At least the rain had stopped for a while. This was the city. No-one peered up and it was unlikely they would be able to see her if they did for the gap was too narrow. It must be awkward at night to maintain privacy if the lights were on. There was no noise and no outside aromas so the place must have double glazing. There were also no trees, bushes, flowers or greenery. Not like the little cottage she had envisioned for her and Madeleine. This wasn't the type of life she would enjoy but she supposed it might suit those who worked long hours in the city and wanted more of the social life with eateries, theatres and night life. She sipped while studying the life outside for it was better than letting what she'd learned simmer in her head.

When her tension eased a tad, she sent her eyes on a journey around the open area of kitchen, dining and lounge. It was larger than she'd thought a city unit would be. Ultra-modern in black, grey and white, it didn't suit her taste, although she wouldn't mind all of the up-market machines in the kitchen. In her motel room, she cooked on a portable electric hotplate and mini oven.

The only splash of colour was from an aqua-tiled splashback in the kitchen with similar shades of the same colour on throws and cushions on the leather lounge and two recliners. Who wanted so many cushions? She never used one. She counted. Twelve cushions. Each would have cost at least twenty dollars. There were far better ways to spend $240. Maybe the owners didn't need to watch each dollar as she'd done for the past nine months. Babies weren't cheap even when Madeleine had only the basics. The cot belonged to the motel. She bought a new convertible pram and capsule along with clothes, clothes and more clothes in incremental sizes. Most of the toys came from friends as gifts when Madeleine was born, as did baby towels, washers, blankets, sheets and other necessities. Rachel always thought Ella had done the secret Santa thing and made suggestions to the town folk but could never be certain although she was forever grateful.

She had already studied the three bedrooms and chosen the smallest with the single bed. The cot went next to it for she was used to sleeping with Madeleine close by and vice versa. In a motel room there was no option. The bathroom had a shower over the bath but it didn't worry her. She could shower anywhere but the big bathtub would be a test for so far Madeleine had been bathed in a plastic baby bath. There would be a lot more water and a lot more splashing for Madeleine loved the bath and delighted in making sure Rachel got as wet as Madeleine. Each of the bedrooms had a different major colour against mid-grey walls and polished wood floors. The room she chose had an emerald-green Doona cover and paler green linen. Green was good.

After the last sip of tea, she rinsed out the cup and sat at the table. One more call. To avoid any more procrastination, she picked up the phone and dialled Ethan Barnes' mobile number.

'Barnes here,' came after a single ring.

'Ethan Barnes?'

'Yes, who are you?'

'Rachel Scott.'

'The name isn't familiar. Do I know you?'

'No.'

'So why are you wasting my time?'

'I have information…'

'I'm not interested.'

'About Kyle Jacobs,' Rachel added as quick as she could.

The silence was profound. 'I'm also a victim of his.' A drawn out *whoosh* whistled in her ear.

'Go on.'

'There's an arrest warrant out for him. The police know the details of his blackmail pursuits.'

'Are you sure because he tried to contact me yesterday?'

'I'm sorry. I haven't had time to ring all of his victims until now. I only found out the details last Friday. I never saw any photos of you but Kyle doesn't have any of them, if that's the way he blackmailed you. The police have them all.'

'Bloody hell.'

'They raided his house, took everything.'

'Why did he threaten me yesterday?'

'Desperation. His account has been frozen and the police are on the hunt for him. They have his phone, computer, hidden camera, files and the photos. Don't give in to him. Contact the police, let them know. Detective Sergeant Justin Smith.'

'Give me a sec to process. The bastard ruined my life.'

'Mine too, I'm sorry. Why didn't you report him?'

'To protect my kids. He ruined my marriage and I lost my job when he sent my wife and boss a couple of photos.'

'Like everyone else, you were drugged.'

'I know but couldn't convince those who mattered. Hell, my brain is in a fog. Are you sure about this?'

'I was there when they found all the evidence. Names were on the back of photos. Details about each person were written in books, which is how I got your contact details. If you can prove your money transactions, you might be able to get it back. It might take a while because there will be a court case and they take ages. But you must contact the police. If I hadn't, he would still be blackmailing victims.'

'You're braver than me. He threatened to kidnap my kids and worse. What did he threaten you with?'

'What happened to me isn't something I ever want to talk about and I don't want to know what he did to others. I don't care how you met but I can tell you we were all singled out well before he made initial contact. He stalked me for months beforehand, learnt too much about me, had me marked as a suitable blackmail target. I've likened his method to the poem, The Spider and the Fly by Mary Howitt.

"Will you walk into my parlour?' said a spider to a fly:
'Tis the prettiest little parlour that ever you did spy.
The way into my parlour is up a winding stair,
And I have many pretty things to shew when you are
there."

'You got it in a nutshell. So, am I safe to ignore his latest threat?'

'I can't promise but contact the detective, let him know. If you're afraid, they might give you protection. It could be a way to draw him out of hiding. Ring today. Now – as soon as you hang up. They will be delighted with the information. Please, don't be afraid to contact him. Detective Sergeant Justin Smith. The police have protected me since I went to them. They want to catch him.'

'Okay, I will. You have no idea how much I appreciate your call. Thank you. I'd like us to keep in contact. Will you give me your number.'

'Umm, not yet. Not until I am certain he's behind bars. I have your number.' Overcome, she hung up and flopped forward on the table. Why did these calls cause her emotions to run rampant? She should be delighted and not feel as though a huge mining mega-truck had run over her a hundred times.

At the loud wail from the bedroom, Rachel shot upright and groaned at the sharp complaints from bruises as she ran along the passage to the rear room. Her heart stuttered at the sight of Madeleine scrunched up and red-faced with the sharp screams more than a normal cry to say – I'm awake and hungry. These were more of the something is wrong variety. She scooped Madeleine up and placed the tense body against her shoulder, one hand giving gentle rubs up and down the equally rigid back.

'What is it? You can't be hungry.' She checked the nappy to find it still dry and clean. 'Come on, give me a hint.' Continual screams were the only answer. With Madeleine over her shoulder, Rachel walked and swayed around the room, along the passage, into the lounge where she nestled Madeleine in her arms and rocked from side-to-side only for the screams to intensify.

'Please, please, please tell me what's wrong,' she crooned. Madeleine drew her legs up. Her little body was too tense. Lying in her arms seemed to make it worse so Rachel put Madeleine back against her shoulder and rubbed the back, around and around and around. The screams softened but didn't give up. Maybe a feed would help. She sat in the armchair and put Madeleine to her breast. She sucked three gulps, paused and screamed.

'Oh, God, what's wrong?' Rachel whispered as she stood again and walked to the gap in the curtain. 'Would you like to see what is outside?' She settled the baby in the crook of her arm so she was little upright. Madeleine scrunched up her eyes and wailed even louder. 'Please don't be ill? I haven't got a car.'

Car. At the idea she hurried to the front door, flung it open, stepped across the passage to Dylan's door and banged with her fist. There was no sound from inside so she banged again and discovered a button which she pressed three times.

'Coming.' The voice was faint before the door opened. 'Rachel, are you okay?'

Her eyes boggled at the bare chest before she could find her voice. 'No, Madeleine. There's something wrong,' she said louder to be overheard above the screams. 'Can't you put a shirt on?'

Dylan snorted and straightened quivering lips. 'I did put my jeans on. I was in the shower. Here give me Sweet Pea.' He didn't give her a chance to pass the baby over for Dylan scooped her into his arms and pressed her head against his heart. 'How long has she been like this?'

'Not long. She's never woken screaming like this before. She's not hungry, nappy is dry, maybe she's ill. Do we need a doctor? I don't know what to do.'

'Take a deep breath. Let me get my key and I'll come over. Her little body is rigid as though she's in pain. It could be a tummy ache.' Dylan went back into his unit and came back within seconds, a sobbing Madeleine over his shoulder, a shirt hooked on one finger and his house keys on another.

Rachel closed his door and traipsed after them with her eyes scouring the long muscled back in front of her. There wasn't an ounce of excess flesh anywhere. The muscles rippled at every movement and, sweet mercy she shouldn't be ogling male flesh when her own flesh and blood was in so much distress. To block out the sight, she turned her head, followed and closed her own door. Dylan settled on the sofa and lay Madeleine, tummy down, along his thighs. With two fingers he gently massaged her back.

'This worked with one of my nieces who suffered from colic.'

'But Madeleine has never had colic.'

'Could be she can't handle the Thai spices you had last night.'

'But she never ate any.'

Dylan raised his eyebrows. 'You don't drink alcohol because it gets in your bloodstream and could affect her. Some foods do the same thing. They can affect the breast milk.'

Heat shot up her neck at her stupidity. 'Far out, I…'

A loud burp interrupted her. It was followed by a long rumble from the other end of Madeleine.

Dylan laughed and picked the baby up to put back against his shoulder while Rachel cringed. The cries lessened to soft sobs until Madeleine dropped her head against Dylan's shoulder. He held her out. 'Your turn. I'll let you change her.'

As soon as she neared, Rachel could tell why Dylan gave her the task. 'Phew, she stinks.'

'I take it we're not having Thai for dinner tonight.'

'I might opt for plain mashed potato.' Dylan's laughter followed her all the way to the end room where she held her nose while cleaning up her daughter. 'I'll never eat spices again,' she said over and over.

When she returned to the lounge with a much happier daughter, it was to find Dylan in a lounge chair with his shirt on and a solemn face. She cursed for in his hand was a sheet of paper she'd forgotten to hide away.

'Do you want to tell me how you found out these details and why you didn't pass them on to me?'

'No.'

'No what?'

'No I don't want to tell you.'

His eyes stared at the ceiling as his shoulders rose. 'I could arrest you for interfering with an investigation.'

'There wouldn't be an investigation without me and I fail to see how I could have interfered.' She sat in the chair opposite but kept her eyes on Madeleine who she settled against the crook of her arm.

'You didn't pass on vital information. How did you find them?'

'The names were on the back of the photos.'

'Contact details weren't.'

'And the police have all the equipment to trace contact details of anyone within a short space of time. It should be a cinch. Adam Hinkler is not a common name, especially when his father is well known.' Not a lie but didn't answer the question she wasn't game to answer.

'Have you contacted them.'

She paused. It would be useless to lie. 'Not all of them.'

Dylan swore. 'Why?'

'I doubt you would understand.'

'Try me.'

'I understand the trauma these people have suffered because I've lived it. I need to go some way to assuage my guilt.'

'What the hell are you talking about? You are not to blame for any of this.'

'I waited nine months before I went to the police. During those nine months these people continued to suffer and Angel got suckered in – all because I was too chicken.'

'You were protecting your daughter and yourself and you did report him at the time.'

'The police dismissed me and for the past nine months these people were devastated.'

'How many have you contacted?'

Rachel ran a hand through her hair. Not telling him will only increase his wrath. 'Most.'

'And?'

She eyed him. 'And what?'

'Don't play games with me. This is serious.'

'Serious is the damage Kyle has done to a lot of people. Serious is Kyle still on the loose. Serious is the money Kyle has blackmailed… Far out, the word isn't good enough to describe what he's done. I encouraged them all to contact the police straight away and told them the police raided Kyle's house and it's possible he can't upload any more photos. And he has uploaded some to the public domain in the past.'

'And you know this how?'

'Two of them told me he had.'

'Damn it, Rachel.' He knelt on the floor in front of her. 'Leave it to the police.'

'Oh, sure. So why don't you explain to me why the police haven't been in contact with any of these other victims. Kyle has – since Friday. I'm not sure how many but he demanded money from… umm… Ethan Barnes, who might need protection because he's not going to pay. His kids are under threat. So why aren't the police protecting them? They've done nothing so far.'

'How do you know?'

'Because none of these victims have heard from the police but the police may have heard from some of the victims in the past few hours. Why?' Rachel glared at him. 'Because I,' she stabbed a finger in her chest and winced,' I did something about it. I warned them. I gave them Justin Smith's name.'

'Ah, hell, Rachel, why didn't you give me these details?'

'What would you have done? There's hardly been time. Be honest. What would you have done?'

'I would have given the details to Justin.'

'Exactly. You wouldn't have contacted these poor buggers to give them the heads up.'

'You should have given them to me over the weekend.'

'No, I couldn't because the notebooks were under the lining of the purple suitcase which I opened last night for those clothes I wore.'

'What notebooks?'

'One for each victim.'

'Why the hell didn't you give them to me last night?'

The tears fell despite her fight to keep them away. 'For the first time in over a year a nice guy took me out for a meal. The first time in nine months I wasn't scared out of my wits when I left the security of my room. The first time in nine months I enjoyed a few hours without looking over my shoulder, terrified I was about to be attacked or verbally abused or put down or told how ugly I was or...' She dissolved in tears and buried her head in one hand. 'I am so useless. I can't get anything in my life right. No matter what I do it's the wrong thing. I can't even care for my own baby.'

'Aw, heck, Rachel.' Madeleine was taken from her arms. 'I'm going to give you a hug so don't panic. I promise I won't harm you.'

Long, warm arms wrapped around her and she was drawn to the floor where Dylan tucked her against his chest and held her head against his shoulder. For the first time in ages, she lost control and the tears kept coming, 'I'm sorry,' she stuttered between deep sobs. 'I never cry.'

'Maybe you should.' As though she was the baby, Dylan rubbed one hand up and down her back.

'It... it achieves nothing.'

'It goes some way to relieve built up tension and it appears you live with a lot of tension. How about I take care of Sweet Pea for a couple of hours while you catch up some sleep. I'll bring her back when she squawks for a feed and I'll bring dinner with me.' He grasped both of her shoulders and held her away so they were eye-to-eye. 'You are a great mother who has had no-one to give you a break since your baby was born. As to not knowing what to do, all new parents learn as they go. This was the first time Madeleine had a tummy ache. Now you know one way to relieve it. You learn as you go. I've got ten nieces and nephews who have taught me most things but I've made a few blunders along the way. Some were funny and some scary. And I'm sorry for giving you a hard time.

Maybe we can discuss these issues after you've had time to yourself and after a feed with no spices. I'm good at mashed potato.' His mouth quirked up at the edges.

Rachel wiped her eyes and nose on the sleeve of her tracksuit top. 'Sounds good but you shouldn't have to care for my baby.'

'It will be a pleasure and you need a break. It will give Sweet Pea and me a chance to get to know each other a bit better. And no guilt trips for you have nothing to be guilty about.'

When she wriggled to get up, his grip tightened. 'Stay there a moment longer to regain your equilibrium.'

'Come on Sleeping Beauty, Madeleine needs her mama.'

'Huh?' Rachel groaned and turned over. A hand shook her shoulder. 'Go away.'

'I will as soon as you wake up to feed your hungry daughter.'

'Huh? What?' A cry had her jerk upright. When she opened her eyes she was disoriented. Where was she? This wasn't her room. 'Where…' A swaddled baby landed on her lap. 'Oh, Madeleine.' A masculine chuckle accompanied the whimper from the bundle. She spun her head sideways.

Dylan sat on the floor. 'You must have slept well. Sorry to wake you but feeding Madeleine is one thing I'm incapable of. Dinner is in half an hour. Knock on my door. Mashed potato is coming up.' He stood and left.

The bundle wriggled and sent out a louder whimper. Still groggy, Rachel lifted the bundle and gave it a hug. Too scared she would fall asleep again if she lay down, she shoved her feet onto the floor and stood. As she shuffled to the lounge she fought to remember how she got to bed and Dylan ended up with Madeleine. The sight of the leather chair brought back a rush of memories. She had blubbed all over Dylan. 'Far out.' Heat rose up her neck while she put

Madeleine to her breast and the tug raced to her inner core. The sensation always overwhelmed her but this time it also gave her a sense of ease and clarity of mind. The entire afternoon's events crowded though her brain cells. She had no idea what the time was but a quick glance at the gap in the curtains gave her a hint. It wasn't yet dark outside but the sun had to be in the last throes of daylight. She didn't want to know how she got into bed but at least she still had her clothes on. She needed a shower and didn't want to think about how her hair looked. She reached up, patted and groaned.

Madeleine suckled for twenty minutes which gave Rachel ten to shower and change. She knocked on Dylans' door a little later than the half hour he'd said but babies didn't account for time. They woke when they were hungry and took as long as they needed to fill their little bellies.

The door opened to a waft of deliciousness and a bare-footed man in black jeans and a grey knitted sweater over a blue shirt. 'Come on in.'

Rachel wheeled in the pram she found parked inside the door of her unit. She remembered Dylan asking for it but had no idea if she had given it to him and wasn't about to ask. 'Smells pretty damn good in here. Nothing like mashed potato.'

Dylan laughed. 'Believe me, there's mash, along with a few other healthy morsels to get some sustenance into a lactating mum. We can't let little Sweet Pea lose weight.'

The unit was much the same layout as the one she'd been in, only it faced the opposite direction and hence back to front. This one was more homely with a lot more colour and the tidy mess of being lived in.

The bold patterned curtains were drawn back to reveal the carpark below and a sad lone tree in the corner. It was still a far cry from the home of her dreams but at least this one had a little more privacy at night. No general public could peer in.

Between the kitchen and lounge area sat a dining table, set for two at one end. Three cork placemats ran in a line down the middle. Water glasses were filled with water and a few ice blocks. A jug of juice had beads of moisture clinging to the outside and a can of low strength beer sat next to one of the place settings.

'Take a seat.' Dylan drew out her chair, the seat upholstered in dark blue. He shuffled the pram at the end where he'd already removed the chair. Before he sat opposite her, he carried three covered dishes from the oven to the table and lifted the lids. She smiled at the bowl of mashed potato he placed in front of her. The second dish contained a colourful pile of mixed vegetables and roast chicken pieces had been skilfully arranged in the third. A sauceboat filled to the brim with gravy was added to the row. The aromas set her gastric juices on a frenzy. She couldn't hold back a grin when Dylan scooped a large spoonful of mash onto her plate.

'Help yourself to the rest. Sweet Pea and I enjoyed our afternoon. We went for a nice stroll to the supermarket in the next block where she told me you loved your vegies and roast chicken was a favourite. And there's not a single spice in any of it. Not even pepper, although there is a pinch of salt in the potato. Sweet Pea reckons potato without a touch of salt is disgusting.'

'I'm overwhelmed. Thank you.' She dropped her head and peeked up. 'Can I ask a question.'

'Go ahead.'

'I don't remember…'

'You fell asleep in my arms. You were exhausted, both mentally and physically. It has been a long day and the accident caused an adrenalin surge, followed by a serious slump. I carried you to bed and tucked you in and I won't apologise for doing so.'

'I don't expect… thank you.' Not sure what else to say, she scooped up a forkful of mash and sucked it off. 'Oh, wow, you sure know how to make mash.'

'Lots of butter to make it creamy. The butter won't harm you when you are feeding a baby. And, let me add, your baby has to be one of the most genial and contented babies I've dealt with. The only time she whimpered was when hunger pangs took hold.' He reached out and grasped her wrist. 'Do you know why?'

Rachel shook her head.

'Because she has such a great mother who tends to her every need the moment she lets you know of her discomfort. She smiles at everything, waves her little arms and legs around in delight and falls asleep without a cry when she is tired. A child couldn't want for a better mother.'

His comments caused a squishy sensation inside. To hide her embarrassment, Rachel dug her knife and fork into the chicken breast, hacked off a hunk, shoved it into her mouth, chewed in awe and swallowed. 'Oh, yum. This isn't a store bought roast chicken. The skin is so crisp and the meat juicy.' She eyed Dylan. 'You cooked this?'

He shrugged. 'As kids we all learned how to cook and I enjoy it.'

'Why hasn't some woman snaffled you up? You would make a great dad, you cook like a chef, you're kind, gentle.'

'And haven't found a woman I want to spend my life with. I thought I had until...'

'She betrayed you, which meant she wasn't the right woman.'

'True. It was hard at the time to accept the concept and took me a while to realise.'

'You couldn't forgive her?' Peas dropped from the forkful of vegies which she shoved into her mouth and chewed. They might not have any spices but they weren't just boiled in water.

'I'm not sure forgiveness is the right word. To cheat on your partner shows lack of respect for the relationship and the partner. To cheat mere weeks before the wedding made it worse and I don't know how long she'd been sleeping with the guy. I doubt it was a one off. I would never have been able to trust her again and to me, trust and respect are two big aspects of a good marriage. Love, honesty and friendship also have to be there. I loved her but I doubt she loved me. How could she if she was so blatant in sleeping with someone else – in my home and in my bed.'

'Have you dated since?' Rachel chased after the peas and stabbed each onto a prong.

'Not for a while afterwards but yes, although not more than once or twice with the same person. Trust has been an issue but also none of the women I've dated have clicked with me in the romantic sense. They've been nice, we've had fun but there hasn't been any deep attraction. Unlike you, I don't class all women as underhanded sneaks because of one experience.'

'I don't…'

'You have been unable to trust any man because of the actions of one.'

'Not true. I trust Pierre and the guys I've got to know well down south.'

'Have any asked you out?'

'Two.'

'Did you go?'

'No.'

'Why not?'

Since she didn't know how to answer, she filled her fork to eat instead and ignored Dylan's quiet rumble of laughter.

When she couldn't fit in another skerrick, she put her cutlery together and pushed the plate to the side. 'This food was so good. Thank you.'

'My pleasure.' Dylan lifted the wide awake Madeleine from the pram and propped her on his lap with her head and neck supported in the crook of his elbow. 'See how she wakes up happy because she is such a contented little girl. That's because of you.' He indicated towards Rachel. 'There are a few other issues you damned yourself with earlier. None of them are true. You understand the type of person Kyle is and know the put downs and insults are because of his shortcomings as a man. The insults about your looks and actions were a reflection on his cowardice. The more beautiful your looked, the bigger the insult to cripple your self-confidence, and you are a beautiful woman and not only in looks. More important, you are beautiful on the inside. And you aren't useless, which you have proved in the way you have kept yourself hidden to protect your daughter and done everything in your power to take great care of her. You are smart – much smarter than Kyle. He has never been able to find you. I know I gave you a hard time about the contacts but I do understand why. I've considered your reasons over the past couple of hours. They are valid. I also rang a buddy on the force to find out why they never acted when you first reported Kyle. They did act but you disappeared without leaving them your contact details. They couldn't find you either.'

'Pierre knew where I was.'

'It wasn't Pierre they were looking for. It was Elise Jacobs and she had vanished off the face of the earth. You checked yourself out of the hospital with no forwarding details. No Elise Jacobs bought a ticket for any bus, train, boat or plane ride. You sold your car some six hundred kilometres north of the city yet you were four hundred kilometres south.'

'I signed the transfer papers. Pierre drove the car north and sold it for me. Olivia drove their car and brought him back after a two-week holiday visiting all the towns with their kids. And Pierre bought another car for me in his name with me as the designated driver.'

'Smart woman. You used Pierre's address on the title transfer as your address and neither claimed to know where you were. The case is still open but couldn't be acted on without you. And there is no email address or phone number in your real name, no social media address, no nothing. Would you like sweets?'

'No thank you. I couldn't fit any more in.'

'I sent a copy of the contacts to Justin's email and made a copy for myself. Please leave it to the police to do their investigation. Justin will pick you up at 8.30 in the morning and will bring you back here. I leave here at 7.30 and will be home close to five. Court sessions usually end at four but can run overtime. Is Olivia coming to care for Madeleine?'

'Yes. I gave her the code to get in. Is that okay?'

'Sure, as long as she doesn't pass it on. Oh, and I put a few essentials in the fridge and on the bench in your kitchen so you can have breakfast.'

'Now I'm embarrassed.'

'No need. I was certain you didn't want to go traipsing around the streets to find food. Sweet Pea, here, suggested a few basics.'

'Did she now?' Rachel lifted her brow.

'Yep, she's as smart as her mother.'

To hide her blush she changed the subject. 'Can I do the dishes?'

'No, the dishwasher will do them.'

'Dishwasher?'

'It came with the unit but only gets used when there's more than a lone plate and mug. I can't abide dirty dishes mouldering while I wait for the dishwasher to be full.'

Rachel stood and reached over to collect Madeleine. 'Thank you for everything. I'll leave you to speak with your dishwasher and get a decent night's sleep after putting up with Buggalugs all afternoon.'

The scene before her caused her lungs to forget how to work. To the far left of what was once her house, stood a perfect room without a roof. Blinds, albeit wrinkled from melting, still hung inside to cover the window. Charred beams and rafters appeared to be still in place although she doubted they had the strength to hold up the weight of tiles, all of which had disappeared. The positive about the scene was if the camera had still been there it would have burnt to a crisp so it was possible Kyle didn't know it had been found. The next room along still had a front wall but the burnt wood hung in a dangerous tangle from the major beam which looked like charcoal. She couldn't see the rooms behind but the rest of the front of the house gave the impression of a jagged streak of lightning where bricks had fallen in a random pattern. The front door had gone but the frame stood tall with no indication a fire had torn through the place, apart from bubbled paint. There's a lot to be said for steel door frames. Where the underground garage had once stood with the main living areas on top, now resembled a bombed out building with flattened layers on top of each other and burnt out appliances and furniture like a jagged rocky outline on the horizon. All were black and still wet from the fire hoses and rain.

In one sense, Rachel was glad the house of horrors had gone. Kyle had done her a service. But it was going to require a massive clean-up to clear the debris away. And expensive, which was why she was here.

She opened the passenger door of the unmarked police car, unfolded from the seat and headed towards the man and woman who stood at the base of the five front steps, about the only undamaged part of the house, but built of concrete they were immune from flames although they were covered in soot and storm debris. Footsteps neared her and she winced when the detective put the flat his hand in the small of her back and guided her forward.

'Good morning, I'm Detective Sergeant Justin Smith and this is…'

'Mrs Elise J… Esquilante,' Rachel interrupted with her hand held out in greeting towards the male. She assumed it was the insurance assessor for it wasn't the coward Kyle.

'Huh, excuse me,' the other woman stuttered.

'And you are…' Rachel scanned the woman's features. It was difficult to tell her age for the tautness of her mouth and whiteness of the creases added a few years. It was obvious she was terrified but tried not to show it. The knuckles of her right hand were white where they clutched the strap of a shoulder bag; the elbow pressed it hard against her side. Rachel masked her features to not let on her thoughts when recognition hit. She'd studied all the photos in detail in case one of the victims had been inveigled into this pretence. Her guess had been correct. 'Madison Hart.'

The woman paled in the same instant her grey eyes boggled. 'How…'

'How did I know? I've seen the photographs.'

The woman shuddered and whimpered.

'I have no idea what sort of hold Kyle has over you but I do know he has been blackmailing you for quite some time. You are not his only victim. I was one as well and there are at least seven others. The police,' she indicated the sergeant, 'have all the photographs and other evidence. There is an arrest warrant out for Kyle and since you are here right now, I presume you know where he is for he had to have been in contact with you over the past forty-eight hours.'

Rachel paused when the woman's face drained of all colour and she shook as though in a force seven earthquake while tears streamed down her cheeks.

Her mouth opened and closed followed by a gulp. 'You can't… he's got my car… forced me.' Madison edged to the side, took a step backwards and gave the impression she was about to flee but the sudden roar of an engine brought her to a standstill.

Tyres squealed so loud it hurt the eardrums and burnt rubber hit the air in the same instant the roar increased to jumbo jet status. All four turned their heads. A blue sedan raced at top speed straight for them.

A full force *whack* sent Rachel flying. A shrill scream was followed a split second later by a loud *whump, oomph* and *crunch*. All the air flew from Rachel's lungs when she landed on the edge of the steps and a lead weight landed on top of her. Agony hit. She gasped for air but couldn't seem to get any to reach her lungs.

'Code three. Send an ambulance,' was said in her ear before the weight lifted from her body. 'Twenty-eight Gloucester Road.' There was a tap on her shoulder. 'Are you okay?'

Rachel managed to lift her head and turn it far enough to see the sergeant get to his feet with a phone held against one ear. His mouth moved as though still speaking but it gaped when he twisted around. When he swore with his eyes staring to her right, Rachel turned her head.

'Oh, sweet mercy.'

Madison was sprawled against the upright section of bricks with the top third of her body hung over the top and the rest dangled down. Blood poured down the bricks. It had to have been the whump and crunch she'd heard at the same time she was hit, not by the car, but by the sergeant. Her mind was so frazzled, she couldn't make out what was real and what wasn't - apart from horrific sight of Madison. Rachel had to close her eyes to get rid of the ghastly vision but it didn't make any difference for the sight had been branded into her brain cells.

'Is she alive?' Rachel swallowed down rising bile.

'I hope not.'

'How on earth did she end up there?'

'The force of the impact sent her airborne. If the wall hadn't been there she would have gone over the edge and landed on the rubble below. I'm pretty sure the impact would have killed her in an instant. I pray it did.' The sergeant stepped closer, put two fingers on the pulse point in Madison's dangling hand and shook his head. 'Are you able to give me a hand after I have taken a few photos?'

Really? But the poor woman didn't deserve such a gruesome end. With eyes shut and hand over her mouth Rachel struggled to sit upright. It hurt to move but she forced the pain away and managed to stand on legs that had turned into jelly. There was little choice but to shuffle towards the ghastly sight, her stomach in desperate need to heave. The sergeant's face was ashen while he moved around the body to take photos from different angles. She presumed it was necessary but it didn't mean she had to like it. She so didn't want to do this but poor Madison deserved better than to be splattered on a jagged wall. Light-headed, Rachel paused to gather courage, heaved her shoulders high on a deep inhale and closed the gap.

Sergeant Smith steadied her when her step faltered. 'I apologise for asking you to do this but we can't leave her like this. If she slips any more, the bricks will shred her face. Hold her around the waist and press her against the wall while I lever the top half off.'

It was surreal to place her hands around a waistline which felt so normal with its warmth and softness when the body was lifeless. With utmost care, the sergeant peeled the shoulders and head away from the jagged bricks and let the top of the woman loll back on his outstretched arm. She was like a rag doll, the skeletal structure holding her together seemed to have been smashed. Her chin and neck had been shredded by the rough bricks and blood poured from the lacerated blood vessels. The gory sight turned Rachel's stomach into an industrial sized agitator. She was so glad the woman was dead for the pain would have been unendurable. It took utmost care to lay the broken body on the concrete porch and arrange her limbs so she appeared to be a normal human being if you didn't take into account the minced neck.

Rachel had to turn away. 'Where's the insurance man?' she asked when she realised the man was missing.

'Down there.' The sergeant pointed to the slope leading to what had been the garage. He followed his finger and knelt beside the prostrate figure. 'He's alive but unconscious.'

The scream of sirens cut through the air. Within seconds two police vehicles pulled up on the paved drive and another two on the verge at the front. An ambulance arrived a few seconds later and was guided onto the property by uniformed officers who hurried towards Justin.

Overcome, Rachel plopped onto the bottom step. She didn't have a clue what she was supposed to do while officers huddled around the sergeant and paramedics tended Madison and the insurance assessor. Everything had happened so fast, Rachel hadn't even learnt the man's name. Even though it hurt to move, she wriggled closer to the wall at the house side of the steps, leant against it for support, drew her knees up and dropped her head on her knees with her arms wrapped around them.

One officer picked up the file of paperwork Rachel had dropped, not that she cared any longer. Several officers sprinted to their cars and sped away. When a body bag was opened out, Rachel turned her head away and clamped her eyes on the ambulance. A stretcher was rolled out of the ambulance and rolled back in with the insurance man partially covered by a blanket and an oxygen mask over his nose. A blood pressure cuff had been wrapped around his upper arm and the two paramedics fussed over him at the same time they fed him into the ambulance. At least he was still alive.

Sergeant Smith approached and sat next to her. He handed her the file, which she dropped on the ground in front of her feet.

'Are you okay? Do you need medical attention?'

'A few bruises but a small price to pay when you consider the alternative.' She indicated towards the body bag, now sealed. It was still too gruesome. 'You saved my life. Thank you seem such inadequate words but thank you.'

'I only wish I could have reached the others but...'

'You couldn't have done any more than you did. It happened so fast. We all have wishes about how we could have done better. I wish I'd never met the bastard but I did. I wish I knew what he was like in his evil soul but I didn't. I wish I hadn't come today but had little choice. This could be my fault for it's obvious Kyle recognised me and figured his latest little scam wasn't going to work.

'It's not your fault. You did nothing wrong.'

'Doesn't mean the regret won't live in my soul for a long time. Neither of us can change the result. It's taken me a while to accept this philosophy. The important thing is to learn from our mistakes and believe me I've made a few major blunders regarding the person who is responsible for this obscene tragedy. This was blatant murder by a depraved lunatic and thanks to your razor sharp reaction there is only one murder victim. It could have been four.' She shook her head to clear away the swirl of confusion. 'I am so spaced out my brain cells don't want to work.'

'Shock might have set in after an adrenalin rush.'

'Possible but it sure feels weird, as though I've been transported to some far off world of unreality. How's the insurance guy?'

'Hit his head. Knocked him out cold but no other serious injuries apart from a bit of missing skin. There will be bruises. He's lucky. The car missed him. He tripped as he ran. He will need to remain under observation to check there's no internal bleeding on the brain but he should be okay. I need to get you back to your daughter but I have to stay here to co-ordinate things. I'll get one of the officers to drive you.'

'What about Kyle?'

'The officers are hunting for him. Thanks to you, we know the name of the victim and we were able to trace the number plate of the car she owned.'

'The one Kyle was driving?'

'Yes. I've sent officers to her home. It's possible we'll find his car stashed there. And he might have been hiding out in her home. The officers will search and find the smallest of clues if there are any. How did you know her name?'

Awkward. How was she supposed to answer without revealing the truth and yet not lie? 'From the photographs. I saw pictures of most of the victims but not all. The names were on the back. Those sort of pictures don't go away. They seem to get welded to your brain cells. What am I supposed to do about the insurance?'

'We'll contact the company, give them the details and assure them you are the real Mrs Jacobs. I assume they have your contact details.'

'My phone number, yes, but the house and insurance have me with my maiden name - Esquilante. What about the other victims? How safe are they?'

'When we have a chance to figure out their details we'll contact them all.'

Wow, another dilemma. 'Didn't you get Dylan's email. He sent you all the details of every victim.'

'I haven't been into the office yet. How did he get them?'

'I umm... retrieved some notebooks from under the lining in a suitcase of my clothes I found in the house when I was here with Dylan.' Well, it wasn't a lie. It might not be the whole truth but it was as far as she would reveal. 'There's one for every victim but I can't be certain. Who knows how many victims there have been over the years. I mean, he changed his name. There had to be a reason. God, this is all too much. There are all contact details and addresses of each person.'

'You should have let us know.'

'I should have, could have, would have but it's been hectic over the past couple of days with getting south and back, working at my job and caring for a tiny baby. Add on the arrival of Kyle down south to create more angst in my life. I wasn't aware you didn't know the details. I opened the case Sunday night and drove here yesterday. But you guys had the names so surely you could figure out their details as well since you've got the means for tracing people.'

The sergeant snorted something like a cross between a laugh and a grunt. 'Like you said, time has been short as was manpower over the long weekend. We all have families we never seem to be able to spend enough time with.' He scrubbed a hand through his hair. 'Sorry.' He stood. 'We'll need you to answer questions about what happened.'

'Surely…'

'And I will have to give a statement as well as the insurance assessor. We are witnesses to a murder. If we don't do it by the book and cover every minor detail, Jacob's lawyer could have a field day and have evidence discredited or thrown out. It won't be me who asks the questions as I'm involved. I'll send someone senior, maybe later this afternoon or tonight. I'll let you know. You might need someone with you when your mind replays the scene. I can organise a specialist…'

'No. Olivia will be with me.'

'Sit here while I organise a car. Don't move from here because this is now a crime scene.'

Rachel sat leant against the low wall, eyes shut until the scene fused into her brain replayed over and over in glorious technicolour. In an effort to get rid of it, she opened her eyes and studied the houses across the road; houses and gardens she recognised. There had been little change over the months. Few would have been home to witness today's carnage for most worked, but some might get a shock when they viewed their respective security data tonight. If the police didn't collect it.

Her mind was like scrambled eggs while she watched two more police cars arrive, officers convene for chitchats and crime scene tape get unwound and attached to various points. After about fifteen minutes a female officer came to her.

'D.S. Smith asked me to drive you home.'

Home. The word reverberated in her mind as she stood and shuffled after the officer. She didn't have a home unless you called a rented motel room a home. She supposed it was better than having to live on the streets and she had to shove some positivity into her mind. There was her present temporary abode – a home for a few days, which was much bigger and far more glamorous than a single motel unit. But it was too colourless and clinical to be warm like a home should be. When she got in the car and glanced at the activity, the twist of fate reminded her how this had once been her home for six miserable months. Well, no, it was never a home for one should be attached to their true home and have a fondness for it. Not four walls and a roof filled with fear, regret, unease and tension. A true home was a happy place. One day she would own a happy place for Madeleine and her. As they drove away, she filled her mind with the vision of her three bedroom cottage with pretty flowers at the front, a lawn and trees at the back under which there was a swing set for Madeleine next to a vegetable patch for her. Around the fence, bushes of native plants attracted birds, insects and lizards. Close, so close. Madison had been within a hand reach, the insurance man next to her. Rachel had shaken hands with the man and Justin stood between them. So close. Kyle had aimed for her, not Madison. Too close. Almost. A fluke. She should be dead, not Madison. Close, close, almost, almost...

Rachel jolted at the shove. 'Ma'am, I have instructions to walk you to your door.'

'Huh?' She straightened at a nudge on her arm. Confused, she turned her head in the direction of the nudge. 'Oh, sorry.'

'Are you okay?'

No. 'Yes, sure. Where…' Recognition hit when the fog in her brain cleared. They were back at the units. She opened the car door at the same time the officer opened hers. 'Thank you for the lift. I appreciate it.' One foot out and she had to grip her fingers into the back of the car seat to balance on a leg determined to not hold her up.

'Ma'am, let me help you. The sarge said you might be in shock.' One uniformed arm went behind Rachel's back and the other gripped her hand.'

It was a worry she hadn't heard or seen the officer move around the car. 'I'll be okay.'

'I have orders to ensure you get inside your unit.' The officer leant inside the car, retrieved Rachel's folder and handbag and held them out.

While she berated herself for letting her brain shut down again, Rachel was led to the front door, where she had to search her brain cells for the code and punch it in. Embarrassed by her frailty after another blank-out, she straightened her spine, lifted her head and pulled her shoulders back to show she was okay. Inside shivered and shook but she made it to the elevator door without stumbling and remembered to punch in the code to get it to move. The trip up took mere seconds, the walk along the passage too long because it was as though each foot stepped in a metre of sponge rubber. She searched every pocket for the key before she remembered Olivia had it. Head down to hide the redness, she knocked.

It was a huge relief when it opened to Olivia who had Madeleine in her arms. 'I have to hold my baby.' Rachel reached out, drew the tiny, swaddled bundle against her chest and hugged her close.

'What happened? Are you okay?'

'There was an incident. Rachel is in shock. Are you able to care for her? I can call in medical assistance if it is needed.'

'No, I'll look after her. What happened?'

'I'll leave it to Rachel to give the details. I have to get back to the scene.'

'Scene? Rachel, what on earth happened? Thank you, officer.'

With her baby safe in her arms, Rachel made it to the sofa, sank down and ran her fingers over every inch of her daughter. The need to ensure Madeleine was safe, was desperate. 'Kyle almost killed me. Drove his car full speed at us. Hit Madison, killed her. Justin saved my life.' After the words raced out, tears overflowed in a deluge. 'So close, so close, so close.'

'Oh, honey. Here, let me take Madeleine.'

The next thing Rachel knew was being wrapped up in arms against Olivia's body. 'S... s... sorry.' Even though she fought the tears they kept on coming. 'I can't cry. It's for the weak,' she stuttered between sobs.

'Tears were created to release and ease strong emotion, so cry as much as you need. You have been stoic for too long. You are safe here. Madeleine is safe. Kyle doesn't know where you are and can't get in even if he did know.'

Rachel couldn't figure out how long Olivia held her, how long the deluge lasted but finally the tears ran dry. With her head bent, she swiped the snot and moisture from her face with the bottom of her blouse and straightened. 'I must look a mess. Sorry.'

'You look like someone who has had a life-threatening experience and you have nothing to be sorry about. I'll get you a drink while you explain what happened. Talk about it. Get it out of your system. Madeleine is asleep in her pram so we have the chance to talk.' Olivia went into the kitchen from where the sounds of hot drink preparation emanated while Rachel related the past hour. Had it only been an hour? A quick glance at her watch told her it hadn't even reached ten yet.

'How long can you stay?' She hoped it was all day because she didn't want to be alone.

'As long as I leave in time to pick the kids up from school.'

'I need a favour.'

'Anything.'

'I arranged to meet someone at 12:30. It's important.'

'Who?'

'One of the other victims. I found something that belongs to him when I went through the house last Friday. I promised I would return it today.'

'You've been in contact with the victims?'

'Most. Not all. Well, the ones I know about. There could be more.'

Olivia returned with two steaming mugs, handed one over and sat next to Rachel. 'This woman today. Who was she?'

'Madison Hart. Another victim. She didn't answer when I phoned her. I guess Kyle must have been with her. She said he forced her. He had her car. The one he used to mow the four of us down.'

'He hit you as well?'

'No, Justin, the sergeant who picked me up earlier, pushed me out of the way but Madison was standing right in front of me – within reaching distance. It was so awful. She didn't stand a chance but I'm sure it was me he aimed at. Oh, God, I'll never be able to get what she looked like out of my brain.' She grubbed one hand through her hair but had to place it back on the mug to steady it when her other hand shook. To calm shot nerves, she sipped and swallowed. Hot chocolate. Not the tea she'd expected although she hadn't looked in the mug. 'Where did you find the chocolate?'

'In the pantry. I'm sure the owners won't miss two spoons of powdered chocolate. Especially under such dire circumstances. Would you like to have a nap?'

'No way. I need to keep busy otherwise the scene will keep flashing in my brain. And I have to go to my bank. How about we leave early and have lunch at the café where I'm to meet this guy.'

'I'm all for lunch with you after all of these long months. I'll call Pierre, see if he can join us. Where do I tell him to meet us?'

'Le Brasserie.' A few more tears threatened at the idea of spending time with her brother. It had been way too long. A loud sniff and shake of her head kept the tears back. No more tears. She was strong, could get through this. The end was mere days away, maybe hours for the police would be more determined than ever to catch the bastard after today's dreadful catastrophe.

'Pierre's favourite.'

'It was mine as well. I was going to treat myself to a real French pastry but now a true French dish sounds perfect.'

'One of Pierre's sayings: a French man can leave France but France will never leave the French man. I've given up trying to cook French food. When Pierre gets a hankering we go to Le Brasserie. Not that I mind. Do you still bake those yummy pastries?'

'Not since I left. No point when there's only me. Besides, Pierre knows how to bake most.' Rachel took another sip and rolled her eyes in pleasure. 'I need a shower and change of clothes.' Determined to think only positive thoughts, she stood and carried the chocolate with her.

'He's here.' Rachel swallowed the mouthful of deliciousness and dropped the fork on the side of the plate of *Boeuf Bourguignonne* before she stood and made her way to the reception desk. 'Adam Hinkler?'

The man spun around and ran his eyes up and down her body. 'Rachel Scott?' Dressed in a dark grey business suit the man exuded strength and not the vulnerability of a comatose naked man being set up in an unbelievable compromising pose. He was much taller than she'd envisioned. How on earth did such a man succumb to Kyle's machinations?

'Yes.'

'Where are you seated?'

Rachel indicated her table where Pierre faced them with a frown and Olivia had turned with a half-smile.

'Who are they? The guy looks familiar.' Adam's frown matched the one on Pierre's face.

'My brother, Pierre and his wife.'

'Esquilante. I thought I recognised him?'

'You know Pierre?'

'Not personally, no. He gave a presentation at a recent mining symposium. The use of industrial solar energy on remote mining sites.'

'His pet project at the moment. He's a design engineer for an alternate energy company.'

When Adam turned back to her, his stare sent a shiver down her spine. 'Didn't you say your name was Rachel Scott? He's French.'

'So am I. I changed my name nine months ago to keep hidden from…'

'Jacobs. He tried to blackmail me again yesterday. Came to my door. Can we sit? Err, somewhere private.' He wavered his hand towards her table.

'Sure, let me get my bag?'

'Why?'

'Your money is in it.'

'Oh, of course.' Adam searched the room and pointed to a far corner table set for two. He was gone before Rachel could agree.

'I know him,' Pierre whispered when she returned to her table and retrieved her small handbag from the pram's undercarriage.

'He recognised you as well. Some mining symposium. He asked for privacy.'

Pierre nodded. 'Yell if you need me.'

'This isn't the man I need protection from,' Rachel quipped before she turned away and joined Adam where she sat opposite. She opened her bag, took out a large brown envelope and passed it across the table. 'The full fifty thousand is there. You can count it to check. Did you contact the police?'

'After yesterday, yes but I haven't heard from them.'

'What happened yesterday?'

'He came to my door, demanded money. It's the first time he's turned up at my place. Might be because I followed your tip and deleted the find my phone APP.'

'What about a tracer on your car?'

'I don't have the same car. I sold it six months back but I checked in any case. There was nothing.'

'Did you give in to him?'

'No told him to get fu… err, lost.'

Rachel sniggered to herself. 'You can say what you mean. I've said worse and you could get a response from the police fairly soon after this morning.'

'Why, what happened this morning?'

'He murdered one of his victims – in front of a police officer and me. Missed me by this much?' Rachel held up two fingers only centimetres apart. 'Sped straight for us. It was… ghastly isn't a good enough description. I'm sure he had been hiding in the woman's place. She said he forced her and was in her car.'

'Forced her to what?'

'Pretend she was the person whose name is on an insurance policy. He burnt down his house. The police also now have all the contact details of all the victims I know about. But I would still be careful. Kyle is an angry man and may want retribution for his evil world falling apart. He is a serial coercive controller. When they lose control they become angry and lash out, like he did today. They try to regain control by making empty promises, threats or emotional blackmail. He threatened you yesterday and didn't get the result he wanted so he could stalk and harass you to intimidate you. To expose his abuse and take legal action may increase the risk of revenge. This is how people like Kyle operate.'

'Is it possible he'll turn up at my place again?'

'Desperate people do desperate things and he is desperate. It's possible. He knows where you live. He could break in while you're not there. If it was me, I'd ask an officer to check it out before you go in.'

'Bloody hell. I don't need this.'

'None of us do. Why do you think I went into hiding for the past nine months? And when he figures it was me who has exposed him and his evil, he's going to be more than peeved with me.'

'Why put yourself in such danger?'

'Somebody has to stop him. I went to court to get back my belongings and the money he stole from me. I doubt he realises exactly how much evidence we found in his house before he burnt it down. Otherwise, why would he have set fire to it? I had no idea about you, or any of the others before last Friday. I mentioned the notebooks I found. They detail exactly how he manipulated each victim after stalking them for months beforehand. Does a shonky business deal sound familiar?'

Adam groaned.

'With each victim it was a different approach.'

'Can I see the notebook?'

'I don't have them with me and the police have asked for them. If you promise to not tell the police about this money I could photocopy yours and email it to you. No, not email. I don't want any evidence on my computer. I'll send it by registered post. But you have to swear to not let the police know.'

'Why would you do this?'

'It's your life he ruined. As far as I'm concerned, you have a right to know how. Police investigations take forever and I doubt they will hand over any evidence to the victims, which is why I snuck out your cash and returned it to you. I could get arrested for doing so.'

'I promise I won't say anything. You're a brave woman, braver than I was – until yesterday. I told Jacobs I reported him to the police. I'm certain he didn't believe me because he threatened to expose more photos. I told him to go ahead so I hope the police do have them all.'

'He doesn't have access to his phone or any electronic equipment from his house. The police have all of the photos and flash drives, which I assume were his backups. They have bank statements and will have the details of how much he blackmailed from each person and the dates, when I give them the notebooks. Make a claim to get your money back. At a guess, I assume they would have gone to his place of work and raided there as well. I hope they did. I could ask.'

Adam pushed the envelope back in her direction. 'I want you to have this money as a reward for ending the bastard's reign of terror.'

Rachel shook her head. 'No.'

'I can afford it.'

'Still no. It belongs to you. My reward will be to see Kyle in gaol: for me to be free to roam these streets without fear, to not be terrified every time I leave the security of my front door. To be able to come back to the city to live and be close to my brother and his family. To not have to hide under a wig and baggy clothes.' She flicked a hand through the strands of false hair and tugged at the long jacket she wore.

'I owe you.'

'You can repay me by standing up to Kyle's threats and work with the police to take him down. No more fear. No more being a victim. Maybe use this money to hire a big burly bodyguard to check out your house and guard you until the bastard is caught. And he will be caught – soon. Desperate people might do desperate things but it's also when they make mistakes. He made a huge blunder earlier today. You don't run your car full pelt at a police officer and get away with it. At the moment he is number one on their hunt list. Now, I need to get back to my lunch with my brother. The first time I've had the pleasure in over nine months.' She stood, reached over and gripped Adam's hand. 'Thank you for believing in me.'

Adam stood. 'Thank you for your bravery. I'd like to keep in contact when this is all over.'

'Deal.' She sent him a smile of acknowledgement and turned away with a strong wave of warmth shooting through her body as she returned to her table, picked up her fork and stabbed a piece of cool beef.

'Pierre Esquilante, I presume you have the same ethics as your sister.'

At the voice, the piece of beef shot down Rachel's throat. As she glanced up she had to cough to get it all the way down.

'I hope so.' Pierre stood and shook Adam's hand. 'Our parent's taught us right from wrong at a young age. They also taught us to stand up for what we believed in and to work hard for what we wanted.'

'My company was impressed with your presentation at the symposium. I'd like to catch up and talk more about it. Can I ring you? I kept your details.'

'Sure, anytime.'

Adam inclined his head towards Rachel. 'Your sister is a gutsy woman. Take care of her.'

'She's pretty good at taking care of herself but while in the city, I keep tabs on her. I can be reached with one finger on her phone if she's in need. We have had an emergency plan for a long time.'

When Pierre sat, he eyed Rachel. 'What did you give him?'

She shrugged. 'Something I could get arrested for if the police knew so if I don't tell you, you won't have to lie for me.'

'What if he tells?' Pierre waved a hand in the direction of the door.

'He promised he wouldn't as my reward for contacting him. I believe him.'

'I think he was impressed with you.'

'I wasn't looking for impressed. All I want is for this to end and the victims have a right to know all the details I discovered. We all knew Kyle was evil but had no idea exactly how evil. I am so glad I escaped when I did. The past nine months in hiding have been worth it when I think about the alternative if I hadn't left the way I did.' She dipped her fork towards the plate. 'Can I finish my lunch?'

There was warmth in Pierre's glance. 'Sure. I need to leave soon. What are you two doing for the rest of the day?'

'I intend to keep busy,' said Rachel. She winced at her words. Now he would want to know why.

'Why?' He frowned.

'You need to tell him what happened.' Olivia placed a hand on Rachel's arm.

She shovelled in another forkful of food and kept her eyes on her plate.

'Elise?'

She screwed her face and kept chewing.

'Okay, what's going on?'

While Olivia gave him the details, Rachel ate until Pierre stood, came to her chair and gently tugged her up from her seat. It was so damn good to have his arms wrap around her.

'As if you haven't been through enough trauma,' he whispered. 'Why don't you come and stay with us?'

She lifted her head and forced a smile. 'Only when Kyle has been caught. If I'm at your place and Kyle finds out, he could harm the kids. He has no conscience, doesn't care who he hurts or how to get what he wants and right now, he wants revenge. I'm safer at the unit until I go back south. There's another person I'd like to visit this afternoon before Olivia needs to pick up your two from school. If she's willing, of course.' Rachel turned to Olivia.

'Of course. With two of us, we'll be safe.'

'Okay, but keep your eyes peeled. I'll pay on the way out. You two take your time to finish your lunch.' Pierre gave Rachel another hug and kiss on her head before kissing Olivia and left them.

Rachel sat but the food had gone cold. 'Can we go?'

'Sure, I can't eat any more. Where to?'

The building hadn't changed since she'd last seen it. Ten storeys high, it was one of the older office blocks at the more historic end of the terrace. A rectangular building with rectangular windows and a large rectangular front door. The only good feature about the plastered brick edifice was its symmetry. A good hose down on the upper levels with a pressure spray might give it a renewed sparkle but as far as Rachel could tell from the list on the signpost, the companies inside were well-established and the rent could be more reasonable than the newer high-end monoliths at the other end of the main street. She had read how a lot of the newer buildings were only half full, which said a lot. With an avenue of mature trees lining the street down this end of town, she would prefer to work here than the newer section where there was almost no greenery.

'You get out and I'll find parking.' Olivia slowed the car, drew against the kerb and came to a stop.

'Don't wait in the car. Make sure you bring Madeleine in where it is safe. I won't be long so you won't need the pram. Level four.'

'I'll wait in the foyer. You go.'

A gust of wind whipped the bottom of Rachel's long jacket upwards the moment she stepped from the car and slammed the door. The cold air on her skin created an immediate prickle of raised hairs followed by a quick shiver while she darted across the footpath, head down to keep her face hidden, and shoved at the heavy glass door. Inside, immediate warmth was a welcome surprise for many of these older buildings didn't have such modern temperature control. Her shoes squeaked across the streaked grey and white tiles until she stilled at the bank of elevators where she pressed the silver button and between glances over each shoulder, searched for arrows to see where each car was so she could wait near the first to arrive. The nervous wait wasn't long. When the door closed and she was the only person inside, her tension eased. There was a faint tang of stuffiness under the sharp scent of some artificial air freshener. She would prefer the stuffiness alone for the chemical sent an itch to her nasal passages. The car jerked to a halt followed by a longish pause. For a second Rachel worried it had broken down until the door took its time to rumble open. The age of the building showed in the condition of the elevator. How often it did it break down. Some maintenance was needed to update or replace it.

It was a relief to get out into a wide passage where two signs faced her. The company she needed had an arrow pointing to the right. She followed and found herself in a foyer-type room big enough for six chairs and a long desk, behind which, sat a receptionist.

'Angel Lombardo is expecting me,' she said to the middle-aged woman who greeted her with a serious face.

'Please sit and I'll let her know you are here. And you are?'

'Rachel. She knows me, I rang ahead.'

The woman who appeared a minute later wasn't the same woman she had last seen only four days ago. This Angel had a haggard face and black hair. The crimson power suit had been replaced by a slim-fitted black skirt, a pretty pale blue, long-sleeved blouse and darker blue jerkin. Flat navy pumps seemed out of place after the pile of stilettos she'd seen when Angel had packed her gear.

'Rachel, I…' Moisture flooded Angel's eyes.

'Hey, are you okay?'

'Not really. It's been a tough weekend. I can't figure out why you want to see me.'

'Can we talk in private?' There was an urge to hug the woman but unsure, Rachel closed the gap and kept her hands by her side.

'Sure, come into my office.' Angel turned and went through the door behind the receptionist.

There was little choice but to follow down a short passage with an office on either side. They turned left, passed two closed offices on her right and entered an open doorway at the end. A large window behind Angel's desk let in a lot of filtered light through a gauzy blind, giving the room an airy and bright sensation. Familiar perfume wasn't as strong as it had been on Friday. Angel tugged a chair from the rear wall and set it in front of the desk before she moved behind the desk and sat in a modern comfortable office chair. 'Why are you here?'

'I discovered a few facts you might be interested in.' She was reluctant to mention names, especially Kyle's for it was obvious the weekend hadn't been kind to Angel, who shuddered with eyes closed.

'I'm sorry if this brings you more angst but I figured you had a right to know what I found. Believe me, I understand how devastated you are. Dylan and I found a lot of downright creepy evidence: so creepy, he called in a couple of detectives after you left on Friday.'

'Oh, God.' Angel swept a hand across her eyes, sniffed and searched for a tissue, which she used and tossed into a bin. 'It can't be any worse than what we already found.'

'Has Kyle tried to get in contact with you since Friday?'

'He came here at closing on Friday. Wanted to talk. The guys here told him I wasn't at work. He didn't believe them but I wasn't. I did call in earlier to give them the lowdown. My friend's fiancé called two other guys to come with me to my place to help me pack my gear and stack it in a van we hired. It took most of the night by the time we stowed it all in a shed. If Kyle came to my home while we were there, I didn't see him and I doubt he would have shown his face with three muscly men with me.'

'Smart thinking. What I discovered were some notebooks and flash drives. I haven't studied them all but now know you and I aren't the only people he scammed and blackmailed.'

'You, but you're a cop.'

'No, I'm not and never said I was. I'm a victim and so far have discovered there are nine of us.'

'Nine!'

'I believe you were set up before you even met Kyle. For about six months he stalked you, planned and instigated the difficulties in his company and recommended you as the person to sort them out so he could manipulate you into a relationship to get your money.'

'Huh?'

Rachel opened her bag and drew out a flash drive. I could be arrested for giving you this but all the victims have a right to know what he did to them. This is a copy of the one I found in a desk drawer. Please, the police don't know I have it. There is also a separate notebook for each victim, which details every nasty, vindictive and illegal thing Kyle has done. There are also photos of all of us, taken while we were comatose.'

'I don't understand.'

'He drugged us all and took compromising photos to use for blackmail.'

'He took photos of me? Drugged me?'

'Sorry, yes. I've seen them.'

'Oh, God, no.'

'The police have them so he can't use them although there were no printed copies of you. It could be because he wouldn't have printed them to use until after you were no longer on the scene. I am certain he would have done so after the non-wedding. Now he can't. The police have all of the evidence, including the camera he had hidden in the ceiling to take the set-up photos. You are lucky he will never get the chance to use the photos of you. The other victims aren't so lucky. For four years he has been blackmailing them with threats so he could amass a small fortune.'

'This is unbelievable. You think I'm lucky?'

'Compared to the others, yes. You got most of your money back. And please, don't tell the police I gave it to you. Why don't you have a look at the flash drive? You might understand better.'

Silence reigned while Angel set up the flash drive in her computer, opened it and stared with her face going pale. 'These were…'

'Months before he set up the initial meeting with you and inveigled you into his web.'

'Dear, God, I sure was suckered in.'

'Like everyone else. He was clever.'

While Angel surfed through the photos, Rachel told her what had happened since Friday. When she got to the bit about earlier, she stalled when the image of Madison surged to the front of her mind.'

'What happened?' Angel paused and turned to Rachel.

The words tumbled out without a pause.

'He did what?'

'Murdered her. Almost hit the rest of us. It… it was ghastly.'

'How safe am I, or should I say, are we?'

'I make sure I have someone with me every time I step out of my doorway. Until he is caught, and he will be – soon, make sure a workmate walks you to your car. Oh, I forgot. You don't have a car.'

'Not yet. My friend drove me here this morning and her fiancée will pick me up on his way home from work.'

'Don't wait outside. Make sure the man is here before you leave the security of this building.'

'Do you think Kyle could attack me?'

'At the moment Kyle is in desperation and revenge mode, which makes him all the more dangerous. He had no conscience this morning. Didn't care. It's a miracle all four of us weren't mowed down. Since

Friday, because the police froze his main account, he has contacted a couple of other victims in an attempt to blackmail them to get money - without success as far as I know. It's probable the police will contact you over the next couple of days. Tell them everything — well, not about the flash drive or how you got your money back. Please, I beg you.'

'What if they ask? I won't lie to them.'

'Maybe you found the money in the bedroom when you packed, which isn't a lie for you were in the bedroom when I gave it to you. Your name was on the bundles. You counted it and realised it matched exactly the amounts he stole. You had the right to take everything that belonged to you from the house.'

Angel buried her head in her hands and groaned. 'Okay. I owe you for showing me the truth about the bastard and appreciate you coming here with this.' She wavered her hand at the computer. 'It's going to take me a while to sort through all of this unbelievable… Hell, I don't know what to call it. She clicked through a few more photos stopped and stared with her face paling. 'Oh my, God, I'm naked.' The next few clicks were slow and received stares. 'How on earth has he got away with this for so long?'

'People were terrified. How does any blackmailer get away with what they do? One of the guys had been threatened with the safety of his kids if he didn't comply. One with public exposure to ruin his father who is in a prominent position. Another works for the government. But it has to stop, which is why I gave you a copy of the photos. They are about you. Kyle uploaded a few photos of other victims on the web to ensure his demands were met. It's likely he would have done the same to you.'

'Did he upload any of you?'

'It's unlikely because he didn't know where I was to make demands and I doubt he would have threatened you until after he dumped you.'

Angel flopped back in her chair. 'I cannot believe I was such an idiot and didn't see what he was doing. Can't believe how he suckered me in. How did I not know I had been drugged?'

'I wondered the same but some of these date drugs don't have residual effects apart from the fact you have no recall. It was the same with them all and it was a different method of manipulation with each person. One was a shonky business deal. Anyone who had more money than he did. In the notebook, he had written next to your name how he could get at least fifty thousand out of you.'

'Fifty thousand!'

'Well, he managed half of it, add on the payments you were making towards the house and the rest would have come from you being blackmailed or from the joint account when you set it up.'

'Good grief. You have no idea how glad I am you turned up last Friday. Thank you.'

'You are welcome. Anything to stop him. And I have to go. If I find any more information I will contact you here at work.' Terrified Angel might figure out who she was, Rachel stood, tucked her bag under one arm and left only to be followed to the front desk where Olivia sat with Madeleine asleep in her arms.'

Olivia stood.

'You came to the house on Friday,' Angel said to Olivia.

'Yes, I...'

'Olivia is my sister-in-law. She came to see me.'

'Oh.'

Rachel didn't like the frown on Angel's face. 'We have to hurry. Olivia has kids to pick up from school.' Rachel shoved Olivia in the back. 'I'll be in contact if needed,' she said over her shoulder to prevent Angel from asking more questions.

'What was that about?' Olivia asked as they made their way to the elevators.

'She doesn't know who I am or who Madeleine is and I don't want her to know in case it gets leaked out.'

With a couple of hours to fill before Dylan came home, Rachel power-walked through the unit and counted steps in an effort to keep her mind away from things she didn't want to ever recall. When the silence became creepy, she counted aloud. She had become used to constant traffic noises outside to the extent this double glazing of windows was something she didn't enjoy. It also kept out the different scents of humanity. Inside might be clean but it was stuffy as though fresh air had never graced the surfaces.

At each round, she paused at the cot, willing Madeleine to be awake but with a full tummy, clean and dry backside and not long having fallen asleep, there was little chance. What could she do? There wasn't even a meal to prepare because she had promised to eat with Dylan and she didn't have the ingredients in any case. Nor would she use the owner's pots and pans without permission. To her, it was an invasion of privacy. Another round, she paused at the kitchen table and eyed her laptop. Maybe – research. She could research Keith Jackson.

Since she wasn't on any social media platforms she typed in the name on Google search. It wasn't of any help, not even when she added Australia to the name to narrow the search. It only brought up well-known people with the same name. She doubted the Keith she wanted details on was well-known, or at least not for the right reasons. *Public Records – Free Online Search* came up. The five headings gave her hope, especially the first one - *Criminal Records. Military* was doubtful to the extent it was ridiculous. *Driving* could mean anything but she figured it would be driving offences. It was a maybe. *Births Deaths and Marriages* was more probable but after a brief search she realised it would take forever and besides, she wasn't sure where Keith Jackson was born. The birth certificate she had copied said England but he could have emigrated any time in past thirty five years. If it was his real certificate. It could be stolen or another fake one. The *Unclaimed Money* section caused her to snigger. No way would he leave any money owed to him – unclaimed.

The ring of her phone ended her frustration until she heard the name of the caller when frustration turned to infuriation with an instant return of the picture of Madison Hart's mangled neck and chin. It was with huge reluctance she gave Detective Inspector Reece Waters the code and directions to her unit. Agitated while waiting for the knock, she swayed from side-to-side in front of the varnished wooden door. Even though she expected it, the three sharp raps sent every nerve strand on a frantic race to see which one could tighten the most.

A deep breath in, she straightened, paused, took the single step to the door and grasped the metal handle. Shoulders back, head high, another pause and she turned the handle. Two officers stood there, one a female officer with constable on her ID card. The inspector held his hat under one elbow and eyed Rachel.

'Mrs Jacobs.'

A shudder raced across her shoulders at the name she hated. 'Please, call me Rachel.' She stood aside, ushered the two in and led them to the dining table where she slammed the lid of her computer to hide what she'd been searching. 'Can I get you a drink? Tea – coffee?' Anything to delay the questions and detailed rehash of a few seconds of mayhem that would never leave her mind.

'No, we've not long had refreshment.' The constable's face was unreadable as she pulled out a chair and sat next to the inspector, who opened out a leather covered notebook, turned on his phone and laid it in the middle of the table.

'We will record the interview so no mistakes are made. Please sit.' He indicated the seat opposite.

With no choice, Rachel sat on the edge of the chair and gripped her hands in her lap to prevent them from shaking. One knee jiggled up and down at a furious pace until she spread her knees and pressed her feet onto the tiles in an effort to control rampant nerves.

The inspector frowned. 'You look worried. All we need is your version of the events of this morning.'

'I'm not worried. What happened, happened. It's more – the vision I can't get out of my head.'

'What vision?' he asked with a frown.

'Madison's injuries. The sound when the car hit her – her scream, the crunch, the whoomph of her last breath. They won't go away.'

The inspector reached over and gripped her lower arm in a friendly squeeze. 'I'm sorry you had to experience such horror, which is why it's important we get an accurate account of the tragedy so we can make sure Mr Jacobs pays for his crime.'

'Have you caught him?'

'Not yet, but we will. Every available officer is searching for him. He had been holed up in Miss Hart's house. His car was hidden in the garage. We found clothing and items belonging to him in the house. From what we could figure out, he had been there for a few days - probably since Friday but we can't be certain.'

'The insurance man. Is he okay? It happened so fast I didn't even get his name.'

'Concussion, bruises and scrapes but he will be fine. A night in hospital for observation. We have already spoken to him but there was little he could tell us apart from the reason he was there and how he ran the moment he spotted and heard the car. He was a little confused about who was who with two women claiming to be Mrs Jacobs.'

'I'd prefer not to be referred to as Mrs Jacobs even though I am and I never claimed that particular name at the time. The insurance policy has my maiden name on it.'

'Which is?'

'Esquilante. Marrying Kyle Jacobs is the biggest regret of my life.'

'You had no idea about him?'

'Not until the day after we married, but I had no idea about the other victims until last Friday, or the extent of his vile behaviour.'

'What do you mean by after the day you married?'

'Up until the day we married he was a gentleman: loving, kind, generous, complimentary – all the aspects you want in a man. I had no idea they were classical signs of coercive control until I researched it later. The day after – there was an instant Mr Hyde and there was never another day of Dr Jekyll. Two days later I knew I'd made the biggest mistake of my life and began to plan how to get out. It took me six life-changing and agonising months.'

'He abused you?'

'In many different ways but I don't want to talk about it – please.'

'It would help.'

'It won't help me nor your investigation into this murder. Can we get to this morning?'

The inspector frowned and paused, but before he could ask a question, her phone beeped with a message. She reached over and flipped the phone around from where she had left it. *On my way*, it read. She ignored Dylan's message, folded her arms and eyed the inspector.

'Start from the moment Detective Sergeant Smith picked you up here this morning. As much detail as you can recall.'

After she closed her eyes, it took a concentrated effort to detail every minute, even what they spoke about on the drive. The constable scribbled notes trying to keep up with Rachel while the inspector kept his finger close to the phone, pressing the pause button when he asked her to repeat or expand on something.

Another ping on her phone and she turned it off, eager to get this over with.

'Exactly what was said when you met with Bradley Armstrong and Miss Hart?'

'Who is…' The thumps on the door brought her to a sudden stop.

'Rachel, are you okay? Rachel,' Dylan yelled from outside.

'What the…?' the inspector said at the same time.

Rachel sighed and suppressed a laugh by biting the inside of her cheek. 'It's Dylan, I'd better let him know I'm okay.'

'Sergeant Marshall?' The inspector asked as he rose and went to the door.

'Yes, he lives in the unit opposite and arranged for me to stay here as it is a relatively safe hideaway.'

When the door opened, Dylan barged in. 'Rachel, oh, err, Sir.' Dylan removed his belt of armour as he took one step in and paused mid-stride with his jaw agape. 'What's going on? Rachel, are you okay?'

'Yes, I'm fine.'

He came in, shut the door and dropped the belt on the floor. 'You didn't answer my message. I thought something had happened to you.' With a questioning lift of his eyebrows he turned to the inspector. 'Sir, can I ask why you are here?'

'An interview about the incident this morning. Please join us.'

Dylan sped towards Rachel. 'What incident?'

A wail from the bedroom silenced the entire room. 'Excuse me.' Relieved to have a break, Rachel stood and hurried to the bedroom where she lifted Madeleine from the cot and wrapped her in a blanket. 'Hey, Sweetie.' She checked the nappy and replaced it with a dry one. Madeleine smiled. 'So you wanted a nappy change so you could join the party. Well, the party isn't any fun. Maybe you and I could hide away in here.'

'The inspector won't appreciate you hiding away.' When Dylan crossed the floor, Rachel noticed how pale his face had gone making it obvious he had been told the facts. 'Kyle almost killed you this morning and you didn't let me know?'

'You were at work.'

'A simple message for me to ring you wouldn't have interfered with my work.' He sounded put out.

'I had Olivia and wasn't in any space to recall what happened let alone talk about it. I don't want to ever talk about it. I want to forget it.' She turned away and buried her head against Madeleine's warm body to prevent another bout of tears.

'I'm sorry. Hell, Rachel, I don't mean to upset you but this is a bit of a shock. Please forgive me.'

Eyes, closed, Rachel lifted her head. 'It's okay. It was so awful and so sudden. Sergeant Smith saved my life by shoving me out of the way in the nick of time. I... I…. Please, can we change the subject?'

'I wish we could but the inspector needs to finish the interview. Do you want me to hold Sweet Pea?'

Rachel shook her head. 'I need her with me.'

'Okay. Come on, let's get this over with.'

Rachel blew out her cheeks. 'I so don't want to do this.'

'Victims never do but it is a necessary evil to get all the facts to ensure the culprit doesn't get away with their obscene crime. I can't believe he would be so stupid to run you all down, especially with a police officer present.'

'Since Justin wasn't in uniform, Kyle couldn't have known police were present.'

'True.' When he put his open hand against the small of her back, she winced. He muttered something as he pressed her forwards until they reached the table where Rachel sat and kept her eyes on Madeleine the entire time it took to answer the rest of the questions.

When the officers left she flopped forwards with relief, her head on one arm while she held Madeleine in the other.

'How about I cook dinner for you?' Dylan squatted next to her. 'You look rung out.'

Rung out weren't the right words. More like exhausted but there was no way she could spend the evening being waited on with nothing to do. Her mind would drive her crazy with vivid re-runs of the body caught on the bricks. Desperate for something to do, she lifted her head. 'How about I cook while you shower. I need to concentrate on anything except this morning.'

'If you're sure.'

'I am. I need to keep busy.'

Dylan stood and reached out one hand. 'The fridge and pantry are well stocked but keep it simple.'

'I can do simple.' With a forced smile, she grasped his hand, glad she didn't wince at his touch for once. Within mere minutes Madeleine was in her pram against the wall between Dylan's kitchen and dining area, where she could watch the movement.

Rachel scanned the shelves in the refrigerator and noticed the left over vegies from the night before. Bubble and squeak was simple, add on the four lamb chops already defrosted. She mooshed the vegies amongst the cold mashed potatoes, found a frying pan and melted a pat of butter. A smaller pan went on a separate hob into which she settled the chops. When the butter began to spatter, she moulded the vegies to fill the pan and drank in the aroma wafting from the stove top. Yum. While keeping an eye on the food she remembered she had promised to phone Laura Jones with an update. She scrolled through the numbers of the victims she was glad she had saved, pressed Laura's number and waited. On the sixth ring, she was about to hang up when it clicked.

'This is Laura's phone, give me the message and I'll pass it on.' At the male voice she would never forget, Rachel trembled and almost dropped the phone before she managed to stab the off button.

'Dylan,' she yelled. When he didn't answer she shot around the bench and pelted along the passage. 'Dylan,' she screamed louder.

'The door to his bedroom opened and a wet head poked from behind the door. 'What's wrong?' A hand holding a towel appeared and he rubbed it across his head and face.

'It's Kyle. He's at Laura Jone's place. We have to save her.'

'Huh? How do you know?'

'I promised I would update her but Kyle answered her phone. Hurry.'

'I thought I asked you to not interfere. Damn it. Give me a minute to get dressed.' The door snicked shut.

Frantic, Rachel raced back to the kitchen, turned off the gas and lifted Madeleine from the pram. Capsule, she needed the capsule. She raced to her unit, strapped Madeleine in the capsule and tore back across the passage to wait for Dylan.

Since the atmosphere in the car was tense, Rachel kept her head turned towards the side window but took little notice of the objects they passed. To her, they were all a blur. It wasn't only because Dylan's words stung. It was more about the bad memories they evoked when he ordered her to stay home, to not become involved in police procedure. After six months of marriage where orders, orders, orders were demanded and being too afraid to not obey because of the consequences, she couldn't handle demands. The argument had been short but intense and only ended when she promised to stand back and not get in the way. All she wanted was to ensure Laura Jones was unharmed.

'Justin is sending officers. They should be there already.'

Still fighting to regain her equilibrium, Rachel ignored the comment but flinched when Dylan's hand landed on her thigh.

'Did you hear what I said?'

'Yes.'

'What's wrong?'

'Apart from a maniacal murderer holding a woman hostage? Nothing.'

'You don't know she's a hostage.'

Rachel swung her head towards Dylan and glared at him. 'How much are you prepared to bet? He has been found out. He's lost control. To regain control these perpetrators lay blame on anybody rather than themselves and use coercion to get the control back. He will do anything to regain control over his victims and in particular - me. He has already murdered one because he lost control over her. He no longer cares who or how he hurts. Murder is the final act of revenge. And it's my fault Madison was murdered and my fault he has Laura in his clutches.'

'How is it your fault?'

'He recognised me at the house this morning. I won at court and bested him, which he can't handle. Angel bested him and will now be a prime target. He is now beyond angry to the extent all he has left is to lash out.'

'You don't know this.'

'I've lived it. It's you who has no idea.' Rachel pressed her hand on the front glove compartment when the car swerved around a corner at speed.

'Sorry. We're almost there. What number?'

'Thirty seven.'

'There.' Even though Dylan pointed, he didn't need to. Three police cars parked at various angles in the driveway and on the front lawn, had blue and red strobe lights flashing. Homeowners from the street stood around in various stages of dress and undress, some still in business clothes, others in layabout wear and a few with belted dressing gowns. One female officer waved the gawkers back as she rolled out tape tied to the front corner post across the street. Dylan drew to a stop on the verge in front of the house, next to an open gate. 'Stay in the car.' As he got out he tossed the keys at her. 'Lock the doors.'

Stung by the orders, Rachel closed her eyes, swore and counted to ten in her mind in an attempt to calm a heart that had doubled its rate in a split second. How could he leave her here unprotected? If Kyle wasn't inside and she bet he wasn't, he wouldn't be far away. Terrified, she searched the area, but there were too many ominous dark shadows and fences he could hide behind. She studied each face of the onlookers, searched for any resemblance in height, build, hair or features but it was too dark to make out any clear features.

Don't panic, don't panic, she willed to her body but her body ignored her and began to tremble. She squealed at the snuffle from the rear seat. 'Oh, God, Madeleine. He can't find you,' she stuttered through teeth that shook as much as her body. Desperate to get out, she clambered over the console, unlatched the capsule and again studied the area near the car, especially the path between the car and front door of the house, now ablaze with lights. All the officers had disappeared inside. Police tape now ran across the road from both boundaries of the property, keeping gawkers away but it didn't mean one in particular couldn't breach the tape and pounce on her and the female officer was no longer in sight. Where was she? Rachel scanned the area but there were no uniforms to be seen.

She was about to open the door when she jolted at a siren. More flashing lights neared. An ambulance. It had to mean one thing. Laura was hurt for if she was dead there would be no emergency sirens. Or perhaps Kyle had been downed by the officers. God, she hoped so. When the ambulance drew to a stop in front of the tape and two paramedics rushed out and grabbed medical packs, Rachel took the opportunity to get out of the car with Madeleine still in the capsule and shadow the two men to the front veranda of the house where she crouched in the corner next to the front door. With the waist high bricked-in end she was partially hidden and couldn't be pounced on. At least here she was closer to the officers and near enough she could rush inside if she was approached.

Within seconds of her sitting, Madeleine whimpered and began to cry. It wasn't a surprise with all the bumps and voices after the lull of car movement which usually sent Madeleine to sleep within a minute or two. The only way to quieten her was to put her to the breast. Too scared to turn and hide a feeding Madeleine from the masses, she pressed her back into the corner, sat with legs crossed and eased Madeleine from the capsule. To hide what she was doing she draped the baby blanket over her shoulder and as far down the tiny back it would reach. To keep Madeleine warm she tugged up the bottom of her hoodie to swaddle the bottom half of the wriggling body. The cold from the concrete veranda chilled her backside and legs until body heat warmed the area.

Across the road, streetlights marched in a straight line. They highlighted the houses close to them and left the fence lines and passages to the rear as vague shapes: scary shapes that could be hiding a maniac. Even from this distance, a haze of insects buzzed close to the lights. This side of the urban street was in relative darkness apart from where strobe lights sent out bright flashes of red and blue.

A sudden scuffle sent her heart racing. One paramedic ran out and belted to the back of the ambulance. Within seconds he was running back to the house shoving the stretcher in front of him. An officer came from the house and helped get the stretcher up the two steps. The rattle of wheels whizzing past, cause Madeleine to jerk and pause. Everyone vanished inside from where a constant rumble of voices emanated, to match the queries and murmurs from the still large crowd.

Madeleine began to nurse again, the sensation calming Rachel's strung out nerves but still she jerked her head in all directions, alert for the slightest threat. The tension in her nervous system might have eased but her brain cells jostled in a mad rush to sort themselves out. Even though it would be stupid for Kyle to hang around, she couldn't get rid of the sensation she was being watched. She prayed it was only the onlookers and not one person in particular.

When the stretcher appeared, it was difficult to see on top but a blanket didn't cover the female face. Rachel blew out her cheeks at the knowledge the woman had to be alive. 'Is she okay?' Rachel dared ask.

An officer stilled and stared at her. 'Who are you and what the hell are you doing there?'

'Is Laura okay?'

'You know her?'

'No.'

'Then how…'

'Rachel, I thought I asked you to stay in the car?' Dylan pushed the other officer aside and stood in front of Rachel with arms akimbo. The muscles in his jaw tightened. She spied a quiver of uncertainty in his eyes, followed by a flash of anger. What did he have to be angry about?

Defiance surged. 'You didn't ask. You ordered and I no longer accept a man giving me orders. Is Laura okay?'

'She has severe injuries but should survive. We arrived in time.'

Rachel raised her eyebrows. 'Good job you didn't make the bet. And Kyle?'

'Gone. This is a crime scene. You can't interfere.'

Furious, Rachel struggled to get upright without dislodging Madeleine. 'Without my so-called *interference,* none of you would he here right now. Laura wouldn't have received urgent medical care and be on her way to hospital. It's more than likely she wouldn't have been found before she passed away. Why wasn't she contacted to let her know Kyle was on the rampage?'

'We rang. She said she was okay.' Justin Smith joined the party.

'You rang?' She winced at the way her voice rose to a screech. 'You didn't bother to come here to check out her house to make sure Kyle wasn't standing over her with a weapon to ensure she said *she was okay?* What about the others? Did you simply make a phone call? Did you visit Angel Lombardo to make sure Kyle didn't have her in his clutches?'

At the intense silence, she waited for the fallout but no-one uttered a word.

'Well, it's a good job I *interfered* and had the nous to visit her to make sure she was okay and give her the heads up to be alert because Kyle was on the loose. Thanks to my warning she now has a big burley man to keep her safe. Kyle tried to get to her on Friday evening. Did you know that?'

More silence with shocked eyes staring at her.

'And what about Adam Hinkler? Did you visit him? Kyle called at his house on Monday to demand money. I know this because I *interfered,* spoke to him and suggested he hire a body guard. And there are Kelly, Ethan and Jordan. Has any officer visited them to see if they are even alive?' She glared at each in turn. 'I'm not sorry I *interfered.* Someone had to.' She stormed from the veranda and reached the open gate before she remembered the capsule. She swore aloud and turned around to be met by Dylan who had the capsule in his hand. 'Don't you dare say a word.'

His eyebrows rose at the same time laughter lines crinkled. 'I'm not game. Let's get you home.' He held out one palm. 'Keys?'

She had no idea where they were; couldn't remember. A pat on all pockets yielded only her unit key but no car keys so she peered through all the windows. 'On the front seat where you threw them,' she said as she snatched the capsule from Dylan's hand and opened the rear door. The only way to sort out the capsule and Madeleine was to put her in it first. With anger still on the simmer, ready to explode, it took a while to calm enough to secure the capsule, wrap Madeleine in the blanket, strap her in and sort out her own clothes so she didn't have one boob hanging out. Too miffed to talk, she plonked herself on the back seat next to Madeleine, slammed the door, clicked her safety belt into place and folded her arms.

It took less than fifteen minutes to reach the units: fifteen minutes while she ignored Dylan because she was not only angry with him but disappointed because he had betrayed the trust she had begun to develop towards him. When they got out of the car, she held tight to the capsule while they rose in the lift to the second floor. She strode ahead along the passage and took out the key to her unit.

'Are you coming in to eat?'

'I'm not hungry?' She opened the door.

'Can we talk?' Dylan asked.

'There's nothing to talk about.'

'Can I ask why you are so angry with me?'

'More disappointed than angry.'

'Why?'

'You left me alone.'

'You were safe locked in my car.'

She kept her back to him. 'You assumed I was safe but there was no way you could be certain. I wasn't safe earlier this morning when I stood so close to a sergeant, his clothes brushed against mine. I wasn't safe in your car with no-one else around. Kyle was in that house less than fifteen minutes before we got there. It was impossible for him to have been far away.' She turned. 'Did you or any officer search the backyard, or the neighbour's yards or the places across the road?'

'The house and yard – yes.'

'But not any other yard.'

'I can't answer because I don't know.'

'Exactly my point. I was a sitting duck. One rush forward with a big rock or brick and the window would have been smashed. I might have been able to escape but – and this is the reason I am so disappointed – Madeleine couldn't escape. You put my daughter's life in jeopardy.'

She stepped inside.

'I'm sorry.'

'Not half as sorry as I am.' She slammed the door and sank to the floor, overcome. Elbows on knees and head in her hands with her eyes closed, she fought to calm tense nerves and not let her body sink into a panicked darkness. 'Stay alert,' she said aloud. 'Don't panic. Think – Madeleine, Madeleine, Madeleine. She needs you. Don't let your mind vanish into space.'

Eyes open, she straightened, swung the capsule around so it was in front of her face. Madeleine was still awake. When Madeleine smiled it brought tears to Rachel's eyes. This time she let them fall. It was better than having a blank out. 'God, Baby Girl, I was so scared he would find you. And it wouldn't take him two minutes to figure it out. And he wouldn't like it.' Desperate to hold her baby, Rachel unhitched her and drew the precious bundle into her arms. 'I love you so damn much.'

'When her phone beeped with a message, she drew it out of her back pocket and read the message. *I'm sorry. Can we talk?* She turned the phone off.

After a restless night, with short snatches of sleep interspersed with long periods with her hand through the cot bars and on Madeleine's body to ensure her baby was still there and breathing, Rachel dragged herself out of bed and took her time to shower in the hope of washing away lethargy. It didn't help the need to sleep but at least she had cleared away lanky hair and the remnants of last night's sweat and grime.

Bath and playtime with Madeleine took twice as long than normal because she couldn't bear to leave the most important thing in her life for a second. Even when Madeleine fell asleep, Rachel wheeled the cot into the lounge area so she could keep her within sight. It wasn't until she sat at the dining table with two slices of buttered toast and a mug of tea, she noticed the piece of white paper poking from under the front door. Logic told her it was from Dylan who had to have been at work for at least two hours.

She stared at the square of white for a good minute before taking another bite of toast, chewed it to mush and washed it down with a slurp of tea. The phone she'd left on the table last night caught her eye. It was still turned off. Will I or won't I, see-sawed through her mind before she pressed the button and turned it on to see at least a dozen messages from Dylan. Most had the word, sorry; all asked her to message him back or ring him to ensure him she was okay. Impossible to answer for she wasn't sure. Was she okay in the being alive or unharmed sense? Sure. Was she okay mentally? Not so sure for her mind had given her little peace during the night and since she'd risen. Emotionally? No, for her emotions were all over the place. Instead of answering she deleted the messages only to discover the piece of white paper seemed to stab at her. Frustrated with the silent message, she picked it up. A key fell from the folds. Mystified, she spread the paper on the table.

I'm really sorry. I have information for you. Please call. I won't be home until around ten as I have uni tonight. Use my place to cook your meals. There's plenty of food. Code for my alarm is 37753.

'I might take you up on the offer since you won't be there,' she said to the key as she glared at it. It was difficult to work out what she thought of Dylan now. He was still being his generous kind self but the trust she'd built up towards him seemed to have vanished. And without trust, there was nothing, which was a pity because she liked him – more than she should or believed she could. Inside her seemed to be permanently bruised.

While she ate, flashes of ideas twirled about what still needed to be done before she could go home. If she could get home without a car of her own. Lord she had to figure that out as well.

Insurance. There was insurance to sort out, not only for the house, but also the car. Well, the car was easier because Pierre had the insurance. There was a loan on the house which she was certain would never be paid by Kyle. What if she didn't get enough from the insurance to pay it off? There were two different insurance companies to deal with but first she needed to find out how damaged her car was. Pete might know. And Ella would worry if she didn't get an update. With the list growing, she found a pen and wrote on the back of Dylan's message. A chat with Pierre and Olivia might bring some peace and they needed to be told about last night and how Kyle might try to contact them. The insidious notion brought on a quick shiver which started at her head and wove down her body. Determined to not let it take over, she stood and shook her entire body to get rid of any residual fear. A few minutes of jogging on the spot set her heart rate higher and eased her angst a little. Since the calls to Pierre and Olivia were the most important, she picked up the phone and settled on the lounge where she could both see and reach Madeleine. Pierre first.

'Hey, Lise.' It was so darn good to hear his voice and the use of his pet name for her sent a warm fuzzy through her innards. It brought… comfort might be the right word.

'Hi, how's work?' She winced at the inane greeting. Get with it.

'The same as yesterday. What's wrong?'

'What makes you think something is wrong?'

'I know you; spill all.'

She laughed, which felt darn good and since he could always tell when she kept things from him, she detailed the events of last night.

'Come on, Lise, the man was probably desperate to get to the scene and didn't think about what he said even though he was right in you not encroaching on a crime scene. He's a cop and you're not. From what Livvy said, he's a good man. Did you know he rang us last night?'

'He did? Why?'

'To warn us to be alert for Kyle. He might have added how he upset you and was forever remorseful. I think he's smitten. How do you feel about him?'

She fought to ignore the squishy sensation inside her. 'Oh, for goodness sake. If he's smitten, it's not with me. More like Madeleine.'

'Not what he indicated, although he did say Madeleine had him wrapped around her little finger. The cutest thing ever, he called her. I think he's spent more time with my niece than I have, which doesn't go down well. I'm jealous. How about bringing her over one night so I can get to know her better?'

'As soon as Kyle is caught. And I send you photos.'

'Photos are good. The real thing is better. I want to cuddle her – and hug you. I miss having you around.'

Tears and a painful pang surged. 'I miss you as well. But soon. Real soon. I want to move back to the city; find a nice little cottage I can turn into a home. With a garden, and trees, and flowers.'

'I'll start looking for a place. How many bedrooms?'

'Three. There's only the two of us but a spare room is handy. A decent yard space is a must. Not one of these massive new homes on a piddly little block where the neighbour's windows are so close it's embarrassing. I've been stuck in a tiny space for too long.'

'In the city or suburbs?'

'Near you.' A faint scuffle came from the passage. 'I have to go.'

'Is everything okay?'

Too scared to answer in case her voice was heard, she hung up, shoved the phone in her pocket and crept to the door. It was hard to make out clear words but she was certain there was a male voice. Dylan? No, couldn't be. He was at work and she doubted he would speak so loud. Besides, who would be there to talk to since there were only the two units on this level? With curiosity and a tingle of nerves, she put her ear to the door. They had to be coming closer because she could make out footsteps, scuffles and some sort of quiet squeal.

'Open the door,' a man's voice demanded and she froze.

'No key.' A quivering female voice answered.

'I know she's here. Which unit. This one?' A thump on her door snapped Rachel out of a daze.

'They away. No-one there.'

'Where's the key?'

'I not clean that one. No key.'

'Then she has to be in this one.' Kyle's voice sent a shiver across her shoulders. How could he have found her?

'No woman live there. Only Mr Dylan.'

'Fuck you. I saw her come in this building with the bastard. She's in there. Open the damn door.'

'No key.'

'Where is it?'

'I not clean there today. Tomorrow this unit. Today I clean down the stairs. I only bring key for down.'

'I don't believe you. Open the bloody door or I'll slit your damn throat.'

Horrified, Rachel sank to the floor with her eyes closed but jerked when something bashed against Dylan's door and an alarm shrieked. It was so loud it hurt her ear drums. When Madeleine made a noise Rachel scrambled up and stumbled across to the cot. She grabbed Madeleine, scampered to the end room and closed the door. 'Hush, little one, hush,' she whispered as she rocked from side-to-side.

Her phone beeped with a message. The last thing she needed was to waste time on the phone but maybe she could message back for help, so she slid it from her pocket and saw there was a message. Dylan. Huh?

'My alarm. Why?'

How on earth does he know? She typed. *Kyle here. Where is he?'*

In passage. Has hostage.

Who?

Cleaner.

Lock U and M in bathroom. 5 mins. On way. I call cops.

Overcome, Rachel spun around in a circle, her mind on a muddled rampage. Madeleine squirmed and snuffled. 'Please, don't wake?' She glanced down to be met by screwed blue eyes and a quivering mouth ready to let loose with a wail. She hoisted Madeleine over her shoulder and rubbed circles around the tiny back. Madeleine whimpered. Not sure what to do, Rachel fled to the bathroom and locked the door. Even though Madeleine wasn't due for a feed, Rachel sat on the toilet lid and put Madeleine to her breast, hopeful it would send her back to sleep. After only a few sucks, Madeleine's eyes stuttered and closed.

Relieved, Rachel grabbed a couple of towels from the cupboard, made a bed in the bath and laid Madeleine in the curved nest. Another towel over the top to keep her snug. Rachel didn't dare move while she stood at the side of the bath with her eyes on Madeleine to make sure she remained asleep while her mind was desperate to find out what was happening outside. She hadn't heard any sirens – she hadn't heard anything with the double glazed windows.

She couldn't just stand here and do nothing, yet she couldn't leave. Think, woman, think. She dropped back onto the toilet seat, closed her eyes and counted to five while she filled her lungs. Another slow five to empty them. Keep calm and think. Madeleine would be safest in the bathroom for it would be the last place Kyle would search, if he managed to get in, and, if she was easy to find he wouldn't bother to search for anyone else. A quick glance at her precious baby. Madeleine had turned slightly with eyes shut and even breathing. In the normal world, she slept well for at least three hours. For Madeleine, it was a normal world so why wouldn't she stay asleep? Happy with the logic, Rachel rose, pulled the small blind down to darken the room and closed the door as she left. Her baby was as safe as Rachel could make her.

Too darn scared to make any noise, she tip-toed to the lounge and screwed her eyes. Why wasn't the alarm still shrieking? Maybe it was on a timer. There were still scuffles in the passage so Kyle had to be there and if there were scuffles, the woman had to still be alive, she hoped. Not sure what to do, she snuck to the gap in the drapes at the front window, peered out and heaved out a breath. Two marked police cars were parked on the footpath but with no lights and she hadn't heard any sirens. Surely they shrill noise would have penetrated. Double glazing couldn't be strong enough to keep out such strident sounds. It was impossible to see the front entry and no officers were in sight. Where were they? Could they get in? Did they know the codes?

'Elise, get out here!' She jumped and whimpered at Kyle's shout. A thump followed but not on her door. Had to be Dylan's. Was it a kick or a fist? What if she didn't go out? Would he kill the poor cleaner?' But what if she did? He would kill her as well for no way would he leave a witness. But she couldn't be responsible for the loss of another person's life and if she died as well, what would happen to Madeleine?

'If you don't come out, I'll kill her.' Well, that answered her question but...

'Let her go, Jacobs.'

Rachel plastered her hand over her mouth to muffle her squeal at Dylan's voice while her heart decided it wanted to act like a jackhammer and drill holes in her ribs.

'Not until the bitch shows her face,' Kyle yelled back.

'Drop the knife. There are officers at all the entries, exits, lifts and stairs. Be sensible and let the woman go. Don't add the loss of another life to make things worse for you.'

'I know she's in here.' A loud thump followed Kyle's words. It sounded more like a kick than a fist.

'There is no-one in my unit. I can open the door to show you if you want but only if you let the woman go.' Dylan must have come closer for his voice was clearer.

'Stay away or I'll use this knife.'

The woman whimpered. 'Please,' she squeaked.

'Okay, but I can't open the door from here. Your choice. You want to see in my unit, you release the woman but I can assure you, there is no-one in there.'

'Then who turned off the alarm?'

'I did. It's connected to my phone, which is how I knew you were here. I can turn it off remotely the same way I can see who is at the door. If you look closely above the door, you will see a small camera. So, what's it going to be?'

'I know the bitch is here?'

'Who are you talking about?

'Elise.'

'What makes you so sure?'

'I saw her come in with you last night. She hasn't come out.'

'The woman in my car last night is a dark-haired, brown eyed lady called Rachel. I saw Elise Jacaobs in court and believe she has light brown hair and blue eyes. You might have seen my car turn into the drive but you didn't see anyone come into this building because you couldn't get into the underground carpark. I know because I checked there was no-one around.'

'Liar!' Kyle screamed and the woman yelped.

Rachel was certain of one thing. She couldn't be responsible for the death of another woman so she shook her wigless head and fluffed up her hair. There had been no need to put in brown contact lenses this morning, not that she'd been in the frame of mind to even think about them. 'You have to do this,' she whispered to herself and put her fingers around the knob on the deadlock.

'Nothing I said was a lie,' Dylan continued. 'Be smart and let the woman go. One yell and three other officers will join me. Show your faces, fellas. They are all armed and will shoot if you harm the woman. There is not a chance in hell you will be able to escape, even if the person you are looking for is with you. How about I move away and you can come closer to the lift?'

At the scuffle, Rachel took forever to turn the knob until the lock snicked. It seemed to echo and reverberate like a big bass drum. To make certain it didn't click again, she paused with pressure on the lock so it wouldn't slip back. It took a monumental effort to will her hand to inch the door open a crack.

Kyle had his back to her, his arms around the woman's throat and the pointy end of a large knife against the side of her head. A pair of creased baggy trousers hung low under the tails of a white business shirt. Never, in all the time she had known him, had he been so scruffy. Neither garment was clean with dark smudges as though he'd slept on the ground or rubbed up against some filth.

Continuous whimpers came from the woman while Dylan encouraged Kyle to keep walking. Her heart stopped when Kyle paused and speared the tip of the knife against the woman's neck.

'I'm not going any further until I see my wife.' He stabbed the knife and blood spurted.

Desperate to stop any more bloodshed, Rachel stepped from the room and tip-toed backwards towards the end wall, away from Kyle. She noticed Dylan's eyes boggle and a slight shake of his head but she had to stop this: she was the only person who could.

'You want me, you release the woman and come and get me.'

Kyle swung around with eyes blazing in triumph. A loud pop and fizz erupted a split second before every part of Kyle's body jerked and jolted and he released his grip on the woman. The knife flew from his hands and he fell to the floor with his limbs still acting like lightning bolts. With what looked like a gun in his hands, Dylan bolted forwards with three more officers on his heels. One kicked the knife so hard it skidded towards Rachel and she jumped over it before it hit the end wall. Another officer dropped on top of Kyle while Dylan yanked handcuffs from his belt.

The third officer grabbed the woman and shuffled her towards the elevator. 'I need medical aid,' he yelled with fingers pressed into the woman's neck. After an initial scream the woman burst into audible sobs and clung to the officer the same way a limpet clings to a rock.

It all happened so fast, Rachel's brain hadn't caught up with the action. She couldn't figure out if Kyle had been shot, if he was still alive or what reality was.

Handcuffs went on and Rachel noticed fine springy wires protruded from the shirt on Kyle's back. Dylan yanked them out and flipped Kyle onto his back. A dark stain spread down the front of the tan trousers. It took Rachel several seconds before she figured the reason. Kyle had been tasered. Delight jiggled her innards There was no-one more deserving of an electric shock. Pity it wasn't plugged into a 240 volt electrical circuit.

'You ugly bitch,' Kyle screamed with his eyes shooting shards of venom towards Rachel.

She had no idea why she straightened, shoved her shoulders back and approached the bastard for the last thing she needed or wanted was to ever get near him again. 'If I'm a bitch then you are a cur but with your lack of intelligence you probably have no idea what the word means. Worthless dog or contemptible person, but you wouldn't know what contemptible means either, even though it fits you to a T.'

When Kyle hissed and bucked around in an attempt to reach her, she stepped sideways.

'And I'm not ugly and never have been. I might not be the most beautiful person on this earth but neither am I ugly. Ugly is someone who stalks and photographs people so he can set up meetings to inveigle them into a his web of deceit and lies. Someone who drugs his victims to take disgusting and compromising photos of them so he can blackmail them. Ugly is someone who cheats, lies and pretends. Someone who is weak and can't control his bladder.' She curled her lip. 'Poor little diddums has wet himself.' She kicked his leg and was rewarded with a snarl.

'You'll pay; you dumb bitch.'

Her laugh wasn't of the funny kind. 'Dumb? Really? I'm much smarter than you could ever hope to be. If I'm so dumb, how come you couldn't find me for the past ten months when I've been living right under your nose? How come I figured out within two weeks how you tracked my phone. If you were so smart, how come you didn't know I had two phones, one which I used for personal calls, especially when I took the tracking device from under the hub of my car and left it where you thought my car was while I drove wherever I wanted. Especially on Saturdays when you were at your so-called golf. Did you really think I didn't know you were meeting up with Angel Lombardo? And you had the audacity to accuse me of cheating. She leant over his contorted with fury face. 'Poor little man has to wrap a sock around his weenie penis to make out he's got something to be proud of.' She kicked the dislodged lump on the top of his thigh and sniggered. 'I'm delighted you get to spend the rest of your life in prison, where you deserve to be, and I hope some big burly bikie uses your backside to rape you, again and again and again so you understand what it feels like to be raped.'

Even though Kyle spat at her, fear flickered in his eye, sending the previous jiggles of delight into a frenzy. He was scared. It felt so darn good. What felt even better was when she wiped the bottom of her shoe in his globule of spittle and spread it over his face with her foot.

'Enough,' Dylan said as he manoeuvred his way between her and Kyle. 'Take him away.'

'Elise you have to help me?'

Rachel couldn't believe the pathetic plea nor the panic on his face. 'Help you? What gives you the idea I would ever do anything to help a low-life bastard like you? The only help you will get from me is when I testify in court, along with Adam, Kelly, Laura, Ethan, Angel and Jordan to ensure your prison sentence is very long. His gasp of surprise at her knowledge brought joy to her innards as did the terror that spread across his face.

'You're my wife.'

Unable to believe he would still beg her, Rachel laughed.

'No she's not.'

Rachel spun around at the words from Dylan. 'What do you mean?'

'His real name is Keith Jackson who has a wife and four-year-old son in Tasmania, where there is an outstanding warrant for his arrest. Your marriage was illegal. Bigamy is another crime we can add to the vast list.' Dylan turned to the officer. 'Constable take him away and read him his rights. Arrest him for first degree murder, attempted murder of four others, including a police officer, abduction and causing injury with a deadly weapon, with other crimes to be added before his first appearance in court.'

Kyle was hauled to his feet but he didn't make it easy. He kicked, screamed and wrestled until he was out of sight but still shouts echoed until the elevator descended.

Disbelief had emptied Rachel's brain cells. She sank to the floor with her arms wrapped around her torso to stop the wave of shivers. Without thinking, she'd revealed things she had vowed to never reveal and now wondered if she was so fractured she would never be complete again.

When Dylan squatted in front of her there was a tightness about his lips she had never seen before. Fear rippled through her gut. 'Yet again, you are in the middle of a crime scene,' he said.

The words sounded like a threat or condemnation. 'Are you okay?' he added with a frown.

No, she wanted to yell. She could never be okay. 'I don't know. I'm kinda spaced out.'

'Probably shock. Where's Sweet Pea?'

'In the bath tub.'

Dylan raised his eyebrows. 'Maybe we should go get her out and sit somewhere more comfortable while we talk. Forensics will be here soon.' As he rose, he put one hand on the back of her shoulder, helped her up and turned her towards the still open unit door.

'Am I going to be questioned again?'

'I have no doubt. The D's might begin to get suspicious of you since you turn up at so many crime scenes.'

Another censure. When she stumbled, he placed one arm around her waist and assisted her to the sofa where she flopped onto he cushion and buried her head in her hands, too overcome to think clearly. The confrontation with Kyle had brought back so many unwelcome visions she'd fought for months to forget.

'Since Madeleine is sound asleep and snug I left her there.' Dylan dropped to his haunches in front of Rachel and shook her leg.

'Huh?'

'Are you okay?' Dylan reached out, paused and drew his hand back.

'I will be,' was the only thing she could think of to say since she didn't think she would ever be okay.

'Are you up to having a chat?'

Desperate to hold back threatening tears, she shrugged. 'About what?'

'Today's little drama to start with. Why did you come out? When I saw you my heart stopped beating.' Not giving her a chance to reply, he sought out her hand and entwined their fingers as he sat on the sofa next to her and leant forward far enough he could catch her eye.

Despite her embarrassment there was a thrill of pleasure at the feel of his hand around hers. For once it didn't scare her to be touched by a man. And it had been so long since she'd felt an inkling of connection from a touch, apart from her family and the few friends she'd made down south. 'I couldn't let another woman be harmed because of me.'

'I wouldn't have let him kill her.'

Rachel turned her head towards him and speared him a fierce look. 'He stabbed her.'

'I know. I was doing my best to talk him down: to convince he there was no way he would escape.'

She sniffed back the threat of tears. 'He was too angry to be talked down or see logic. I thought you shot him.'

'You have no idea how much I wanted to but I've been with the force for nearly fifteen years and have never shot a person. I've used the taser many times but shooting a real bullet is not something any officer wants to do. If there had been no other option, I would have, for he certainly deserved it. But in the front of my mind was what would happen if I missed. There was every chance a bullet would have hit Lina or you, when you appeared. I wasn't willing to take such a chance. Either way, it doesn't matter now. He has been caught and it's unlikely he will ever walk free again. The charges are too serious. It will take us a while to figure out every charge we can lay at his feet – there are so many. And Tasmania want him as well.'

'What did he do there and how did you know?'

'Justin and I agreed to have an officer do some research, which is another thing I wanted to discuss with you. The Jacobs birth certificate is fake. The passport is genuine but the paperwork he used to get it, isn't. The passport will be rescinded. As to what he did? The list is long but not as long as the current list here. Forgery, blackmail, stealing, false pretences, wife battery and I believe there was physical abuse of two other women. I don't know the nitty gritty details.'

'He's still married?' She winced at the idea.

'Yes. The wife applied for a divorce but they couldn't find him to serve the papers. He left when she announced her pregnancy.'

'What does all of this mean for me?'

'It means you are in a bit of a legal mess but the marriage isn't legitimate. It will take legal advice to untangle the web.'

'What do you mean?'

'The house is in your supposed married name. As is the insurance policy.'

'No, they are in my maiden name.'

'How come?'

'The house was purchased before the supposed marriage when I changed my surname. All the documentation was signed before then so is has my legal name at the time.'

'Lucky for you but there is the joint account with your married name. You will need a good lawyer to sort everything out.'

'Terrific.'

'It's a good job one of my brothers-in-law is a good lawyer.'

'I can't...'

'Yes, you can. I already asked him.'

'Why?'

'Because you are in a pickle through no fault of your own and need help.'

'It is my fault.'

Dylan put one finger on her chin and turned her face towards him. 'How can you think any of this is your fault?'

'I let myself be suckered in.'

'By a master of deception and you weren't the only one. All of his victims are intelligent people. You more so because you figured him out within days and did something about it. It took Kelly Barker two years as his girlfriend to come to her senses. She escaped his clutches with a permanent A.V.O. after she reported his behaviour to her father, with whom she now lives for protection.'

'She wouldn't speak to me. She hung up.'

'How many did you contact?'

With a shake of her head, Rachel tugged her chin free and willed her heart to settle. 'All of them.' She turned back and glared at him. 'Someone had to.'

Dylan shook his head with a wry smile. 'I'm not going there. It got me into enough strife with you, last night. And my next question might get me into an equal amount of strife but I need to ask it.'

A frisson of fear snaked across her shoulders. She shuddered and plastered on a smile. 'What?'

His shoulders rose on a hiss as if he was searching for courage. 'Something you said out there.' His fingers wavered towards the door. 'You inferred he raped you. Did he?'

The tense silence was palpable.

'Rachel?'

Eyes closed and close to tears, she nodded slowly and dropped her head. 'After the wedding night, which was the first time we slept together, almost every night for six months.'

'Sweet mercy.' His hands were gentle but firm as his arms curved around her body and drew her against him. Bits from his belt prodded but for some reason they gave her comfort. It was so darn good to be held by this man who she more than liked, despite her conscience telling her she couldn't let her defences down.

'There are no words to express how sorry I am that you had to endure such evil. This is why you are so afraid of a man's touch.'

A knock at the door prevented an answer she didn't want to give. Dylan released her and went to the door. 'Bring him up,' she heard before he stepped further into the passage from where mumbles came from different voices.

Bring who up? Surely not Kyle. The thought caused her to curl into a ball on the sofa. It was difficult to understand why this dread had settled in her gut when she should be overjoyed the bastard had been arrested. A shudder took hold when footsteps neared.

'There's someone here to see you,' Dylan said as he approached.

She dared to peek. 'Pierre? What… how…?'

'You hung up on me and didn't answer any of my messages or calls. I was frantic with worry. What happened? Why are all the cops here?'

Rachel leapt from the sofa and flung herself at her brother's chest, too overcome to answer but Dylan explained while she lapped up the sensation of being hugged tight by her brother.

'You went out to confront him? Why?' Pierre held her at arms-length. His face was fierce.

'I could tell he was too angry to be placated. He would have killed the cleaner. I couldn't live with the knowledge another innocent woman lost her life because of me. I heard what Dylan said, knew there were armed officers. I did peek before I went out, to make sure I was relatively safe.'

'Weren't you scared?'

'Terrified but there was little choice.'

'There's always a choice.' Dylan came closer. 'Even though you scared the pants off me, your appearance made Jacobs turn which gave me the chance to taser him. The shock forced him to release the woman. Your actions, despite being dumb, ended the stand-off. You two chat here while I talk to the Forensics team after which, I need to get back to work.' He turned to Pierre. 'Rachel has to remain here until an officer gets her statement when she will be free to go. It could take a while but I don't like to leave her alone after such an ordeal. Tonight, I have uni and won't be home until about ten.'

'I can pick her up after work and take her home for dinner. The kids will be overjoyed.' He turned to Rachel. 'You can stay with us.'

'I'll drop by your place on my way home because I have some paperwork for you about Rachel's car. I believe it is registered in your name.'

'Yes, as is the insurance.'

'Whether Rachel stays or comes back here can be decided then but she needs to be here tomorrow for there will be legalities to tie up. The past few days have thrown up some doozy problems to sort. If we don't get every minute detail recorded accurately, Jacob's lawyer will be like a ferret to find a way to get him released.'

'I'll come back here. I don't care how long it takes to record everything if it means he is never on the streets again. And please, everyone, call me by my real name. Rachel Scott has now retired to the ether, from where she came.'

'Elise,' both men said.

All evening, it was as though she had been in some surreal world. She still hadn't come to terms with being able to eat a family meal at the same table with Pierre, Olivia and their children, Jessica and Armand, without the worry of being found and attacked. The pleasure and weird sensation had overwhelmed her most of the night. Maybe she was still in shock or still suffered from PTSD. Can the condition pass so fast when the source was no longer there? Or did it linger for too long after? She didn't understand how it worked. And as for Madeleine, the poor girl had been cossetted and cuddled on a continuous roundabout of doting close family who barely gave her a second out of someone's arms. The only time she and Madeleine had been together had been when hunger pangs took hold.

At last, peace reigned. The three youngsters were tucked up in their beds while she lounged back in the comfiest of recliners, sipping hot chocolate of the French variety. Olivia sat opposite with eyes closed and probably exhausted while Pierre seemed content. They'd had fun tonight. Like old times and it felt so darn good inside her.

'Livvie,' Pierre stood and shook Olivia's arm. 'Go to bed.'

'Uh?' Olivia opened her eyes and glanced around, 'Oh, sorry.'

'Go to bed,' Pierre levered his wife upright.

'What about…' Olivia wavered a hand towards Elise.

Elise placed the mug on a side table and crossed to Olivia. 'You have a had a long day, go to bed. And thank you for all you have done for me this past week.' She turned to Pierre. 'You go too. Dylan won't be long.'

Pierre gave his wife a peck on her cheek followed by a gentle shove in the direction of the bedroom. 'I usually stay up until about 10.30. in any case and Dylan has some paperwork for me.' He indicated the seat. 'Sit down and finish your chocolate.'

'If you make this sort of chocolate every night, you might find me here forever.' She sat, sipped and sighed in pleasure.

Pierre dragged his seat closer to her. 'You are always welcome to stay.'

'I know but I want a home of my own.'

'I began a search. There are a few possibles. It depends on what you can afford.'

'Which depends on what I can get from the house insurance, which in turn depends on legalities with this bigamy mess.'

'You could rebuild on the same site.'

'Too many bad vibes. The block is large enough for a developer to build several units. It's worth more as a block. Which reminds me, I might need all the paperwork I gave you for safe keeping. Am I glad I had the nous to secrete my personal papers out when I did.'

'Do you need them tonight?'

'Yes because I need the bank statements and receipts to prove how much I deposited on the house. If I can get the same amount back and add in what I've saved this past year, I won't need much of a loan to buy…'

Knock, knock.

'There's Dylan.' Both stood at the same time.

Pierre waved her down. 'I'll get it.'

Still in uniform, minus his belt of bits, Dylan looked tired as he entered the lounge and sat on the divan. He held out a plastic file to Pierre. 'This is all the paperwork you need for the car claim. There's a copy of my police report, the mechanic's report on the condition of the car, Pete's report on the drug and alcohol tests, photos of the car and I can get a copy of my dashcam if it is needed. Oh, and the driver's insurance details are there.' Dylan turned to Elise. 'The car is a write-off. You managed to bend the chassis and crumple a few engine parts together. It would cost more than the car is worth to repair it and I wouldn't want to drive a car with a repaired chassis. I queried why the air bags didn't inflate. They were missing. Was the car new?'

'No,' said Pierre. 'Second hand. I bought it from a dealer.'

'Well, I wouldn't use the same dealer. The car had been in a prior bingle.'

'Not what I was told.'

'There are a few dodgy dealers out there.' Dylan turned to Elise. 'When you find a replacement, I could come with you to check it out if you want. How was your evening?'

'Beyond pleasant. Super is a better word.'

'Are you ready to go? Oh, there's something I wanted to ask you both. Once every couple of months my entire family get together for a pot-luck dinner. It's my turn to host the shindig. You are all welcome to join us. Saturday. The gang begin to arrive around four and are usually gone by eight-ish. It's mainly B.Y.O. Every family brings a dish of food to share and what they want to drink.'

'Thank you for the invite but Olivia and I have a prior engagement.'

'The invite stays open.' He turned to Elise. 'Are you ready?'

'Sure, I'll get Madeleine.'

The drive home was so quiet, Elise began to worry. 'Is anything wrong?' she asked to break the tension.

'No, why?'

'You're unusually quiet.'

'Sorry, I'm plain tuckered out. Will you come to meet my family on Saturday?'

'Umm… I can't.'

'Why not?'

She couldn't understand why her heart lurched and the nerves in her gut clenched so tight. 'The same reason Pierre can't go.'

'Which is?'

Eyes closed, she turned her head away. 'Can we discuss this when we get back to the unit?' You're a big fat chicken, Elise Esquilante.

'Now I'm worried. What is it you can't tell me?' He pressed the remote to open the gate to the unit parking space and they drove in. Once the engine ceased it's murmur, Dylan unbuckled the capsule and carried Madeleine to the unit door where he handed her over but kept a hold of the handle. 'Are you going to tell me what's going on?'

'Come in for a minute.'

Dylan didn't release his grip on the capsule until they were in her unit and the door was shut. Capsule on the ground, he turned her to face him. His expression was so serious she gulped in trepidation. 'No more procrastination.'

'Pierre and Olivia are driving me home on Saturday.'

With his eyes raised to the ceiling Dylan groaned. 'And you were going to tell me – when?' His eyes dropped and stared into her soul. He shuddered and held out his hand, which she took and grasped. 'I had hoped I had more time.'

'More time for what?' Heat raced through Rachel's veins at the same time a squishy sensation settled in her stomach.

With eyes closed, he shook his head. Eyes open again he grasped her other hand. 'I still can't figure out why... Heck, I like you – a lot. More than I thought was possible to like a person after so short a time. I was attracted to you the first time we met at the court house and the more I learnt about you, the deeper the attraction. Do I understand it? No. What I do understand is how I can't let you go without exploring the attraction.' He rubbed the back of his neck. 'Hell, I'm doing this all wrong aren't I? But time is short and you want to go back south. To be honest, I don't want you to go. I want to spend as much time with you as possible, go on dates... but I don't have a clue how you feel about me?' His eyes were like those of a begging puppy before he hauled in a breath and whispered a swear word. 'I understand you have a road to journey as you heal but I want to walk beside you along that road, to give you support and a shoulder to cry on when the going is tough. You are a keeper and I want to be the guy who gets to keep you. I adore Madeleine and would love to be her father.'

'Her father! Even though she's not yours?'

'DNA doesn't make a father. Just because a child doesn't have your DNA doesn't mean you can't love the child or be the dad a child needs. We don't share the DNA of our ultimate partner in life but we love them unconditionally.' His eyes shot skywards. 'God, help me out here?' A long sibilant hiss of frustration escaped as he dropped his head and stared into her eyes.

With her innards intent on doing crazy things, all she could do for a minute was stare back. She blew out her cheeks. 'Dylan, will you hold me?'

'Hold you? Are you sure?'

She nodded.

'You won't freak out?'

She shook her head. 'No.'

It took a few seconds before Dylan beamed, carefully wrapped his arms around her and drew her close. 'You have no idea how much I've wanted to hold you in my arms, and I have to say, you fit perfectly.' He moved his shoulders back and peered down. 'Will you let me kiss you?'

Even though every atom in her body shouted yes, past experience caused her to bite her lip. 'As long as you are gentle.'

'Why wouldn't I…? Damn, he was rough with you, wasn't he?'

All she could do was nod because if she spoke, she would break down.

'Let me assure you, I have never, and will never, lift a finger to hurt a woman. It's not how I was raised and not in my make-up. I promise.' He took one of her hands, raised it to his mouth and brushed his lips over her knuckles in the lightest of kisses. 'Gentle enough?'

Close to tears, she nodded slowly. A tiny thrill of anticipation centred in her gut. She so wanted this.

His hands were gentle as he reached out to caress first, her cheek and the curve of her jaw. He caught her eye in silence. 'Okay?'

The tiny thrill turned into a shiver of delight as a tear of pure pleasure escaped on her nod.

He tilted her head up to his and lowered his mouth to brush over her lips in a barely there kiss. He must have felt her breath catch in her throat for he drew back with a silent question in his eyes.

The need to touch, to taste, overwhelmed her to the extent a few more tears escaped.

He brushed them away with a knuckle. 'Your tears scare me. Tell me to stop if it's too much.'

'It's not enough.'

'Then why the tears?'

'I'm overwhelmed. I can't explain. They are the happiest tears ever but I don't think I'm ready.'

He dropped his hands and looped them behind her back as he drew her close and rocked her. 'You and I are in the same boat.'

'What do you mean?'

'Both of us have been betrayed, making it hard for us to trust. If we end up together, how can I believe you would never be unfaithful to me?'

'But I could never be unfaithful to my partner.'

'Do you want me to believe that?'

'Of course.'

'Yet you find it hard to trust me enough to believe I would never hurt you.'

'It's not the same.'

'In a basic sense it is. Think about it. Please tell me you'll stay.'

'I have to go back for a while. I owe the gang down there more than I can explain. They all opened their hearts to me and silently ganged together to keep me safe. I can't walk out on Ella in an instant. I owe her at least the four weeks' notice to leave so she can advertise for a replacement. And I can't not thank the entire group or say goodbye. Plus, I need time. To be honest, as much as I like you and want a relationship, I don't think I'm ready.'

'I understand. This week has been rough on you. You've been through even more turmoil to add to your past trauma. It will take a while for you to recover but I'm willing to wait because you are worth waiting for, as long as you can give me a bit of hope.'

'I can, because I am desperate to get back into the real world and you are one of the nicest people I've ever met. I just need time. Pierre is searching for a small cottage for me to buy when all the insurance has been sorted. I'll be back here in a month.'

'It will be a long month for me. How about you let me take you and Sweet Pea on a real date tomorrow night.'

With her heart filled with warmth, she smiled. 'I'd love to go on a date.' She stood on tiptoe, pressed her mouth against his and felt him smile against her mouth before he stood back.

'What are you doing tomorrow?'

'I'm going to take Madeleine in the pram and explore the city without any fear.'

Dylan gave her hand a gentle squeeze. 'I wish I could join you but enjoy the day, although the D's will want to spend time with you to tie up legalities. I'll ask them to phone you with a time. Sleep well. Dream of the future with no more fear and if I'm lucky, you will include me in your dream.'

To prevent the itch in her eyes developing into tears, she forced her lips to turn up at the corners as she opened the door. 'Goodnight and thank you for everything,' she said without turning around.

'Night,' she heard as she shut the door.

It was impossible to describe the sensation when Elise stepped from the front door of the unit block and pushed the pram towards the main shopping mall of the city. The sense of freedom abounded, along with joy, but after so many months of constant fear there was still an underlying trepidation she couldn't seem to shake. When she squinted at the brightness of the sun, she lifted one hand to shade her eyes. With the weather so bleak when she'd left the motel down south, she hadn't thought to bring sunglasses but boy, was the warmth welcome and for the first time in days there wasn't enough wind to rustle the leaves on the few street trees as she passed under each. Every step brought a tad more confidence until she paced with haste, lifted her head high and shoved her shoulders back. Propped up so she could enjoy the sights, Madeleine gurgled and waved her arms as though she also enjoyed the freedom.

In less than thirty minutes, they were in the main shopping precinct where Elise swung into every shop, dawdled along aisles and studied every item, not to purchase but simply to relish the privilege of not being too damn scared to have such free rein. It took a display of garments on sale to realise she donned the over-sized hoodie out of habit. She stopped mid-stride, whipped it off and shoved it under the pram carriage. It would go in the first bin she found but it meant she'd need another jacket for warmth. Every cell in her body jiggled with joy while she tried on a few jackets and settled on a dark aqua fleece with a zipper all the way down the front. Even better than the bright colour was the fifty percent off price since it was the end of the season.

Next was hot chocolate and a *pain au chocolat,* which wasn't as good as her dad made but wasn't terrible either. The ring of her mobile was an unwelcome intrusion, especially when she answered it to find Detective Sergeant Justin Smith was about to spoil her day with a request to interview her.

'I'm in the city. I can be home by one.' Which would give her time to eat and feed Madeleine who hadn't whimpered once so far. Time agreed, she paid for her new top, steered the pram out and stuffed the black hoodie in the bin outside the shop door.

On the way home, a dress in the window of a shop caught her eye. A date with a new man required a new outfit so she went in, chose three garments to try on and walked out with a Cheshire Cat grin. The elegant paper bag she placed at the foot of the pram lightened the heaviness in her heart all the way back to the units. After hanging the outfit on the back of the bedroom door, she fed and changed a now sleepy baby and sat in front of the slightly wider gap in the curtains with a mug of tea, a banana and a bowl of Greek salad. She didn't know if it was only her own lighter mood but the pedestrians outside seemed to move faster and be happier than the last time she'd sat there to study them.

Her mood darkened at the raps on the door. It took stern self-talk to open the door and invite Justin Smith, along with his partner, Constable Rick Thomas, to sit at the kitchen table. The questions were as expected, boring and long-winded. It was only the knowledge that the slightest hiccup in misinformation would give the bastard's lawyer a crack to open wide and give the bastard a chance of leniency, that kept her spirits up. A niggle of unease wriggled across her shoulders when Justin opened out a file and withdrew a pile of papers with his fingernail.

'Is this your signature?' he asked with the end of a pen pointed on the bottom of a type-written sheet.

She stared to study it. 'No, even though it looks a bit like my writing. Why?' She eyed Justin.

'Are you certain?'

'Positive.'

'How can you be sure?'

'First, I never signed this and second, the spelling is wrong.'

Justin's mouth gaped. 'What do you mean?'

'There is no 'e' on the end of Esquilante. I do know how to spell my own name. What is this?'

'A land transfer form.'

'Excuse me?' She snatched the paper from under the pen and flipped the page to read from the beginning. The actual form appeared to be genuine but the writing wasn't hers. 'I've never seen this before. Where did you get it? And my middle name is spelt wrong as well.'

'It was with Jacob's belongings we took from the house he'd been staying in. There's another document. Your last will and testament. Dated the day after your so-called wedding.'

'Are you kidding me? Can I see it?'

'Yes, but we don't want you to touch it.'

'Why not?'

'Fingerprints. If it was genuine, your fingerprints would be on it?' He pointed to the paper she'd grabbed. 'Like they now are on this document.'

'Oh, damn, sorry.' Both men's faces said what words didn't need to say while her own face heated to incineration point. With eyes on the ceiling she emptied her lungs and filled them again, long and slow. 'I presume I left all of my worldly goods and money to one Kyle Jacobs.'

'You did.'

'Of course, but since he failed to dispose of me, it holds little relevance. He came to the units to kill me, didn't he?'

'Not that he's admitted it but we presume so.'

'The will wouldn't have held up in any case because my recent will leaves everything in trust to my daughter. My brother, Pierre, is the executor and has a copy. And the land transfer? To Kyle?'

'Yes.'

'Which could easily be challenged because Kyle Jacobs doesn't exist. Did he really think he would get away with this?'

'I'd say he was going to give it a good try.'

'I'll add this to the list to discuss with a lawyer. Will he be able to get a copy of these documents?'

'Get him to contact me. Your lawyer is entitled to any evidence that will be used in court.'

'Is there anything else I need to know?'

'Not all of the money in the secret account was blackmail proceeds. A fair chunk was stolen.'

After what she'd learned to date, this revelation didn't surprise her. 'By the way, how is Laura Jones?'

'The injuries are severe. She's had surgery. It will take a while but she should be okay.' His smile was wry. 'Thanks to you we reached her on time. How did you know?'

'I promised to ring her with an update. When Kyle answered her phone, it didn't take genius status to figure out it wasn't a good sign.' A sigh escaped on the lift of her shoulders. 'I need to ask this even though you will tell me not to interfere but do the other victims know Kyle is no longer a threat.'

'Yes and you will be pleased to know we visited each, in person, to inform them and get statements. It will take months, but they have all agreed to be witnesses when this goes to court.'

'Will he be let out on bail before the court hearing?'

'No. He committed first degree murder and attempted the murder of a police officer – me, along with the attempted murder of you, the insurance assessor, the cleaner and Miss Jones. Due to his prior criminal activity in Tasmania he is a proven flight risk and bail would be set so high he would never be able to pay it, especially with frozen accounts and all of his accounts have now been frozen. It's possible he will be held in solitary confinement until after the court case.'

'Pity.'

Justin raised his eyebrows. 'Why?'

'I would love it if someone nasty gave him the same treatment he's meted out to others.'

Both men eyed each other with quirking lips. 'Which is why we want to keep him alive long enough to face justice,' said Justin.

Elise didn't need any explanation.

Both men stood. Justin gathered together all of his bits and pieces. 'I have no doubt we'll be in contact more times than you'd like over the next few months but it will all be necessary to ensure there isn't a skerrick of wriggle room to escape life in prison without parole. Thank you for your time and your help. And I'll need those journals you spoke about.'

'As soon as I get back south.' But not until she had copied what she wanted. It was a relief to shut the door on their backs.

After a half hour of fast paced rounds of the room to rid herself of angst, she spent time on the phone speaking with Ella. The rest of the afternoon required a long soak in the bath, attention to her hair to make it look elegant enough to go with the new outfit so she could begin her new life with a potential new man on an actual date she could enjoy without fear.

www.ingramcontent.com/pod-product-compliance
Lightning Source LLC
Chambersburg PA
CBHW070540120726
47909CB00007B/2197